The Loves of a
D-Girl

ALSO BY CHRIS DYER

Wanderlust

The Loves of a D-Girl

A Novel of Sex, Lies, and Script Development

CHRIS DYER

A PLUME BOOK

PLUME
Published by Penguin Group
Penguin Group (USA) Inc., 375 Hudson Street, New York, New York 10014, U.S.A.
Penguin Group (Canada), 10 Alcorn Avenue, Toronto, Ontario, Canada M4V 3B2
(a division of Pearson Penguin Canada Inc.)
Penguin Books Ltd., 80 Strand, London WC2R 0RL, England
Penguin Ireland, 25 St. Stephen's Green, Dublin 2, Ireland
(a division of Penguin Books Ltd.)
Penguin Group (Australia), 250 Camberwell Road, Camberwell, Victoria 3124,
Australia (a division of Pearson Australia Group Pty. Ltd.)
Penguin Books India Pvt. Ltd., 11 Community Centre, Panchsheel Park,
New Delhi – 110 017, India
Penguin Books (NZ), cnr Airborne and Rosedale Roads, Albany, Auckland 1310, New
Zealand (a division of Pearson New Zealand Ltd.)
Penguin Books (South Africa) (Pty.) Ltd., 24 Sturdee Avenue, Rosebank, Johannesburg 2196,
South Africa

Penguin Books Ltd., Registered Offices: 80 Strand, London WC2R 0RL, England

First published by Plume, a member of Penguin Group (USA) Inc.

First Printing, May 2005
10 9 8 7 6 5 4 3 2 1

Ⓟ REGISTERED TRADEMARK—MARCA REGISTRADA

LIBRARY OF CONGRESS CATALOGING-IN-PUBLICATION DATA

Dyer, Chris.
    The loves of a D-girl : a novel of sex, lies, and script development / Chris Dyer.
      p. cm.
    ISBN 0-452-28492-9
    1. Young women—Fiction.   2. Screenwriting—Fiction.   3. Women screenwriters—
Fiction.   4. Motion picture industry—Fiction.   5. Hollywood (Los Angeles, Calif.)—
Fiction.   6. New York (N.Y.)—Fiction.   I. Title.

PS3604.Y46L687   2005
813'.6—dc22

                                                                        2004023767

Printed in the United States of America

PUBLISHER'S NOTE
This is a work of fiction. Names, characters, places, and incidents are either the product of
the author's imagination or are used fictitiously, and any resemblance to actual persons, living or dead, business establishments, events, or locales is entirely coincidental.

For Franca

D-Girl *or* **D Girl** *n Slang* \dē̆ gûrl'\ [Origin Hollywood, Calif. (1930s? 1940s?)] **1 :** A female executive who toils in the movie business, often fruitlessly and always without credit, procuring and developing screenplays, books, plays, articles, and other literary properties for cinematic adaptation, and sometimes even production. **2 :** Short for *Development Girl*. **3 :** Variant of *Story Editor, Director of Development, Vice President of Development, Creative Director,* or any impressive-sounding title her boss will let her get away with.

1

F ADE IN ON A FAMOUS ACTRESS AS SHE GLIDES ACROSS A
grandiose Hollywood stage. Over her entrance, someone's heart pounds a steady, ominous rhythm. She must be a
serious actress, one known for her command of craft, not a
starlet or an ingenue. She must be able to project intellect
and she must be known for making films of artistic substance or social import, at least occasionally, because she is
stepping up to the podium to present the Academy Award for
Best Original Screenplay. Meryl Streep, say, or Julianne
Moore. Susan Sarandon if the political winds aren't blowing
too high. Any number of English actresses will also do,
preferably a dame, as the British are always imbued with literary pedigree in Hollywood by mere virtue of their citizen-
ship and their intimidating accents.

The famous actress pauses briefly, perfectly, just long
enough to acknowledge the respectful applause from her
peers without appearing conceited. She is such a natural, she
can even make good of the between-season TV writer's

"clever" intro. Because she is so smart and so well prepared, the famous actress can also be counted on to pronounce correctly the names of the nominated writers many American box office stars might not even recognize as they zip across the teleprompter. Why, the famous actress is so natural and so smart and so well prepared, she doesn't seem to be reading at all.

Angle on Lizzie Hubbard, she of the pounding, ominous heartbeat. She looks elegant in her borrowed Cerruti gown, without appearing too glamorous, as it is useless for a lowly screenwriter even to try standing out in a room filled with so many fussed-over movie stars and Hollywood wives. Understatement is the only way to go. Besides, Lizzie knows that she is the long shot tonight. She is the youngest screenwriter and the only woman among the five nominees, one of whom is a well-known, much-hyphenated actor. He is largely favored to win, having the advantage of a household name that all of the Academy voters can recognize on their ballots, even the sound editors and the makeup artists.

When the famous actress gets to Lizzie's name, Janie Hubbard squeezes her daughter's hand, as if the entire Kodak Theatre were about to take flight. Lizzie is glad that she brought her mother and so proud that she could share this once-in-a-lifetime moment with her. The camera picks Lizzie out of the crowd, catching her with a slightly pained expression. Janie squeezes tighter, Lizzie's cue to smile. It's a closed-mouth smile full of humility and gratitude just for being here in this expensive dress, in front of these cameras, with her mom, while one of the brightest stars in the

Hollywood firmament is broadcasting her name around the planet.

The famous actress struggles comically with the unyielding envelope. It's shtick, but it's adorable shtick when she does it. That's how smart and how natural and how good at her job she is.

Lizzie's heart beats louder. It feels as if it is trying to bust out of her rib cage with all the indignant rage of Susan Hayward wrongly imprisoned in *I Want to Live!* To quiet it down, Lizzie reminds herself over and over again that she is the dark horse here, the favorite to lose according to the Las Vegas odds-makers.

She does not realize that she has beaten those odds even when her mother lets loose with a squeal and locks her in a clinch. Janie is already crying, and Lizzie is momentarily concerned for her. That's when she notices that the orchestra is playing the theme song to her movie, her heartbeat has been drowned out by applause, and everyone is beaming at her proudly, as if she has just now mastered the alphabet for the very first time.

Janie guides her daughter out of her seat, and Lizzie begins her stunned march to the stage. On the way, well-wishers congratulate her. Her producer rushes at her, stealing an awkward kiss. So does the leading man, those bitchy rewrite battles conducted entirely through the producer now forgotten, if not forgiven. It all happens in a blurring rush and Lizzie can think of only one thing: to lift the hem of her gown as she ascends the stairs.

Suddenly, Lizzie finds herself center stage, where the

famous actress is embracing her as if they were old friends and there's a cold, hard, naked statuette in her hands. Lizzie stares into the blinding lights, the cameras craning and fawning for her and the expectant audience all hers, too. She takes this in for an awestruck moment, then she barks out a laugh and says, "I just won a freakin' Oscar!"

It's an unguarded moment, the kind the audience loves, but the roar of their laughter comes as a shock to Lizzie, who is briefly thrown off her prepared speech. She regains her composure and goes on to thank the producer "who truly believed in the script and fought so hard to get it made," the director "who brought it to life so lovingly," her parents, and her teachers.

"Well, not all of my teachers," she improvises. "Not the professor who gave me a B-minus in my Screenwriting workshop."

More titters from the audience.

"I never got a B-minus in anything until I met him! And where's his shiny Oscar?"

The audience laughs again, always grateful when a non-performer exhibits any stage presence at all.

"And I certainly didn't get here with any help from my first boyfriend—or any of my boyfriends, for that matter—and certainly not from my first boss."

The conductor cues the orchestra, a signal that Lizzie has gone over her allotted seconds.

"Oh . . . oh . . . I'm sure there are people I'm leaving out. Wait . . ."

The theme song builds insistently.

"Oh, come on! This is the only chance I'll ever have to be up here so just give me a few more seconds," she pleads. "Just pretend I'm a movie star."

The conductor relents at a cue from the director and a cringing discomfort sweeps across the audience and living rooms around the world.

"Thank you," Lizzie snarls into the orchestra pit. "I also have to thank my agent, for all her help and . . . hard work . . . and y'know what? No, I don't. I could have done it without her—because I *did* do it without her."

The theater hums with murmurs of disapproval.

"I mean she wouldn't even take my calls until she knew there was a producer *and* a star interested in the damned script, which I shopped around myself, thank you very much. That parasite."

Boos and hisses rise from the audience.

"Oh, you're booing me? *You're* booing *me*?"

They are indeed booing her, with increasing gusto.

"Oh, that's just great. I haven't heard this many hacks since I was a candy striper in that TB ward," she spits, as the orchestra seizes the theme song full force, and an usherrette takes her by arm.

"Get your hands offa me, you overgrown Barbie doll!" Lizzie screams, as she swings her Oscar at the woman.

Several security guards rush out from the wings. Under the cover of a three-second delay, they restrain Lizzie, now frothing and fuming. They drag her off-stage, where she passes Billy Crystal, adjusting his bow-tie and getting ready to make it all better with a prefabricated one-liner—

Smash cut to the real Lizzie Hubbard, a pencil projecting from the thick wedge of curls that grows to her jawline. She sits at her office desk, eyes closed, chewing on the arm of her smart, stylish glasses, a habit she has been meaning to quit ever since an astigmatism was detected in a compulsory seventh-grade eye exam. She is off on an extended daydream.

In addition to garnering an Oscar and settling some professional scores, in the past three hours Lizzie has also redecorated her apartment with a budget beyond her means and stretched her dollar, along with her vaguely stiff muscles, on an Uruguayan beach she read about in a budget travel magazine. For a brief moment, her mind has even alighted on a possible solution to the problems in the second act of that screenplay she wrote in college, before she came to work for Gil Gorman Productions and stopped writing altogether.

Her job hasn't always allowed her such indulgent luxuries as daydreams, but the company is no longer buzzing from the producer's successes of the 80s and 90s. It is in fact near to collapse, and Lizzie is counting the days to her severance pay. While her boss is out hustling to save his faltering regime, Lizzie's mind, once colonized, occupied, and brutally exploited by the hostile forces of her day job, is free to pursue its own happy liberties, which are now rudely interrupted by an e-mail alert.

Lizzie's eyes sting. She has been reading much too much, she reminds herself, as she squints at a message from Daniel, her college boyfriend.

Staying friends with her ex seemed so sophisticated to Lizzie at the time of their breakup, so modern, so mature.

Besides, it wasn't a hostile split. Lizzie simply felt that they had been together too long for people so young and they had different agendas for their lives. Daniel, a Creative Writing major, craved the country and wanted to start a family immediately; Lizzie, a one-time student of Dramatic Writing, has never suffered from maternal yearning and finds the country all too green and out-of-the-way.

Lizzie stares at the e-mail and its perky kick-line of exclamation points. A collection of Daniel's stories is being published by a small but well-respected press. Lizzie should feel happy for him, and in a sense, she truly does. He has real talent and a dedication for writing that Lizzie can no longer muster. Daniel has made all the sacrifices a good writer can—and probably should—make, going for years without things that people with more mundane callings take for granted, like medical insurance, paid vacations, retirement plans and savings accounts. He has earned his good fortune.

But Lizzie can't deny a twinge of envy either. After all, Daniel has his wife, a hale beauty with a perpetual country glow, to support him through his struggle with her busy veterinary practice in Vermont. She is the kind of woman who always looks good, even with one arm buried up to her elbow in the birth canal of a dairy cow. The kind of woman Lizzie decidedly is not.

Lizzie sits there, wondering if there isn't a bit of vengeance in Daniel's regular dispatches of literary triumph and domestic rural bliss, his postcards from the road not taken. She wonders if each one of his exclamation points isn't meant to rub her nose in a decision she made years ago, and she finds herself wondering, too, if there isn't something to be said for the clean break.

Angle on a large, businesslike clock. It is 2:51. Lizzie's boss is late getting back from the airport.

Gil Gorman has been in L.A. all week playing legal matchmaker between the troubled but talented star Christian Rydell and Laszlo Baranszky, the slick, powerful criminal defense attorney. The movie star violated his parole and a multitude of California state laws after drunkenly driving a stolen car through the wall of a day care center. Luckily for the children, it was a holiday and the center was closed. Unluckily for Gil Gorman, Rydell had just signed on to *Split Second,* the project that the producer has been counting on to revive his moribund career and save his endangered studio deal.

Gil has a call scheduled with the studio president for three o'clock. Lizzie could do the right thing, swallow her envy, and use these few precious minutes before Gil returns to fire off a congratulatory e-mail to Daniel. Or, she could use them to stockpile office supplies.

Track with Lizzie as she bustles out of her office and into the copy room. She has seen too many movies; you can tell by the way she throws open the double doors to the supply closet a bit too grandly, like Loretta Young in *The Men in Her Life,* or Greer Garson in *Blossoms in the Dust*. She wonders how people ever lived without Post-its, as she stuffs the brightly colored wads into the pockets of the sweater she chose this morning for just this purpose. She congratulates herself for her foresight and for remembering to order extra packages of her favorite pens, too. She crams some Scotch tape and staples into her pockets as well, because she knows that time is running out.

After seven long years of toiling in feature film development, Lizzie is keen to all the signs of a producer's demise. The incoming calls are few; the outgoing many. The company's preference in package delivery degenerates from UPS or FedEx, to Airborne Express, to the U.S. Postal Service. The once Himalayan pile of promising submissions dwindles down to a mere Murray Hill of the picked-over and the pathetic until all that's left are musty, cursed old projects tossed into and out of turnaround; or worse, unsolicited long shots that come from "weekend screenwriters" who live in places far, far from the action, places like Schenectady, Spokane and Wahoo, Nebraska. The company begins "streamlining" its staff, doing away with the little extras like receptionists, office assistants, and the freelance story analysts who scramble together the most meager living reading all the submissions that everyone else is too busy, or too important, or too manic to read. In their place, a reservist force of perpetually disoriented interns is recruited from the most expensive universities in New York and Los Angeles, the unofficial training grounds for the movie business. They fumble through the daily operations of the company one semester at a time, binding scripts, mailing rejection letters, booking tickets, fetching bagels and botching copies, rarely ever to be seen again after their unpaid tours of duty are completed, their grades filed, and their precious letters of recommendation procured.

Lizzie has been watching Gil Gorman Productions die an especially slow version of this death for nearly four of her six years with the company. The situation has left her as Gil's de facto personal assistant, reader, receptionist and gofer, her impressive executive title notwithstanding. Although officially Gil's director of development, or D-Girl, these days Lizzie is a director of development in much the same way that the blacksmith in Colonial Williamsburg is really a blacksmith, the pirate at Treasure Island a genuine swashbuckler. She has the office, the business cards, and the personalized stationery, but there is no actual development for Lizzie to direct.

Pockets full and lumpy, her arms cradling a jumble of notepads, paper clips, and other whatnots, Lizzie stands face to face with the copy machine, the Hope Diamond of office booty. She is wondering how she might outfox the building's security cameras and roll it past the doorman when she hears the front door slam with a thunderous clap.

Enter Gil Gorman, or barrel in really, as the overweight, overextended, and overbearing movie producer never merely enters any room.

"Hubbarrrrrd!" he calls, by way of a needy reflex.

"You bellowed," Lizzie deadpans, as she finds him huffing and panting and struggling helplessly with his briefcase, his rolling luggage and his oversized umbrella.

"Where's my call from Van Allen?" Gil demands, oblivious to the armful of goodies Lizzie is carrying.

"The phone hasn't rung since you left."

"Why not? Have you called the telephone company to make sure it's working?"

"I think they're getting tired of that. Besides, in exactly

three minutes, Van Allen's assistant's assistant is going to call to tell us that he is running late and needs more time."

"Hmpf!" Gil sputters, as he always does when he knows that Lizzie is right. He chug-chugs past her into his office, where he drops his bags with an operatic sigh.

"I'll take my eyedrops while we wait!" he declaims.

Lizzie shudders and groans.

One hour later, the loot has been safely stashed, the boss's eyeballs have been lubricated, and the all-important call from on high has been delayed, as predicted. All is quiet at Gil Gorman Productions, save for the ticking of the clock, the faint purr of a dozing hard drive, and the sound of Gil Gorman himself, heaving, shifting and fidgeting about like a bored zoo animal. Lizzie, in headset, eagerly awaits the call that might finally announce the cancellation of Gil's housekeeping deal and her subsequent emancipation. She makes a note to investigate customary severance pay, a term that has taken on a poetic, almost holy, meaning to Lizzie in the last few years.

A telephone ring breaks the silence. "Hubbarrrrd!" Gil harmonizes, just off the beat.

Lizzie answers the phone, doing her best imitation of the breathy actress/receptionist who was one of the first casualties of Gil's foundering career. After running the obstacle course of Garth Van Allen's assistants, Lizzie connects Gil to the studio honcho who pays the rent, writes the paychecks and controls the green light Gil so desperately needs to move his projects forward and stay in the movie-making game.

Intercut between Lizzie and Gil in those endless moments

between the time the assistant says Van Allen is on the phone and the time that Van Allen is able to tie up other, more promising matters and is actually on the phone. Gil paces and sweats, while Lizzie files her nails with a Powerpuff Girls emery board she scored at a publicity screening. She will miss these little giveaways once she is free, she has to admit, but not all that much.

Garth Van Allen finally picks up, and Lizzie and Gil both listen hard for any hint of sympathy or regret that would signal bad news, but Van Allen is as cool and uninflected and inscrutable as ever.

Gil congratulates him on "the numbers" for *Total Mayhem,* which means that he has not actually seen the studio's weekend box-office slayer, but wishes he had made it.

"We're very proud of it," Van Allen mumbles.

Lizzie stifles a snicker and stabs the mute button. She has seen the movie, at yet another industry screening. It is just about the only way that Lizzie ever sees movies these days, and over the years she has come to consider these events more occupational hazard than perk. Van Allen's movie is nothing more than a glorified video game, a coldly conceived, run-of-the-mill actioner that doesn't exactly instill pride.

Van Allen changes the subject. "We haven't seen any submissions from you in a while, Gil, and I wonder where you are with *Split Second*?"

This is it, Lizzie thinks. She holds her breath as she awaits the ultimatum she has been longing to hear for years: "Show us a marketable, castable movie that can sell some

12

real popcorn once and for all, or pack your bags and leave, you freeloading, dead-weight, has-been!"

"It's out to Killian Louth now," Gil feints, invoking the Irish megastar and two-time Oscar winner who has recently pulled out of a high-profile production, the only kind he ever gets involved in, or pulls out of.

Lizzie rolls her eyes, another bad habit she has been meaning to kick.

"Hmmm," says Van Allen, barely covering his own skepticism. "When do you think you'll hear from him?"

"Sam Waterman says the agency is completely behind it and he's on Killian every day. I really think we should make him an offer while the window is open. Force his hand."

"Let's gauge his enthusiasm first, Gil. If he's on the fence, maybe we can make an offer. But Don Flynn is on the fast track with *Contents Under Pressure,* and they've already got Crowe and Diesel attached. I don't want to go up against that without some genuine commitment."

Here it comes, thinks Lizzie, as Gil sags a bit.

"You need to focus on your other projects," says Van Allen. "Take something off the back burner, turn up the heat. What else have you got?"

Gil picks a thick, beat-up script from the pile on his desk.

"I found a great script, Garth. I'm close to closing on it now. It's called *The Way.* It's got action, fantasy, drama, a love angle, an uplifting message. It's a smorgasbord with a full dessert station. Nobody goes home unhappy," he filibusters. "I really think it could be a classy franchise for the studio. I'm very excited about it, Garth. Very excited."

Lizzie attacks her keyboard, searching for the submission in her database. She scrolls past *The Vortex* straight to *The Wayfarer*; there is no match for *The Way*.

"Great title," Van Allen says. "Provocative and mysterious."

Lizzie is mystified by this and it's impossible for her to glean either sincerity or cautious diplomacy from Van Allen's monotone.

On his end, Van Allen consults his Palm Pilot. Since he's contractually obliged to give only a sixty-day notice of nonrenewal on Gil's deal, he figures there's no harm in riding this out, hopeless as it seems. "Who's the writer?" he asks.

"It's a very talented young guy just out of film school," Gil vamps, squinting at the script's messy cover page. "His name is Nick Inkersham."

Lizzie types in the writer's name a few different ways, and faces more blank screen.

"Who represents him?" asks Van Allen.

"He doesn't even have an agent yet. He's using an attorney. That's how new he is. We could get this for a song. I'm not saying it's perfect, of course. It needs some work, but hey, they all do."

Lizzie realizes that this isn't the call she has been waiting for at all. Once again, Gil seems to have bought himself some time with the Killian Louth gambit, even if it's only a few days, and it is Lizzie's turn to sag at this discouraging turn.

At some prompt from one of his assistants, Van Allen suddenly runs through a slick, but abrupt good-bye. Lizzie hangs

14

up and barely has to time to slump before her interoffice line chirps at her.

"Cherry Orchard!" she chirps back.

"Very funny, Hubbard. Send a copy of *Split Second* to Sam Waterman at CTA for Killian Louth to consider."

"They already passed on *Split Second* in February."

"Then change the date on the title page and tell them we got a new draft."

"Desperate times call for desperate measures, huh?"

"Get off my phone, Hubbard."

"I thought you'd never ask."

Lizzie, grateful for something to do to kill the work week's interminable final hour, goes about doctoring the title page of *Split Second,* the script that was orphaned when Christian Rydell paid his impromptu visit to that day care center. It is a story about a UPS driver who discovers that a maniacal terrorist has shipped a bomb special delivery to the UN. A calculated but well-crafted nail-biter, it all takes place in a single day.

Gil paid the screenwriter top dollar for his pitch, sure that such a blatantly commercial story would be the summer blockbuster that could jump-start his career. Unfortunately, another D-Girl liked the idea so much, she stole it and brought it to her boss, Don Flynn, producer of such testosterone-pumping crowd pleasers as *Combustible, Fire Hazard, Slippery When Wet* and other titles that dare the audience to risk their ticket purchases. They changed the UN to the Capitol, the UPS driver to a FedEx man, and called their story *Contents Under Pressure.*

Despite his head start, Gil has been losing the high stakes race ever since Don Flynn got commitments from Russell Crowe and Vin Diesel to co-star, making it even harder for Gil to recast his picture or get the green light he deserves, and badly needs. If Killian Louth signed on to his project, however, the studio would be happy to reenter the race and would even relish all the free pre-production publicity it would snag, but without a star with serious box office clout, Van Allen's just not going to take the risk.

Gil knows that he has only bought himself a small slice of time. In a rare instance of self-reliance, he begins to hunt and peck out a number on his telephone.

Cut away to a white, otherworldly fog, underscored by a strange, slurping, sucking noise. This is broken by the sound of a ringing telephone, and suddenly, out of the ethereal cloud stumbles Nick Inkersham.

Pull back to reveal the Perkmeister Café in Madison, Wisconsin. Untidy college kids drink coffee, stare at laptop screens and free newspapers and scratch themselves listlessly. Nick, their scruffy barista, fans his way through the frother's steam cloud and grabs the phone, but it slips from his grasp.

"Shit!" he says, wiping his hands on his apron, while the dangling receiver emits a string of faraway, agitated "hellos".

"Yo, woah, yeah, sorrysorrysorrysorry," Nick says, finally picking it up.

"Yes," says Gil, already wondering what he's gotten himself into. "I'm looking for Nick Inkersham."

"You got him."

"It's Gil Gorman. Laszlo Baranszky passed your script on to me. I'm halfway through it, and I think it's a great read."

"Wait. Is this Tad? Dude, don't be yanking at me while I'm working."

"No, no, this is Gil Gorman. Calling from New York. The attorney, Laszlo Baranszky, gave me your script to read. He tells me he got it from a former intern at his firm."

"Okay, Gil Gorman who produced like *The Scheme of Things, The Cool Blonde, In a Warm Country, Four Englishwomen by the Sea*?"

"Yes," Gil admits, always happy to be reminded of his greatest hits.

The cashier barks out an order for a soy chai latte and Nick shushes her.

"I love the title of your script, too, Nick. I find it very . . . provocative and mysterious."

Nick's whole world suddenly stops. After five post-collegiate years of suffering through ego-crushing jobs, tactless rejection letters and the condescending smirks of deeply unimpressed writing teachers, a genuine movie producer is pouring compliments into his ear. His moment of vindication has finally come, and Nick has not felt so breathless, so ineffably exhilarated, or so far outside his own body or the corporeal world since losing his virginity at seventeen.

A honking sound jerks him out of his trance. "Do you get to New York very often?" asks Gil, in an accent that screams Ronkonkoma, Long Island.

"New York! No, no I haven't been to New York in . . . a

while," Nick lies whitely, not having been to New York since a junior high weekend field trip to the Statue of Liberty. "But I'm long overdue."

"Well, I am always looking for fresh young writers and I'd love to sit down to talk to you about *The Way* as soon as possible. Is it still available?"

"Completely."

"Do you have any other scripts or pitches?"

"Oh, lots. I've got this one thing I've been working on about a race car driver who—"

"Beautiful. Well, I'd love to hear about those, too. I'll tell you what, Nick, I'm going to give you the number of my development director, Elizabeth Hubbard. She's away from her desk right now, but contact her on Monday and she'll set up a meeting for us all to get together and hear some pitches. How's that?"

"Tha-tha-tha-that's great."

Not used to compliments and abashed to the verge of tears, Nick jots down the number on his forearm. He stammers through a good-bye with Gil, then wrestles free of his chai-stained apron.

"Hey, where's my latte?" he hears an anonymous voice wonder as he dashes for the door. He thinks that he hears the cashier call him a slacker, too, but it feels good to run, as he clocks a quick distance away from the drab café. Nick isn't sure where he's running to, or even why he's running at all, but it feels like the right thing to do, and the cool spring air is bracing and full of hope as it rushes against him.

* * *

On Friday evenings Gil's posture always takes on a slight stoop. His shoulders sag forward and his large head angles downward, as if fighting a private wind. It might seem to be a physical symptom of overwork, as if Gil's backbone, so tightly coiled all week long, suddenly snaps like a time-released spring every Friday at exactly six o'clock. In fact, it is an outward expression of Gil's deep-seated contempt for the weekend. What everyone else appreciates as a time for play, or rest or spiritual reflection, Gil Gorman considers something to be suffered through, a period of culturally enforced stasis that must be endured until he can get to Monday's phone calls.

This is exactly how Gil feels now as he lumbers into Lizzie's office, already wearing his raincoat, his briefcase overstuffed with enough work to keep any other mortal busy for a month.

"Hubbard, this writer will be calling you next week to set up a meeting," he says, plopping Nick Inkersham's script on her desk. "I want you to cover his script over the weekend."

"I don't work on the weekends, and I don't do coverage," says Lizzie, appalled at the mere suggestion that she would spend her time preparing a dry reader's report, the industry standard for evaluating screenplays.

"Since when?"

"Since two promotions ago, when you agreed to it. I'll get an intern to cover it on Monday."

"We need to get to this right away. This is a hot young writer. You heard how enthused Van Allen was."

"Only if 'enthused' means 'catatonic'."

"Van Allen is a devoted Buddhist. He's very serene."

Lizzie peers at the script and notices the writer's Wisconsin address.

"Who submitted this?"

"I got it while I was meeting with Christian Rydell today."

"It came from a penitentiary? Gil, I'm sorry, but I am not reading a screenplay that was slipped to you through the bars of a jail cell by an actual felon."

"It didn't come from an inmate, Hubbard. It came from a lawyer."

"That's even worse!"

"Coverage on my desk Monday morning, Hubbard, or don't bother coming in at all," Gil snarls over his shoulder as he slouches off to face the weekend's purgatorial cruelties.

"Then I guess this is good-bye," Lizzie says to his back, and she sends the script fluttering across the room like a startled pigeon.

Unlike Gil, Lizzie absolutely lives for the weekend. Already, she can feel this one slipping away from her, like so many before it. Lizzie would cry, if she could remember how, but it has been a long while since her workaday life has been tragic enough, or sweet enough, to warrant tears. Instead, she lays her head on her desk and stays that way, unblinking, for a long existential minute as the fluorescent lights hold an endless sharp note. She is feeling much too much like Monica Vitti in *Red Desert,* or any one of Antonioni's torturous excercises in contemporary anomie, when the door buzzer breaks the spell.

Enter Iago Betencourt, the Brazilian bike messenger who runs packages between the studio's corporate offices uptown and Gil Gorman's office in Tribeca. Iago always comes at the end of the week to deliver checks from the payroll department. Since the rest of Gil's paid support staff was let go a year ago, Iago has become the closest thing to an office confederate Lizzie has left. His visits, which once were standard water-cooler gripe sessions, have evolved into something much deeper and more complicated in the past few weeks, when they have ended with Lizzie and Iago having fast, frantic sex on her desk. Although their encounters have their undeniable, if fleeting, pleasures, they are wholly gratuitous and not at all professional, and in the sheepish afterglow of last week's indiscretion, both agreed never to do it again.

As Lizzie steels herself, Iago steps past the unmanned reception post calling her name in his soft, accented English. An inner voice writes on the blackboard of her conscience: *Mustn't fuck the messenger, mustn't fuck the messenger, mustn't fuck the messenger . . .*

Lizzie meets Iago in the hallway, blocking off entry to her office. With his sinewy build, his sharp Roman nose and his sleek bicycle helmet, Iago looks like some classical rendering of Mercury come to life. Lizzie wouldn't be at all surprised to find little wings quivering at his ankles and the thought almost cheers her, but she still feels sad and deflated, and Lizzie is one of those people who cannot mask her own feelings. Whenever she is discontented her eyelids get heavy, her jaw sets hard, and her mouth goes as straight as a hyphen drawn to stress her displeasure.

"Lizzie, what's wrong?"

"Oh, nothing you haven't heard before."

"Ah, my little Lizzie. I wish that I could wash it all away like the waves of the mighty Atlantic." Iago is also a part-time poet.

"You're very sweet," she says, digging her paycheck out of the package he has handed over to her. She tears it open and scrutinizes it carefully to make sure that the payroll is indeed still rolling.

"Is it Zhil?" he asks.

"Of course it's Zhil . . . Gil. He's making me write coverage on a script this weekend. Coverage! On an unsolicited script! Like an intern or a reader. I'm supposed to be the director of development here! It's so humiliating."

"You are proud, Lizzie. Like the lion."

"I *am* proud like the lion, and I'd like to tear him limb from limb like the defenseless little lamb."

"Such anger isn't good for the soul. You know this. You need to find some creative release."

Lizzie understands just what Iago is getting at, and she starts to back him slowly down the hallway, all the while maintaining her inner chant: *Mustn't fuck the messenger, mustn't fuck the messenger, mustn't fuck the mess—*

"It is much too long you are working in this place for this man. He is not an artist like you, Lizzie. Artists, we are like different species, with different needs . . ."

"Oh, he's an artist, all right," Lizzie stalls, trying to avoid any conversation concerning her "needs." She turns up the voice louder and louder: *Mustn't fuck the messenger, mustn't fuck the messenger, fasten muck the massenger . . .*

Lizzie makes the mistake of looking into Iago's sad, dark eyes, the kind that seem to hold a deeply cultivated soulfulness and superhuman powers of sensitivity, even if they're actually just a lucky gift from a gorgeous gene pool.

Mustn't fuck the messenger, pheasant must the passenger, peasant fuss the packager, fuck it . . .

Lizzie throws herself at Iago and they go crashing backward through the door of the script library, smearing each other with panicky kisses, as Iago's helmet hits the floor with a hollow *thwok-wok-wok-wok-wok-wok*. Suddenly all arms, they grapple and grope and clutch at each other, each trying to follow the other's lead. Lizzie backs him into a sagging shelf, setting off an avalanche of long forgotten screenplays. He backs her into an opposite shelf, murmuring lush Portuguese phrases into her temples, her curls, her throat, her clavicle. To Lizzie, it all sounds like *boorzhazhow, boorzhazhow, boorzhazhow.*

Lizzie orders him to the floor like a testy bank robber, then dives on top of him, mashing his body into the mound of fallen scripts. Iago tears off her sweater. She tears off his jersey. They both tear off her skirt. Lizzie grabs his wrists and pins him down, as everything stops but their breathing. He is letting her make the next move.

Mustn't, mustn't, mustn't . . .

Iago's eyebrows pitch a plaintive, pointed arch, two caterpillars straining for a kiss, and Lizzie heaves a sigh that clears her head. She can't use him this way. It's getting her nowhere. It just isn't right, she decides, as Iago tilts his hips upward, pressing against her a bit . . .

Mustn't, mustn't, mustn't . . .
And then a bit more.
Mustn't, mustn't, must . . .
The best thing about bicycle gear is how easily it peels away from the flesh, as slippery and compliant as the skin of a ripe fruit.

2

INSIDE EVERY APARTMENT BUILDING IN NEW YORK THERE dwells at least one "Sandy Dennis character," or so Lizzie maintains. Hopelessly locked into the routine of her daily existence and permanently drunk on her own anonymity, she is the kind of New York woman who came to the city so that she could "have it all," but got so much less than she had ever expected. Forced to reassess her own worthiness in an overflowing pool of talent and ambition, she is the type of woman who has long lost sight of the pluck and idealism that first brought her here to conquer the city and set her chosen field on fire. Profoundly unfulfilled, but fully insured, the typical Sandy Dennis character is defined almost entirely by her less-than-glamorous second- or third-rung job. She's the kind of career woman all those first-rung career women never talk about when they are delivering their commencement speeches at Wellesley, Smith and Bryn Mawr.

Lizzie has observed that with this unenviable social and professional position comes an exclusively urban psychobehavioral syndrome. A woman suffering from it is rarely seen in the company of others, if ever at all. She tends to live alone, or with any number of cats, and she tends to smoke incessantly, the city's aggressive anti-smoking laws be damned. She is typically plagued by some combination of phobias, unusual allergies and unclassifiable chronic aches, along with antiquated afflictions like neurasthenia, and a chunky alphabet soup of newfangled disorders like ADD, ADHD, SAD, CFS, SID, HSP and PTSD. If she is not deeply dependent upon the help of a psychotherapist, she is positively promiscuous in her search for the right one.

If life were a movie, she is the kind of woman who would be played by Sandy Dennis, the method actress who so perfectly captured the twitching, stammering tics and mannerisms of the insecure, hypersensitive, discontented female of the species ectomorph in every role she ever played.

There are male versions of these women, too, of course; though unfairly, not as many. Lizzie thinks of them as "Don Knotts characters."

As she scales the four flights of stairs to her Brooklyn Heights walk-up, Lizzie passes her building's resident Sandy Dennis character, a frail little woman with lank, colorless hair and a chalky pallor. She hugs the wall like a mouse as she squeezes past Lizzie, expertly avoiding any eye contact. She is talking to herself under her breath, as she often does, obviously telling someone off, but good, and looking quite pleased with her own imaginary performance. Lizzie doesn't bother with a hello, which would only be met with a quick, blank-faced glance anyway.

Although this tends to happen several times a week, today the non-encounter unsettles Lizzie tremendously. She picks up her pace and rushes into her apartment, where she charges straight into the bathroom. She flips on the light and looks in the mirror. Sure enough, her left cheek is looking a little pale and for the first time she notices that her hair seems slightly washed out, as if the pigment were fading.

"Oh my God," she says to her reflection. "It's the Sandy Dennis syndrome! It's happening to me!"

Flashback to a younger Lizzie, with the same wedge of curls that do indeed seem to be a richer, deeper shade of chestnut brown. There's even an unmistakable flush in her cheeks, a genuinely hopeful glow. She sits in the reception area of Gil Gorman Productions, now also flush. She has been working for Gil as a freelance story analyst for six months without ever having met him, all of her assignments being handled by his D-Girl, Judy Tolliver.

Lizzie has no idea why, but today Gil has requested a face-to-face meeting, booked through his assistant with great urgency just this morning. She is nervous, as Gil's reputation for being punishing on his staff is well known. He has even been the subject of an assault-and-battery charge for lobbing a paperweight at a previous assistant. Judy, however, has assured Lizzie that she would never have to deal with Gil directly and that Judy herself would intercept any paperweights lobbed Lizzie's way. Lizzie is worrying that her coverage isn't up to snuff and wondering how she is going to pay her rent and her student loans if she is about to lose this job, when Gil's assistant enters and tells her that Gil is ready to see her.

Lizzie follows the assistant back to his office and finds Gil, still twenty-five pounds overweight twenty-five pounds ago. He is having his way with a pastrami sandwich, talking on the phone and leafing through a script as if it were a junk mail catalogue—his version of being ready to see someone. Lizzie takes a seat and squirms for a moment, not knowing exactly where to look, a professional smile hardening on her face.

"That's right, that's right," Gil grumbles into the telephone without looking up at her. He makes some grunting noises that serve as a good-bye and pushes the sandwich and the script aside. He reaches for Lizzie's last reader's report.

"So you're Elizabeth Hubbard," he says charmlessly while scanning the report.

Lizzie springs up from her seat and offers her hand. He looks at it a moment, then gives it a limp shake.

"Yeah, I thought this script was a piece of shit, too," he says, offering Lizzie one of the greatest compliments any producer can give to a freelance reader who has passed on a weak piece of writing, but this pink-cheeked Lizzie is still too inexperienced to understand this.

"Oh, I wouldn't go that far—"

"So, Hubbard . . . You don't mind if I call you Hubbard, do you? I have too many names in my head and last names are much easier for me."

"Well, I prefer Lizzie, or even Elizabe—"

"Great. I called you in here, Hubbard, because my development director left today."

"Judy's gone? Where did she go?"

Gil gives her an impatient look that says "How am I supposed to know?" and forges on. "So tell me about yourself. Why are you reading scripts? You know there's no living in it."

Lizzie chuckles, then realizes that this is not a joke. "Well, I need the work. Y'know, rent and student loans and all that, and reading scripts is good for me. It keeps my story muscle in shape. Plus, it's flexible, so I can work it around my writing schedule. I'm a writer."

Gil looks unconvinced.

"A screenwriter," she adds. "I write screenplays."

"Have I read your script?"

"I don't know. Judy did. It's called *The Seat of Our Pants.* It won the departmental prize at NYU last year. That's how she found me."

Gil jots the title on his sandwich wrapper as a reminder to check the files for coverage on the script. "What's it about?"

"Well, it's about three generations of this family of Italian tailors—"

"What's the genre?"

"Uh . . . well . . . I . . . guess it's kind of a crazy family story. Although some people would probably call it a dramedy, but I—"

Gil crumples the sandwich wrapper and tosses it away. "Look, there's a development job open," he says, getting down to real business. "I need someone who's got a sharp eye for material and a realistic sense of the market."

"Oh," says Lizzie, genuinely caught off guard. "That's very flattering, but I really haven't thought about—"

"Think about it. Right now."

"Well, I'm really a writer. I've gotten myself into debt pursuing my dream," she says, instantly regretting such a corny phrase. "So I really want to be true to it. I'm afraid if I take a full-time job I won't have the time to write and I want to be fair to myself and give myself a real chance."

"If you're a screenwriter, then why aren't you in L.A.? That's where you go if you're a screenwriter. If you're a fish, you don't live in the desert. Right?"

"Well, I've considered it, but I prefer New York for now. It suits me."

"Yeah, I hate L.A. too, but that's where the action is."

"I don't hate L.—"

"How do you plan to write screenplays if you're scrambling for money reading them?" Gil badgers. "You'll never make the connections you need to make toiling in obscurity as a freelance reader. If you come to work for me you'll get to know people who can help you: agents, producers, talent. Important people. On both coasts. You could even pick up some producing skills. That's what screenwriters should do anyway, learn to produce their own scripts and stop complaining about guys like me."

"But writing is such a solitary act. Producing is all collaboration and schmoozing and raising money and managing people. It goes against a writer's nature."

This prompts the first "Hmpf!" Gil ever shot at Lizzie, and he quickly changes his tack. "Look, I could start you as a story editor at thirty-five, plus two weeks' paid vacation, full medical and a retirement plan."

Lizzie quickly does the math and knows this is actually more than she has been earning patching together an unpredictable living reading scripts, catering functions and working at minimum wage odd-jobs.

"Oh that's very generous of you, and very, very tempting," she says. "I'm deeply flattered and grateful for the offer, but I really have to stick to the writing."

"Who said you have to stop writing? It's a nine-to-five job. Your evenings and weekends would be yours and yours alone," he lies. And Lizzie falls for it.

Dissolve to the older, more experienced Lizzie, clutching the sink and still staring down her reflection in the mirror. The blanching part of the Sandy Dennis syndrome seems to be happening before her very eyes.

"Oh, no," she gasps. "This is how it starts. I'm working at a job that I never wanted in the first place and I'm having vindictive fantasies and passing neighbors in the hallway without saying hello and forgodsake I'm talking to myself!"

"All I need now are six or seven house cats and a carton of smokes!" Lizzie blurts into her telephone later.

On her end, Judy chuckles. "You're too neat to be a Sandy Dennis type. Aren't their apartments always cluttered and disorganized?"

Lizzie scans the room and seizes on a small pile of newspapers meticulously bundled for recycling. "Y'know, my place is looking a little messy."

"Oh, c'mon Lizzie, you're addicted to your Swiffer and you know it."

A seasoned D-Girl who has worked at nearly every independent production company and studio development office in New York, back when the studios *had* development offices in New York, Judy Tolliver is the city's uber D-Girl. Well connected, well respected, and remarkably adaptive to the whimsical changes of the local film scene, she has held twelve jobs in the course of her twenty-year career, five of them in the last seven years alone, including one stormy, short-lived stint at Gil Gorman Productions. In any other profession, this might be taken as a mark of ineffectiveness or unreliability, but in the New York development world, it is a testament to Judy's resilience and blamelessness. Because of this, Judy plays mama bear to the rest of the city's ever shrinking litter of D-Girls, which even includes a few D-Boys. Judy is the go-to person whenever anyone needs sage advice, a new job, a sharp reader, a dependable assistant, or even just a sympathetic shoulder to cry on.

"I just don't think I can take another day of it, Judy. Tell me you know of some other job openings?"

"Believe me, if I knew of one, I'd grab it myself. There's just nothing out there right now. All the script development is happening out of L.A., the studios are using freelance book scouts and the indie directors are driving their own projects here. We're all doomed for extinction."

"I can't make it to extinction. I have to quit."

"You could do that, but speaking of 'doomed for extinction,' you know just as well as I do, Lizzie, that it's only a matter of time before Gil's housekeeping deal expires, and he's not going to get another one. He hasn't had a hit in nearly a decade. You've hung on this long. What's another month or two? With your severance pay you can take some time off and write your own movie. I give him two more months. Tops."

"That's what we thought a year ago, and look at me. I really don't think I can hold off this encroaching Sandy Dennis thing much longer."

"Spoken like a true drama queen. Look, there's nothing wrong with you that a long, indulgent health-and-beauty day won't fix. Do you still have that spa certificate we gave you for your birthday?"

"Yes. Thanks so much, Judy. You're a peach."

"Well use it before it expires, forgodsake. When you come to cocktail hour on Thursday, I want to see you looking rosy and carefree."

"Hmm, does this spa perform gentle, healing boss-removal?"

Judy snorts out a laugh, then hangs up, but even talking to the level-headed and congenitally cheerful Judy hasn't done much to lift Lizzie's mood. She considers calling Iago, who has been generous enough to offer her his pager number in case she is "suffering too much, like a battered frigate in a tempest." The little slip of paper is tempting her, crooning her name in soft bossa nova tones from the dark, breath-minty depths of her purse. But Lizzie has never seen Iago outside of the office before and she is afraid of establishing another precedent, no matter how much fun it might be in the moment. Besides, she doubts that she would have the energy for another athletic sex match.

Instead, Lizzie does what she usually does on Friday nights. She orders Special Double Happiness from her local Chinese restaurant and chases it down with half a bottle of bargain bin wine.

Two hours later, woozy from the wine and the week's indignities, Lizzie realizes that she has been staring uncritically at a marathon of *elimiDATE* reruns she has seen before. Disgusted with herself for having wasted another Friday night and ashamed at the cliché of discontented urban singlehood her life has become, she resolves that she will not lose another weekend to her unhappiness. She decides to get the unsolicited screenplay out of the way tonight so that she can start working on her own writing, and maybe even her love life, tomorrow.

She picks it up and reads the first page once, then twice, then one time more before plummeting into an extended program of fitful dreams, all starring the late, great Sandy Dennis.

A great clanging and ringing and gonging of pots announces the arrival of morning in a one-bedroom attic apartment in Madison, Wisconsin, where Nick is busy orchestrating an elaborate breakfast. Lemony sunshine throws a spotlight onto the production. Bacon sputters and hisses in a skillet while the coffeemaker huffs over its morning duty.

A pretty, sleepy-headed young woman pads into the kitchen. She is wearing fuzzy slippers she should have thrown away years ago and staring at the ex-boyfriend she should have thrown out months ago.

"Nick, it's seven o'clock," says Didi. "On a Saturday."

"Oh, sorry, Didi. I couldn't sleep," says Nick, furiously whisking a batch of eggs.

"Well, *we* were doing just fine," says a bleary young man, yawning from the bedroom doorway and scratching his left buttock.

Tad is Nick's best friend—or was until three months ago, when he became Didi's new boyfriend. Since then, Tad's sleepovers have become more regular and the walk-in closet Nick has been using as a bedroom until he can get back on his feet has been shrinking by the day, along with Nick's self-esteem.

"I'm sorry, guys. I was just making breakfast for the three of us, but it can wait if you want to go back to sleep."

"No, no, no, keep going," Tad insists, snatching half an orange prepped for the juicer. Nick slaps his hand away.

"Since when do you have trouble sleeping?" Didi wonders.

"Since I got this New York problem."

"What's the problem?" she asks. "Some producer likes your script."

"Some producer? This is Gil Gorman. *The Cool Blonde*? *The Scheme of Things*? *Four Englishwomen by the Sea*? And he wants to meet with me to hear some pitches."

"Okay, Nick," she presses on gently. "But I still fail to see the problem."

"The problem is I have a golden opportunity but I don't

have any way of getting to New York, 'cause I don't have any money."

"Should've thoughta that before you ran out on your job," Tad mutters.

"Keenly observed, Sir Isaac."

"Guys," says Didi, pleading for a truce.

Tad slouches, chastened; Nick goes back to cooking.

"Nick, I think you just need to settle down and wait to hear from these people," Didi says, full of sweetness and concern. "You're getting much too worked up over this and I don't want to see you crash from the disappointment."

"What disappointment? I couldn't be happier, and I have earned my elation. You were never very supportive of my writing, Didi. Never."

Tad collapses into a chair and groans.

"Shut up and eat this," Nick snaps, serving him a picture-perfect plate of French toast smothered in a colorful medley of fresh fruit, with a side of crispy bacon. Nick slams the maple syrup on the table for good measure.

Didi tries again. "I'm just saying that you shouldn't let yourself get over-excited, Nick. Like that time you got wait-listed for UCLA Film School and you bought that car and that new laptop?"

Tad barks out a "HAH!" and Didi shoots him a stern look. Nick removes the fork from his own steaming hot breakfast and presses it onto Tad's bare arm.

"What the . . . !" Tad shrieks and jumps up from his chair. "Are you crazy?"

Like a hurt little child, Tad shows Didi the four pink lines branded onto his forearm. "Look!" he says, begging for favoritism.

"Okay," says Didi, throwing up her hands. "I give up."

"No, I give up," Nick says. "I can't go on this way much longer, Didi, and let's face it, neither can you. This was supposed to be temporary, but I can't keep sleeping in the closet with the belts and the luggage anymore."

"I can move the belts," says Didi, ever the conciliator.

"I don't care about the damned belts! It's me! It's us! It's this twisted situation! I have to get out of here and get on with my life!"

Everything stops, as Didi and Tad freeze in a moment of inexpressible remorse for having hurt someone they both still care about.

"Okay," says Didi. "But you should eat your breakfast first. It's really good."

"Yeah. Yeah, dude. Great job," Tad mumbles, hiding behind his bangs and sawing away with his knife.

The next day, Nick is squeezing himself into a tiny window seat on a low-cost flight from Milwaukee to New York.

Someday he will write a movie about all this, he thinks, a small, character-driven story about three college friends who become incestuously entangled. He knows it's not an original idea, but love triangles and coming-of-age tales are evergreen. Perhaps it will be his directorial debut. Small, personal, heartfelt stories are perfect for that sort of thing.

Nick grabs his notebook from the pouch beneath his tray table and begins jotting down ideas. He doesn't want to forget the way that he and Tad sat together on the air mattress in the cramped closet while Tad strummed on Nick's old out-of-tune guitar as if nothing between them has changed since high school. He doesn't want to forget how Tad mentioned some money he had, almost as a second thought, or even how Tad steered the conversation toward the script, and New York and Nick's big chance. He doesn't want to forget how truly excited Tad got, or how his expression softened in a moment of unmistakable tenderness for his old friend, before he went back to torturing the neck of the poor, innocent guitar.

Nick can't wait to write this scene. He can already picture it. There will be no apologies, no literal moments of forgiveness, no hard and fast resolutions. The characters will never acknowledge that the best friend has always loved the girl more than the struggling young writer ever did, and that they are temperamentally better suited to each other. They will never admit that the writer always dreams too big, and that it has always scared the girl, who craves more security and stability from her partner, or even that the writer and his college sweetheart had outgrown each other long before they split. Instead, the scene between the writer and his best friend will be full of pregnant subtext and subtle, but profound behavioral gestures, all totems of the intense and ineffable love between men.

No, that's really a play, Nick thinks, *maybe a one-act,* as the plane noses up into the sky. Lost in his own heady inspiration,

Nick is too busy scribbling away to notice the familiar landscape below as it slants and slips and slides off the shelf of his world.

On Sunday afternoon, Lizzie is still reading the script she swore she wouldn't read on Friday. She has put it down several times, determined not to go one page further, but the script is so egregiously unprofessional and so gallingly impenetrable that it has become a challenge, a test of her endurance and professionalism just to get through it.

The story begins as a gritty urban adventure about a kid trapped in the subway tunnels beneath New York, before an overblown and out-of-control sense of surrealism takes over. At two hundred pages, it is eighty pages longer than the standard format and it is only the first installment in a proposed seven-part series. Parts of it are actually handwritten, and much of it even has footnotes. Maps, glossaries and family trees are included, but they only serve to confuse matters. It would be absurdly expensive to make, difficult to market, and even harder to follow.

By the time Lizzie has finished it, and the young hero wakes up to discover it may have all been a dream, she actually feels nauseated. Once her stomach settles, she finds herself hot with rage for having lost another weekend of her life to a piece of amateurism so irredeemable she would not have assigned it to an intern, or her worst enemy. For a moment, Lizzie actually considers calling the writer's number listed on the cover page to tell him everything she despised about his ill-told tale and why she thinks he should consider another line of work altogether. It takes a couple of calls to Judy to convince her that it would be terribly unfair to the poor writer, and that Gil is really to blame.

As usual, Judy is right, so Lizzie resorts to the only course of revenge at her disposal—the coverage.

3

O<small>N MONDAY MORNING, GIL IS HUNKERED OVER HIS</small> desk, wagging his head and firing off little "hmpfs!" at Lizzie's scathing report. The only thing a producer hates more than a good piece of coverage on a lousy piece of work is a lousy piece of coverage on something he considers promising. Suddenly Gil explodes with a wall-rattling *"Hubbarrrrd!"*

Cut to Lizzie in her office. Feeling quite smug, she counts down, "Three, two, one," and Gil is standing in her office door, trembling and waving her report in the air.

"What is this, Hubbard?"

"Hm-m-m-m," says Lizzie, faking a squint. "That looks like the coverage you requested on that unsolicited script."

"It's a pass!"

"Is it ever. Let me tell you, it stunk up my apartment so badly I'm going to have to call an exorcist."

"Don't you think you're being a little hard on this, Hubbard?" Gil fumes, scowling at the report through his reading glasses. " 'Wayward . . . chaotic . . . undisciplined . . .

nonsensical'? 'The Middle East would be easier to fix than this script's troubles'? . . . 'No sense of human psychology whatsoever, as if the writer never actually met a human being before'? . . . 'No discernible genre though it gives new meaning to the term *disaster film*'?"

That's an old one, but a classic, and it always makes Lizzie smile.

"You call yourself a professional? This isn't a professional reader's report, Hubbard. It's subjective and smart-alecky and arrogant!"

"I'm not a professional reader. Remember that interview six years ago?"

"I am very disappointed in you, Hubbard! Very disappointed!"

Lizzie rolls her eyes.

"What am I supposed to do with this? I can't get anyone else interested in the project based on this crap! I can't show it to the studio, or talent, or agents! And I'll tell you another thing, Laszlo Baranszky would not submit a script that was 'a sure-fire formula for cinematic ipecac.' He is one of the most brilliant lawyers in this country and he raved about this script."

"Maybe you should get him to do some weekend coverage for you."

"Oh, ho-ho-ho, Hubbard. Very funny. You're going to need that sense of humor in the unemployment line."

"There is no unemployment line anymore, Gil. It's all done by phone. Believe me, I've looked into it."

"Well I hope your phone is working, because this company is in trouble, and reports like this aren't helping. We need material, and we need it fast." It's a hard truth Gil admits aloud for the very first time.

"I have a good mind to make you rewrite this, Hubbard, but it needs a professional touch, someone who knows what he's doing, so obviously I'm going to have to read it and write it up myself."

Gil blows back into his office, slams the door, and throws himself into his chair. He has no intention of reading the script himself. In the movie business, the amount of power one has is proportionate to the amount one reads. Those on the lower rungs—interns, story analysts and story editors—read constantly until their minds are wearied, their eyesight fails and their dreams become a jumbled collection of hackneyed plot devices and puerile male fantasies. Executives and producers read what has been filtered through these underpaid drones, and studio chiefs read only when a property has already been deemed "hot" by someone with real authority. Stars, who have the most power, read the least of all, and only when it is convenient to their whims, or when in recovery for plastic surgery or substance abuse. Although he may be in dire trouble, Gil refuses to step down any of the rungs he worked so hard to climb in the last twenty-five years.

He glowers at Lizzie's coverage and reads her eviscerating comments over and over again, meeting each one with a saucy little "hmpf," because he knows that it's all true.

While Gil steams behind his door, Lizzie spends a leisurely morning on the job, reading the paper, Internet shopping and answering personal e-mails. At lunch time, Gil rumbles past her office without a good-bye. As soon as she hears the front door slam, Lizzie brushes a pile of scripts off her sofa and goes down for a hard-earned nap. Working for a failing company does have its perks, she reminds herself, just as her telephone has the nerve to ring.

"Hel . . . uh . . . Gil Gorman Productions," announces a drowsy Lizzie, finding her fake receptionist's voice.

"Hi. This is Nick Inkersham calling for Elizabeth Hubbard."

Lizzie flips through her mental Rolodex, trying to locate this vaguely familiar name, but nothing comes up.

"She's not in. May I take a message?"

"Yeah, I submitted a script called *The Way* and Gil Gorman told me to call her to set up a pitch meeting."

"Oh, that bast—" says Lizzie, suddenly springing awake. "Uh . . . can I have someone get back to you, Nick?"

"Not really. Do you know when she's due back?" Nick asks over a racket of sirens and traffic.

"There's no telling. But if there's a number where you can be reached, Gil will be in later this afternoon and I can have him return your call," Lizzie says, meaning to make sure that Gil personally passes to this amateur.

"It's a little tricky for me right now. I'm not at home. I'm in New York."

"Well, can he reach you on your cell, or in your hotel?"

"I don't have one."

"A cell, or a hotel?"

"Neither."

44

Lizzie finds this very strange, and stranger still comes a sound she hasn't heard in ages—an electronic woman demanding another twenty-five cents.

"I'll have to call back later," Nick yells, before the line goes dead.

"Who calls from a pay phone?" Lizzie asks the dial tone. "What a loser."

Although Lizzie dislikes her job through and through, passing to writers is the part she dislikes the most, and this time she is determined to leave this grim and thankless task to Gil. "Let him clean up his own mess for once," she mutters, as she goes back to her well-deserved nap.

Moments later Lizzie feels a warm, sweet slumber taking over her body when the phone rings again. This time it is Andrea, Garth Van Allen's assistant's assistant, calling for Gil. When Lizzie tells her that Gil won't be back until later, she detects a nervous, urgent tone beneath Andrea's usual over-studied perkiness.

"Is there some message I can give him, Andrea?" Lizzie asks, fishing for hope.

"Well, I'm really not at liberty to discuss it, but it's very important."

Lizzie is now certain that Andrea is trying to hide something. "Is it something *I* should be concerned about?"

"Mmm. Possibly."

"Is it bad news?"

Lizzie can almost hear Andrea deliberating. "It's not too good," says Andrea softly.

"Is it *the* bad news?"

"I can't say," Andrea blurts in a voice that says it all.

Cue up a chorus of heavenly angels as the room fills with a golden otherworldly light. Salvation is at hand. Lizzie is paralyzed with profound emotion, and she has that faraway, beatific look reminiscent of Jennifer Jones in *The Song of Bernadette*, or any number of actresses who have burned at the stake playing Joan of Arc, from Falconetti to Ingrid Bergman to Luc Besson's girlfriend. Lizzie is finally being delivered from her six-year hell. She will recover from this tragic loss of youth and this traumatic test of her mettle, emerging older and wiser and stronger, a better woman for having suffered so nobly. From here on in, everything she does will be truly fulfilling, and it will all be done for a higher purpose beyond the mere procurement of rent, health insurance, two weeks' paid vacation and fifteen sick days, non-retroactive. Lizzie will go on to do extraordinary things; she can feel it deep in her soul.

"Lizzie?" Andrea knows that she has given away too much and she is trying to get back to business, but Lizzie is too moved to speak. "Hello? Lizzie?" Andrea's smooth young brow wrinkles with concern as she checks her headset's connection.

"Lizzie? Are you still there? Lizzie? Hello? Hello? Hello?" Andrea's voice deepens, becomes more insistent, more abrasive. "Hello-o-o! *Hello-o-o! Hubbar-r-r-rd!*"

Lizzie jerks awake from her nap.

"Is this what I pay you for?" asks Gil, looming over her.

"You don't pay me," Lizzie reminds him. "The studio does."

"Hmpf!" he says, watching as she straightens herself out. "I tried calling you, but I kept getting the after-hours voice-mail."

"Oh, I'll have to check with the phone company," says Lizzie, furtively switching the telephone back on.

"Hubbard, you'll never guess who I bumped into at lunch this afternoon."

"You're right; I won't."

"Killian Louth. Himself. He was meeting with his editor. Did you know he was writing a children's book?"

"Who isn't? What's it called? *Goodnight, Moonshine*? *The Little Lap Dancer That Could*?"

"I don't know, Hubbard. I told him all about *Split Second* and he wants to read it."

"I thought you were trying to spring Christian Rydell from the hoosegow?"

"That's a lost cause, Hubbard. He's too much of an insurance risk at this point. But imagine if we can get Killian Louth attached!"

Lizzie imagines it, and doesn't like it one bit.

"He doesn't want to wait for his agent to send it from L.A., so messenger a copy up to the Gansevoort immediately."

"Gil, you know just as well as I do that Killian Louth is not going to read it this week if it's not a formal offer."

"Hmpf! You are such a defeatist, Hubbard. Do you know what happens to defeatists? They get defeated. He said he wants to read the script this week, so we send it this week," he decrees. "Did I get any calls while I was out?"

"Yes, Nick Inkersham called."

"Who?"

"The guy who wrote *The Way*? Remember? The 'brilliant' script Laszlo Baranszky submitted?"

"Oh, yes, yes." Gil says, his interest now squarely focused on replacing the difficult and messy Rydell with the difficult and messy, but bankable, Louth. "Call him back and tell him we're not interested in pursuing the project further."

"You told him to come in for a pitch meeting!"

"Then take him out for a meeting. But drinks, not lunch. Maybe you should just have him up here for coffee."

"I am not listening to this guy's pitches over drinks, lunch, or coffee! His screenplay destroyed whole parts of my brain that will never be regenerated!"

"Fine, then handle it however you see fit, Hubbard. You know it all," he says, waddling into his office. "Did Van Allen call?"

"No, unfortunately," Lizzie groans, and grimaces at the reminder of yet another happy ending that was all just a dream.

Establish a teeming midtown sidewalk, the tired, the poor, the huddled masses yearning to get to their jobs on time. Zoom in on Nick, lost in the dense pack, as he clumsily struggles against the tide of bodies and ducks into a Starbucks. He catches his breath and cases the busy room. He is up to something.

Nick grabs a choice seat near an electrical outlet, then extracts an empty Starbucks cup from his backpack and places it on the table in front of him, along with his laptop and notebooks. He can't afford the coffee here, but he can't resist the free electricity or the view of the street. This has been his routine for the last two days, since he decided that the YMCA just isn't conducive to creativity or worth the few precious borrowed dollars he has left. Instead, he has been stealing bits of sleep in subways and city parks whenever he can, working at Starbucks for as long as he can, and taking in New York's nonstop urban miracles in between.

Ever since he can remember, Nick has imagined his professional deliverance happening in the blandly even 70s cop show light of the Southern California sun. He never expected to meet his glory in these sooty, shadowy canyons, but he finds working in the New York Public Library, coffee shops and all-night diners truly inspiring. Even without money, the city is thrilling and wondrous to Nick, and he finds all that raw life force thrumming in the streets wildly contagious. He already has some ideas for rewriting *The Way* and expanding its sequels, and he has been honing some new pitches, too. He knows that someday he will look back on this escapade fondly as just another part of those romantic, penniless days full of youthful hope and great expectations.

If only Gil Gorman or his development person would return Nick's calls, everything would be perfect. Nick has called four times now, but the only person who ever seems to be in that office is the standoffish receptionist with the strange, breathy voice. He wonders why someone with such a telephone manner would get into that particular line of work, and just who would hire her in the first place.

An acne-faced barista steps from behind the counter to

clear some tables. Nick takes a "sip" from his "coffee," laying it on thick with an appreciative "ahhhh," but it's lost on the kid who shambles by morosely, his spine bowing under the burden of a chronic post-adolescent low-grade funk. Nick wishes he could comfort this poor kid, tell him that surely there are better days ahead, that he won't be a barista forever, and whatever is troubling him now will surely reverse itself; but mostly, Nick doesn't want to blow his cover.

Nick decides to give Gil Gorman another day, and somehow he knows in his gut that his patience will be rewarded. Maybe it's the overwhelming sense of possibility that the city has transfused into him, but since getting Gil's call, Nick has renewed faith in the universe and his fellow man and he has never felt more sure of himself in his life. He just has to keep his eye trained on the bright horizon, he coaches himself, as he cracks his knuckles, sips some invisible house blend, and starts plucking away at his keyboard.

Conventional wisdom says that you should dress for the job that you want, but how should you dress for the job that you don't want? Wearing a splurge-bought Donna Karan suit accessorized with a bag she scored at Daffy's and a pair of Havaianas that Iago brought back from his last trip home, Lizzie is entertaining this conundrum as she flip-flops into another D-Girl cocktail meeting.

When Lizzie first started working for Gil, these get-togethers used to happen monthly. As the New York development scene has constricted, along with the D-Girls' enthusiasm for their jobs, they have become quarterly affairs.

There is even talk of downgrading them to annual events, or doing away with them entirely. Lizzie is not only in favor of this motion, she is the driving force behind it.

At their usual booth in the back of a dim hotel bar in midtown, Lizzie finds her regular gaggle of D-Girl irregulars, along with their token D-Boy, Ryan Chang. He runs the development office of Yearround Spring, a company owned by a well-respected character actor turned well-respected independent producer.

"Hi, guys. Sorry to be late," says Lizzie. "What did I miss?"

"Ryan was just doing good news/bad news," says Judy.

"Well Jenna-Five isn't here so I already know the good news. Hold off on the bad till I get a drink."

"I already ordered one for you," says Stephanie Greene.

After managing a string of see-and-be-seen downtown lounges, Stephanie was hired by fashion designer Raul Sant'angelo (nee Marvin Krongelb) to develop a splashy, exclusive boutique property in Manhattan where he could create an entire Sant'angelo mise-en-scène. Tricky zoning laws and a capricious change of heart seized him mid-project, however, and he decided to pursue a sideline in the "liveliest art" instead. The cognoscenti gave his production company two years to live, but Stephanie, who was suddenly thrust into the movie business, has defied them all by keeping it afloat for five, thanks to her hard work and Raul's couture, ready-to-wear, perfume and home products lines.

Stephanie finds Raul the ideal boss, as he is almost always in Paris, Milan, Miami, Buzios or Lago di Como, leaving her plenty of time to tend to her own robust social life. Like so many veterans of the food and beverage business, Stephanie is a positively athletic drinker, one seemingly immune to hangovers and even drunkenness.

"God bless you," Lizzie says, as the waiter sets a chunky glass of whiskey in front of her. Lizzie sips, then takes a moment to let the warm current mix into her bloodstream. "Okay, Ryan, I'm ready."

Ryan takes a fortifying breath. "Well, the bad news is that Yearround's string of critically acclaimed productions has finally caught up with it. The office will be closing at the end of the month," he announces sadly.

"Oh, no," says Judy.

"Goddamn it!" says Stephanie.

"Why, why, why?" cries Lizzie. "Why can't it be me?"

"I'm sorry, Lizzie," says Ryan, a dying man graciously comforting his death-bed mourner. "I know how much you wanted this for yourself."

"Oh, no. I'm sorry, Ryan. It's selfish of me," Lizzie admits. "I know how much you actually like your job."

"Wow," says Stephanie. "Maybe it's time for all of us to move to L.A."

In a rare moment of silence, four dedicated New Yorkers try to imagine themselves living in Los Angeles, each one wondering if her, or his, driver's license might still be valid.

"This business," says Judy, as they all reach for their drinks in perfect synchronization and swig heartily.

"Sorry I'm late," coos Jenna Wahl, suddenly standing at the table. The former Miss Delaware runner-up looks too pert, as always, her face makeup-counter fresh and her hair tight as a gasket. "I got tied up with a new draft of *Contents Under Pressure*. Russell asked for a rewrite. You know how it is."

In fact, they don't know how it is to have a box office titan like Russell Crowe dictating your life and lending your job some semblance of security, and they all just stare at her blankly.

A creative kleptomaniac and professional ingrate, Jenna was once Lizzie's reader, but when she landed a plum story editor's job at Don Flynn's company, she took Gil's pet project to Flynn, along with her letters of recommendation. For her severe hairdo, her varnished skin, her coat-hanger shoulders, her cyborgian sangfroid, and her heartless ambition, she is known by the other D-Girls, none too affectionately, as Jenna-5.

"I was just telling everyone that Yearround Spring is closing at the end of the month," says Ryan, breaking the ice.

"Mmmm," Jenna mewls, scrunching up her brow with condescening pity. She stands there waiting for them to make room for her. Convinced that she's not going away, they all shift over a bit, and Jenna takes a seat.

"Well, something will open up," says Judy, already calculating some way that she can help Ryan. "It was another strong year at the box office, so more work and money might flow back East. I'll start making some calls for you tomorrow, hon."

"Thanks, Judy, that's really kind, but I'm going to take care of the baby full-time. We can afford it. It just involves some belt-tightening," he rationalizes. "My kid is never going to be one year old again and frankly I'd rather spend time with him than in some insane development job."

"I'll drink to that," says Stephanie, raising her glass in a toast. "Now all I have to do is find a kid who'll put up with me for sixty, seventy hours a week."

They laugh and clink.

"Your wife doesn't mind being the breadwinner?" asks Jenna-5.

"Why should she?" says Ryan.

"Oh, no reason. I guess I'm just old-fashioned," she says as she turns to the waiter, standing ready to take her order. "I will have an Appletini," she informs his belt buckle, imperiously.

"Amateur," Lizzie sniffs.

"Hm?" says Jenna, challenging Lizzie with a chilly smile.

"Oh, she was just talking about this screenwriter who's been hounding her," says Judy, thinking on her feet. "A real amateur."

"That's too bad, Lizzie. I just have my assistant handle pests like that," Jenna tells her former boss and the person who gave her the first break she ever had, knowing full well that Lizzie has been working without an assistant for over a year.

"So," says Lizzie, slamming her drink on the table a bit too hard. "Has anyone given any more thought to cutting these wing-dings down to once a year?"

Barely touching her drink, Jenna-5 cuts out of the cocktail hour early, carefully complaining about a "whole day of meetings" ahead of her. After she leaves, the D-Girl get-together takes on the mood of an Irish wake, raucous and melancholy all at once.

The next morning, Lizzie is awakened by the sound of someone rapping hard on a steel pipe before she realizes that it is coming from inside her whiskey-logged skull. She considers calling in sick, but even Lizzie is too conscientious for that, believing that hangovers aren't actually an illness, just dues.

When Lizzie arrives at work, Gil seizes her as soon as she's in the door and orders her to confirm his afternoon appointments. Emboldened by Killian Louth's "interest" in *Split Second,* Gil has set up a series of meetings to capitalize on this morsel of promise. For the fourth day in a row, he has also refused to take Nick Inkersham's calls, insisting that Lizzie handle the situation. She has been just as adamant in her refusal to be his hatchet woman, and they are now locked in a standoff.

At noon, Gil charges out for his first meeting and the office goes quiet as a chapel. It would be the perfect time for Lizzie to work on her screenplay, or her résumé, if only her head didn't ache so. Instead, she draws the shades, switches the phone into Do Not Disturb mode, and crawls onto her beloved sofa. It feels incredibly good just to close her eyes and shut out the glaring, blaring world, and it occurs to Lizzie that the sofa might be the one thing she will actually miss about this job, once she is finally free of it.

The door buzzer shatters the calm, and Lizzie suddenly remembers that Iago is due for a pickup. She groans as she gets up to buzz him in, then she slouches out to the reception area to meet him. In the lobby, however, she is surprised by a tall, unshaven, unkempt stranger with dirty hair and a mad glint in his eyes.

Cue the sound of slashing, stinging strings, as Lizzie's life flashes by in a series of a rapid cuts: her first trike; the tap shoes she loved more than tapping itself; her pet goldfish whirling counterclockwise down the toilet bowl; her first bra that itched so much; her first kiss; her first hickey; the SATs; college; her first orgasm; all of it—right up to last night's mini-binge. Lizzie doesn't know exactly how she wants to die, but she is certain that it's not at the hands of some crazy-looking ragbag in this utilitarian office with all of its glum associations.

"Hi, I'm Nick Inkersham," says the intruder, dropping a battered duffel bag to the floor and offering her a handshake. "Are you Elizabeth Hubbard?"

"More or less," she says, heaving a sigh of relief and shaking his hand. She collapses into a chair and massages her aching temples.

"I'm not sure if you got my messages, but I've been calling like crazy. The receptionist said you weren't available, so I'm sorry if I'm interrupting your work. You're probably working on some big project, or hammering out a deal, or something."

Lizzie would roll her eyes at this, but it would hurt too much.

"Mr. Gorman told me to set up a pitch meeting with you after he read my script. *The Way*? Maybe you haven't even read it yet, but he called and was really excited about it, and I'm excited, too," says Nick, overstating the obvious.

"It's very nice to meet you, Nick, but Gil isn't here and you should really speak to *him* about your submission."

"But he told me to talk to *you* about the pitch meeting."

"He's a very busy man," she lies. "Sometimes he gets confused, and I'm much too hungov . . . up . . . hung up . . . on this deal . . . that I'm . . . hammering out."

Nick looks at her, detecting a familiar note in her voice. "So, where's the receptionist I've been talking to all week?" he wonders. "I was hoping to meet her in person and thank her for her patience."

Lizzie turns to look at the empty receptionist desk. "She had an appointment. With her podiatrist. Weak feet. A congenital thing," says Lizzie, unable to resist the ever increasing velocity of her own lies.

"Okay, then maybe I should wait for Mr. Gorman to clear this up because I came a long way for this meeting and I'm sure that he said to speak—"

"You can't."

"I can't?"

"Shouldn't. You shouldn't do that," she says. "There's really no telling when he'll be back in the office, and his schedule is booked solid."

Lizzie knows that if Nick is still here when Gil gets back, he will order her into a meeting with Nick on the spot. This will cut into her recovery time and another cherished weekend, and no doubt result in her reading more scripts and hearing more pitches that nobody has any intention of ever producing.

"That's okay. I don't have anywhere to be and I brought some work with me," Nick says, readily producing a laptop from his bag, as well as a fraying folder overstuffed with papers. "Is there an outlet? My battery's low."

Lizzie looks at Nick, with his baggy-assed pants and his beat-up sneakers and his built-not-to-last luggage. Feeling a powerful surge of pity, she tries a new approach.

"Listen, Nick, I really don't want you to waste your time. We're always interested in finding new writers," she says, trotting out some standard, uninspired pass-speak. "I'd love to hear about whatever you're working on. Just write up your pitches one paragraph each and have your agent send them to me."

"I don't have an agent, but I have a friend who interned for this lawyer, Laszlo Baranszky—"

"But he's a criminal defense attorney. You really should find an agent."

"But I have some stuff I can give you right now, or I'd be glad to make some pitches. I've got three. I practiced all week and timed myself. They're twenty minutes each," he says with great pride.

"I'm sorry. I just don't have the—"

"C'mon, three pitches in an hour. It's a bargain, right? What's an hour?"

"A lot," says Lizzie, losing patience.

"Okay, but you haven't even read my script."

"Yes, I have."

"Oh," says Nick, pulled up short. "You have?"

"Yes, and based on your submission, Nick, I really don't think you're what Gil is looking for."

"Then why would Gil say that he liked it?"

"Who knows why producers say anything? But trust me, Nick, you don't want to get caught up in Gil Gorman's desperation."

"Why would he be desperate? He produced *Four Englishwom*—"

"Because he's a movie producer! Their lives are lived in shades of desperation and his is very dark right now. So dark, he just picked your script off the top of a pile, called you to say he liked it, then asked me to read it."

Despite the countless tales of venality and mendacity that color the history of the movie business, no one trying to break into it ever really believes that it is as corrupt or as absurd or as maddeningly illogical as it really can be. All too often the uninitiated take this version of the business as heavily embroidered legend spun by people who are in the habit and business of spinning legends, and Lizzie watches as Nick's first hard lesson in Filmmaking 101 sets in.

"So, what did *you* think of my script?" he braves.

"Honestly, Nick? I think that screenwriting is a bad habit undertaken by too many insecure writers who believe that it will be faster and easier and more profitable than writing books."

"That's so cynical."

"It's cynicism based on life experience."

"So you don't think *The Way* would make a good movie?"

"Since you're pressing the issue, I have to tell you that I don't think *The Way* would make a good movie, if it could even be made at all, which it can't, so the point is moot."

"Well, what would you do to make it better?"

"I would put it aside, Nick, and I would go back to She-boygan—"

"Madison."

"Okay, Madison, and I would find an honest, bearable nine-to-five job that left me with enough time and energy to write stories that are personal, and mine, and not blueprints for some crazy producer or some soulless corporate machine or some hambone actor to ruin. Maybe you could be a park ranger. That seems like a fairly low-impact job to me. Or library science? Have you considered that?"

Nick has heard enough. "Okay, well, thanks for reading the script," he says, snapping his laptop closed and collecting his things. "And thanks for that guidance counseling session, too. I'll have plenty of time to count those pearls of wisdom on my way back to Sheboygan!"

The door slams shut behind him and Lizzie winces, then slumps in the chair. She knows that in situations like this one, you've got to be cruel to be kind. It's much more merciful to tell a writer the truth rather than humor him when it is obvious that he doesn't have the talent or the cunning to succeed in the movie business. She figures that she has just saved Nick a decade, if not a lifetime, of frustration and heartbreak. Still, it takes a lot out of her and she feels a bit guilty for having been so harsh with him.

Lizzie wonders how she ever got this way when she too

was once just a kid who came to the big city with nothing but a laptop and a dream. Working in such a culture of ferocity is bound to make you ferocious, she tells herself, but it's no comfort whatsoever.

Lizzie makes her way back to her office, and the door buzzer sounds again. Of course, someone like Nick Inkersham isn't going to go away this easily.

"Great," she says, pressing the door release. "Now he really is going to kill me." But Lizzie feels that the least she can do is hear him out. She steels herself for the inevitable comeuppance, but before she is even out of her seat, Iago is standing in the doorway, glistening and panting and beaming at her.

"Iago," she says, clearing her desk with a grand sweep of her arm. "Just the man I wanted to see."

4

THE NEXT MORNING, LIZZIE ARRIVES AT WORK EARLY
and finds the light already shining out of Gil's office,
an unwelcoming sign that the mania driving him all week
has built to a Friday pitch.

"Hubbard, I'll talk to Nick Inkersham," he proclaims.

"Good morning to you, too," says Lizzie, leaning in his
doorway. "And you don't have to worry about it; I already
passed on his script."

"And who told you to do that?"

"You did."

"Well that was unwise of you, Hubbard. You were in on
that call. You know that Van Allen admires the hell out of
that project, and I'll have you know that he called me last
night. Directly. On my cell phone. To inquire about it."

Six, or perhaps even five years ago, the younger, greener
Lizzie might have found this bit of news utterly mystifying,
and even exasperating. But she has become so inured to the
whiplashing twists of the movie business that she barely

even blinks. The only thing that does truly surprise her about this development is that the chronically helpless and hopelessly low-tech Gil was able to take the call from Van Allen without anyone's assistance.

"Rewrite your coverage immediately. And I want nothing less than euphoria and ecstasy from you in this report. Hosannahs, Hubbard! Hosannahs *and* hallelujahs," he rants. "And get Nick Inkersham on the line before he takes his project elsewhere."

"I really don't think you have to worry about that," Lizzie says with a roll of her eyes as she trudges back to her office.

Lizzie spends the rest of the morning muttering obscenities under her breath and rewriting her coverage on *The Way,* hyping up its "potential" as much as she can without sounding totally insane. It is a very delicate balancing act indeed, and in a perverse way, Lizzie is actually proud of her ability to pull it off, like a slick politician expertly managing to spin his way out of an economic depression or the inadvertent launching of World War III. Every five minutes or so, Gil barges into her office to check on her progress. Even when she's finished, she tells him that she has got pages to go, just to watch him suffer.

Meanwhile, Lizzie tries to hunt down Nick. She calls the Wisconsin number from the title page of his script, but she reaches a surly café cashier who says Nick owes her nine dollars. She puts a call in to Laszlo Baranszky's office, but his secretary knows nothing about the script at all. The secretary promises to try on her end "as soon as Laszlo is back from St. Tropez," which Lizzie understands as an efficient, diplomatic way of informing her that her request is very low priority indeed and she shouldn't hold her breath waiting. Lizzie reviews her phone logs from the previous week, but after reaching a cranky operator at the West Side Y and a remarkably helpful pedestrian at a pay phone on the corner of 46th and Ninth, the trail goes cold.

Lizzie waits until lunchtime to deliver this bad news—along with her strenuously bowdlerized coverage—to Gil. Food is the one thing that Gil loves as much as work, and Lizzie knows that feeding time is the only time of day when he is even remotely tame and approachable. Just after noon she finds him at his desk ravaging a meatball sandwich, right on schedule, and she places her report prominently in front of him.

Gil peers at her over his glasses, his face bloated with meatballs and distrust as he carefully, elegantly wipes his hands with a napkin.

"Hmpf," he says, when she tells him that at least for now, Nick Inkersham cannot be found.

"Everybody can be found," he declares, scrutinizing her comments, dabbing at the corners of his mouth, and emitting little burps and grunts of contentment as he reads along. "Now get out of my office, Hubbard," Gil grumbles without realizing that Lizzie has already left the room.

The only thing more humiliating than having some arrogant low-level development person tell you that your script is worthless, is having to catch a bus from the Port Authority Terminal afterward. That's where Nick and his traumatized ego have spent the worst night of his life, dodging security guards, panhandlers, and a mixed assortment of suspicious lurkers who narrow their eyes at him like hungry cats.

When his bus arrives the following morning, Nick takes his place with all the other passengers fleeing the city for reasons no doubt as discouraging and humbling as his, but despite his misery, he isn't appreciating the company at all. Corralled together in a poorly defined line, they all squeeze through the gate and into the cavernous garage where the noxious bus fumes add nauseating insult to their injuries.

Nick reels from the smell and staggers up to board the bus. The baggage handler grabs hold of his duffel bag, but Nick can't let it go.

"Yo, is this a tug-of-war or something?" the man wants to know.

Nick is barely aware of him. Instead, he is looking at the fleet of buses lined up to shuttle the crushed and defeated armies of would-be actors and writers and artists and models and dancers and designers back to the hinterlands, where they can all readjust their perspectives and aim their sights lower.

Okay, so maybe I'm not the best writer in the world, Nick thinks to himself, *but how dare that woman say those things to me! How dare she patronize me the way she did! And how dare that producer lead me on!*

"They're not going to get away with it!" he blurts.

"Huh?" says the baggage handler, as Nick yanks the bag away from him, turns around, and struggles against the crush of jostling, clamoring bodies. Their lofty creative pursuits and dreams of fame and glory already forgotten, they would be happy now just to score seats as far from the toilet as possible.

Cut to Nick now, as he battles a ferocious elevator that has his duffel bag locked in its colossal jaws.

"Hold it! Hold it!" says an anxious-looking fat man racing down the hall.

Tugging his bag free, Nick stumbles backward as the doors close.

"Damn it!" says the fat man, stomping his foot like a spoiled child.

It takes a moment for Nick to recognize Gil Gorman in the flesh, as the producer has gained so much of it since his last Oscar appearance ten years ago.

"Gil Gorman, I've been trying to reach you all week."

"You have?" says Gil, unpleasantly surprised and wary of the unkempt, unshaven vagabond standing before him.

"Yes, I'm Nick Inkersham, and I'd—"

"Nick Inkersham! Nick, Nick, Nick! Well, I would like to have a word with you, too, my friend!" says Gil, reflexively slipping into his unctuous producer persona. "Let's go back to my office. Here, let me help you with that," he says, graciously lifting Nick's leaden duffel bag and instantly regretting it. He leads Nick into the office and past the reception area, talking all the time and overwhelming him with a cataract of compliments.

Lizzie is just getting ready to leave for the weekend, admiring her neat-as-a-pin, nearly bare desktop, when Gil stops at her door, showing off Nick like a proud parent.

"Hubbard, look who I found!"

"Well, lucky you," she drawls.

"I believe you've met my associate, Elizabeth Hubbard."

"Yes, that's what I wanted to talk to you about," says Nick, who has been thrown off his purpose by all the talk and the kowtowing.

"Yes, great idea. Let's talk. Would you like something to drink, Nick? Hubbard, why don't you bring us some coffee?"

"Because of a little thing called feminism, that's why," she says, channeling Eve Arden.

Gil forces out a laugh that's much too jolly as he nudges Nick into his office and kicks the door closed behind him.

Not at all fond of surprises, Lizzie always likes to know what is happening, so that she might better predict what *could* happen. This isn't usually difficult working on the other side of a cracker-thin wall from someone as habitually loud as Gil, but whenever he closes his door and brings his voice down to a more human volume, it makes Lizzie nervous to the point of paranoia. She scampers out into the hallway, wondering how much a stethoscope costs and where she might purchase one.

Intercut between Gil, in game mode, and Lizzie, the outsider, with her ear pressed to his office door.

"I can't begin to tell you how much we love your writing," Gil gushes at Nick, and Lizzie rolls her eyes.

"You do?" says Nick.

"Oh yes, it's just so fresh . . . and wild . . . and just . . . just . . ."

"Who's we?" Nick wonders.

"Oh, all of us. Garth Van Allen is really interested in you. You do know who he is?"

"I've heard of him," says Nick, who recalls the name from somewhere high on *Premiere*'s annual power list. "But if everybody liked my script so much, how come you're passing on it?"

"Who's passing?" Gil says, miffed at the very injustice of such a thing.

"Well, your development person said just yesterday—"

"Oh, never mind her," Gil says, swatting at the air. Then, lowering his voice to a conspiratorial stage whisper, which is the closest to a real whisper he ever comes, Gil leans across his desk and says, "Frankly, I think she needs her dosage adjusted."

"Oh!" yelps Lizzie, like Doris Day in *Pillow Talk*.

Nick reacts, but Gil ignores her.

"Psychiatrists will just prescribe these drugs to anyone," he carries on. "I'm telling you, it's harder to get a MetroCard. It really is a national epidemic. But she's very hard working and she's been with me a long time, and I'm nothing if not loyal."

Seething, Lizzie gives the door a good hard kick. Nick flinches, but Gil powers on. "I want you know that, Nick. I stick by my talent and I fight for my talent. Ask anyone I've ever worked with."

"Well, I appreciate that, but I don't think your associate is as crazy about my script as you are."

"Nonsense, Nick. Listen to this," Gil says, as he proceeds to read from Lizzie's fresh, made-to-order coverage. " 'The script shows real promise. . . . an inventive imagination . . . truly original storytelling, daring even . . . characters no audience has ever seen before . . . given the state of current cinema, there could be a wide audience for this material.' "

Lizzie flinches at the sound of her own carefully spun lies. It is too much for her to take, so she stomps back to her office, slamming the door behind her.

"Could I get a look at that?" Nick asks Gil.

"Oh, well, you should know that coverage is a totally confidential thing. Normally I wouldn't let any writer look at a reader's report, but this one glows so brightly, you might want to put on your sunglasses," Gil says, handing the report over to Nick, who pores over Lizzie's comments.

"Well it also says that 'the premise needs some focusing,' and 'the characters tend toward the one-dimensional,' . . . and 'the cluttered plot requires some considerable restructuring,' " says Nick, reading Lizzie's dire prognosis.

"Minor points, minor points. That's just the reader being thorough, covering her ass, so to speak. Listen, I've been in the business now for twenty-five years and I've never seen a perfect shooting script, let alone a perfect submission. But you're missing the most important point, Nick. Read all the way down to the final word. Standing proudly there, all by itself, at the bottom. What does it say?"

" 'Consider'?"

"Exactly! That is the reader's recommendation, and let me tell you, Hubbard does not give out gold stars like some kindergarten teacher. She's tough stuff."

"Yeah, I learned that already."

"Oh, don't let her scare you. She's got a sharp editor's eye and a keen story sense and I think you're going to enjoy working with her. Here's what I'd like to do, Nick. I'd like to have Hubbard throw together some notes over the weekend and work with you to make this script better."

"I thought Garth Van Allen liked it already."

"He does. He loved the title and he called me personally to inquire about it. On my cell phone," Gil boasts with a misplaced pride that is totally lost on Nick. "But we all agree that it needs some work, Nick. You did a great job, but now it's time for all of us to put our egos aside and help the script become the best movie it can possibly be, like loving, selfless parents. In the end, it's what's best for everyone. You, me, the studio, the audience, the world really," Gil hyperbolizes, as he leads Nick back toward Lizzie's office.

Gil taps lightly on her door before opening it, showing Nick how considerate he can be. From her desk, Lizzie smirks at his performance.

"Hubbard, how does your Monday look?"

"Pretty bleak, all of a sudden. Why?"

"Nick would love to get your notes on his script. So why don't the two of you get together on Monday?"

"You're not going to be there?" Nick asks, concerned.

"Oh, no. Hubbard's the story person here, and she doesn't like me interfering."

"I'll make an exception this once," says Lizzie, knowing that Gil has no intention of reading the script before it's rewritten. "I'm sure that Nick would love to get your expert opinion on his script, too."

"Let's not overwhelm the poor man, Hubbard," Gil says through a smile so broad it looks painful. Then he turns to Nick and says, "So we'll see you on Monday, first thing."

"Eleven," shoots Lizzie.

"First thing at eleven," says Gil, finalizing the deal.

Not sure what just happened, but surely liking it, Nick gives Lizzie a cocky little grin and says, "I'll be looking forward to it."

Lizzie squeezes him a near-smile that tells him he shouldn't.

Janie Hubbard has been wringing her hands and sighing ever since Lizzie left home eleven years ago. A small, fretful woman, Janie has not set foot in New York since the 1964 World's Fair, when she was just a teenager. For Lizzie's college tour and subsequent graduation from NYU, Janie dispatched her infallibly obedient husband, Phil, a big, friendly dog of a man who loves the city almost as much as Janie fears and loathes it. Nevertheless, Janie considers herself a bit of an expert on New York, its people, its attractions, its excesses, and especially its dangers. Her idea of the city comes exclusively from gritty TV crime dramas, believe-it-or-not infotainment programs and Lizzie's weekly calls home, which Janie tends to distrust almost as much as those news reports of the city's ever-plummeting crime rates.

Over the years, Lizzie has learned to edit her phone calls to her parents, so as to avoid the inevitable reminder that she can come home anytime she's ready, as if she were merely at summer camp suffering through a stretch of bad weather. It doesn't matter that Janie and Phil sold Lizzie's childhood home in Ohio and moved to Arizona ten years ago, so that Phil could fulfill his lifelong dream of running his own motel. Janie indulged him, mostly for the warm weather and the low crime rate, but also because the motel, which needs constant attention, makes a convenient, inarguable excuse for not visiting Lizzie in New York.

Like so many other people who don't know the city first-hand, Janie also imagines that New Yorkers spend most of their free time at the Statue of Liberty, or taking in Broadway musicals; that is, when they aren't actually fleeing roving gangs of bloodthirsty, heavily armed evildoers. To justify residing in such a "treacherous" place and to avoid the one-way invites to a "home" where she in fact has never lived, Lizzie does nothing to disabuse her mother of the brighter part of this fantasy. In fact, she tends to feed it.

"So, have you seen any shows?" asks Janie, her voice thin with worry.

"Oh, yes, I'm on my way to a matinee right now," says Lizzie, as she enters the criminally overpriced dry cleaners on her corner.

"Oh, that's nice. What are you going to see?"

"Um . . . *The Lion King*," says Lizzie unimaginatively.

"Again?" says Janie with a laugh. "Well that must be a good one. I'd love to see it."

"Well, why don't you come to New York," says Lizzie, regressing to adolescent brattiness. "We can go together."

Janie launches a fleet of excuses, including the upcoming

motel inspection, then turns a bit bratty herself. "So, have you been dating?"

"Oh, lots, but nothing serious." Even Lizzie can't quite sell her office quickies with Iago as dates.

"Have you heard from Daniel?" Janie asks eagerly.

In her sophomore year of college, Lizzie informed her mother that she and Daniel were moving into a cramped studio apartment together. Janie, unlike many mothers, was greatly relieved, believing that Daniel would help to protect her daughter from the plunderers, marauders and latter-day Huns who she imagines terrorize the city's neighborhoods. When Lizzie and Daniel split up three years later, Janie was positively distraught, and she is more prone to wistfulness for Daniel than Lizzie is herself. An incurable romantic, Janie refuses to stop believing that someday Lizzie and Daniel will get back together, despite his wife, children and livestock.

"Uh, Mom, can we skip that topic for now?"

"Well, you don't sound very happy to me these days."

"I'm happy, forgodsake," Lizzie says, raising her voice through gritted teeth. "I'm going to see the damned *Lion King* for the eighth damned time."

The woman in line ahead of her moves her child away protectively, while outside a police siren wails.

"Oh, God, what's that?" says Janie, seized with panic. "Are you all right?"

"Yes, Mom, it's just some cops on their way to a donut sale."

"Oh," Janie says, not getting the joke and not entirely convinced either. "Well . . . how's work?"

"Busy. Working on a new project this weekend."

"Something interesting?"

"I'll say."

"What's it about?"

"It's sort of hard to describe."

"Oh. Well, have you met any stars?"

Janie is convinced that the only reason one would risk living in a "high crime" place like New York or L.A. is to see and meet celebrities. She loves to hear that Lizzie has been involved in meetings with famous actors, or at least breathed the same air at premieres and screenings.

"I saw Lauren Bacall at a screening last week," Lizzie says, relieved to be telling the truth.

"She's still alive? How did she look?"

"Good. Great."

"Oh, that's good. She must have an excellent plastic surgeon. We brag all the time to the guests about you."

Like almost everyone outside the movie business, Janie believes that Lizzie has a dream job, one that allows her to read for a living and attend screenings and premieres, and sometimes the after-parties. As scary as it all is, it also seems terribly glamorous to Janie, deep in her climate-controlled, culture starved, desert fortress. Lizzie doesn't have the heart to tell her mother that almost all the scripts she reads are mechanical and banal at best, that the screenings are just as poor and that her dream job feels like a waking nightmare. Nor does she mention that all the movie stars she has ever met, or observed, almost all seem like nervous, insecure people who have gotten into something that they only *thought* they wanted. Although she may be an adult, Lizzie is still Janie and Phil's daughter, and on some primal level she still wants to please them. She supposes that she always will. And what harm can it do to indulge her mother's sweet misconceptions if they make her so happy?

"So what fabulous things are you doing with the rest of your weekend?" Janie asks.

"Oh, y'know, *Phantom . . . Hairspray . . .* the Statue of Liberty . . . Central Park . . ."

"Oh, honey. I wish you wouldn't go to that park. You know that wilding thing the kids do really scares me."

Lizzie is about to debunk the idea that "wilding" is something kids have done anywhere in the world, but then she remembers that she has no honest intention of visiting the park this weekend anyway, and she knows there's no arguing with Janie when it comes to New York.

"The park is out, Mom. I'm deleting it from my calendar right now."

"Oh, good. Now here's your father."

"Thank you, thank you, thank you," Lizzie mouths to the heavens.

"You're welcome, you're welcome, you're welcome," says the clerk, handing over her dry cleaning.

Lizzie spends the rest of Saturday afternoon dissecting Nick's script, taking it apart bit by bit, trimming out subplots, extraneous characters, and long-winded speeches that could sedate even the most hypermanic audience members. She breaks only for a lunch of leftover Special Double Happiness and works until her eyes burn, her neck aches and her brow ties itself into a tight little knot. Still, there's at least another whole day of work on it.

When Daniel calls later, missing the city and eager for news of it, Lizzie indulges him all too readily. She glamorizes her weekend just as she did for Janie, lying about how much she loves her job, praising performances she has only read about in the newspapers and turning her nose up at "over-rated" exhibits she has not seen and restaurants she has not tried.

Daniel sighs wistfully. He goes on to tell Lizzie about the first signs of spring and the roar of the brook that rushes past his property. He gives her an update on the new writing studio he is building with his very own hands, and Lizzie feels her face get hot with covetousness, for the writing studio, not Daniel.

"We're so lucky to live in Vermont," he says, as he launches into an oral essay on the quotidian joys of family life and the simple, pastoral pleasures of the country writer. Mercifully for Lizzie, they are interrupted by the less than joyous wail of his enraged ten-month-old baby, and they promise to talk again, soon.

Feeling terrible for her lies and needing to confess, Lizzie calls Judy, who can't deny that this kind of behavior sounds like a primary symptom of the Sandy Dennis syndrome.

"If the job is making you this unhappy," Judy sighs, "maybe it really is time to quit, never mind the safety nets."

Cut to Lizzie, striking a circus pose in a tacky sequined costume high atop a trapeze pedestal. Somewhere down below, a crowd roars with encouragement. The trapeze comes swinging at Lizzie, who grabs it with gymnastic expertise. She goes flying out over the void, swooping and arcing and generally showing off, as another trapeze artist in a matching unitard comes sailing toward her. Lizzie finesses her release, spinning through the air and makes a grab for his wrists, but they're not there.

"Hey, what the . . ." Lizzie says, free falling toward a cold hard floor, which is racing up to meet her—

"Lizzie? Are you still there?" Judy asks.

"Oh, yeah, Judy. It's just that I've really gotten used to my weekly paycheck, and my regular medical checkups, and my paid vacations, and my sick days. I'm afraid that my struggling bohemian years are all behind me."

"Well, the least you can do is give yourself a break from your daily tortures," Judy says to her inconsolable sister in D-Girlhood. "And go to that day spa already!"

On Lizzie's last birthday, Judy and the other D-Girls gave her a very generous gift certificate to The Floating World, a sleek, fashionable Soho spa. It has been languishing in Lizzie's purse, out of sight and mind, ever since. Following Judy's orders, the next day Lizzie decides to cash it in. She books a massage appointment, then swelters in the sauna, trying to sweat out her anxiety. Still, she still can't keep her mind off her work, and she fidgets impatiently through a seaweed facial wrap.

Lizzie brings Nick's script with her into the lounge while she waits for her massage. She begins scribbling notes all over it, loudly ripping out whole pages until the cool, haughty receptionist gives her a disapproving look for upsetting the precious mood of the place.

"Oh, sorry," says Lizzie, whose apology is met with a placid smile full of hostility and the supercilious attitude of the New York service worker. So Lizzie just sits there, in silence, wondering how anyone can find this whole spa scene so relaxing.

"Mike will see you now," says the receptionist, after a brief eternity.

"Mike?" says Lizzie, surprised to hear a man's name.

"Oh, I'm sorry. Didn't you schedule a massage?" the receptionist says, pretending to search her schedule.

"Yes . . . I just thought . . . I assumed . . ."

"Hi, are you Lizzie?" asks a handsome man in a skin-tight T-shirt and linen drawstring trousers, looking as if he just stepped off the cover of a men's fitness magazine.

Lizzie stammers an awkward hello.

"I'm Mike Fontana," he says, giving her hand a warm squeeze. "Follow me."

"O-kay," says Lizzie, gathering her things.

Mike shows Lizzie into a small, dimly lit room furnished only with a massage table, an oil dispenser, and so many votive candles that Lizzie can't help wondering about the fire code violations. Mike is not concerned at all, and he motions Lizzie to hop up on the massage table.

Mike speaks with a slight Brooklyn accent, which makes him seem sweet and boyish, an eminently likable regular guy. Because he didn't come to the city to reinvent himself, he gives off none of the airs or pretensions of the typical transplant. New York is his by birthright, and Lizzie finds it refreshing.

"So," he says, smiling at her. "Tell me about your body."

Lizzie struggles for an answer. "My body? Well, what's there to tell? It's been with me ever since I can remember."

"I mean any injuries, aches, pains, tender spots I should know about?"

"Tender spots? Just a gift certificate that was about to expire."

Mike smiles again, and his blue eyes catch a twinkle from the candle glow.

"So this is the first time you've had a massage, huh? I can always tell."

"Busted," says Lizzie, putting up her hands in surrender.

"Well, relax. It's your lucky day."

After they have established that Lizzie's job is very stressful, involves too much reading, writing, and sitting, and is much more interesting than it sounds, Mike steps out so that Lizzie can undress, which at the moment means removing the excessively plush five-pound robe that the spa provides. She wraps herself in a sheet, per Mike's instructions, and lies down on the table, staring out through the odd little face hole and admiring the carefully chosen slate tiles.

After a gentle tapping on the door, Mike enters and dims the lights another notch. The slurpy noise of massage oil being pumped out of the dispenser breaks the mood for a moment, then Mike takes a couple of deep breaths. He peels the sheet down to the base of Lizzie's spine and begins to rub the oil into the flesh of her back. Lizzie instantly tenses.

"You might want to relax your arms by your side," he says.

Lizzie realizes that she is clutching onto the head of the table as if it were a life raft, and she lets go with an embarrassed "Hah!"

"Just let all your weight go," Mike says, while guiding her arms slowly down to her side. "Trust me. Let me move your limbs."

He talks her through some deep breaths, then begins massaging her shoulders and working his way down her back, using his arm like a rolling pin. At first, this feels supremely silly to Lizzie, then it feels supremely good. When Mike is finished with her back, he draws the sheet up to her neck. For a disappointed moment, Lizzie worries that the hour has already passed, until Mike peels the sheet back lengthwise, exposing the entire left side of her body.

Angle on Lizzie's eyes, widening at the sudden shock of cool air on her bare bottom.

"Are you warm enough?" Mike asks.

"Mm-hm," says Lizzie, trying to sound casual.

"You store a lot of tension here," says Mike, kneading her left buttock like a mound of dough.

For once in her life Lizzie is speechless, even when Mike begins digging into her gluteus maximus with the tip of his elbow. There is no denying, however, that he has a point, and suddenly an unexpected warm current courses through her body.

Mike performs the same routine on Lizzie's right side, then turns his attention to her toes, stretching each one individually and manipulating it in tiny circles. He moves on to her legs, which go limp under his command, and when he's finished, he lays each one down ever so gently.

By this point, Lizzie is adrift in a state somewhere between semi-consciousness and blissful idiocy. She is no longer aware of herself, her nakedness, or this ridiculously fit man having his way with some of the most obscure, private, and long-neglected parts of her anatomy. She doubts that any Sandy Dennis character anywhere has ever enjoyed such attentive, expert pampering.

Mike asks her to turn over slowly and he shifts his focus to Lizzie's arms and hands, squeezing and stretching each finger with a great love for detail, then rubbing the tender pad of flesh between her thumb and forefinger. He delicately lays each hand down at her side as if she were made of spun sugar, then makes his way up to her neck. He cradles her head in one hand, while his other hand battles the forces of tension that have been holding her neck hostage for years. With the tips of his fingers he rubs away at her temples and her eyebrows and her cheeks and tiny little tendons Lizzie never even knew existed, and they all surrender to him willingly.

Suddenly, in this dark, untroubled nether zone where she has been floating for the last hour, Lizzie feels something else that she has not felt in years—a warm single tear trickling from the corner of her right eye. It is soon followed by another, which races to her earlobe, and another, which steals the lead. Lizzie's face scrunches and reddens. Her throat catches, and in an instant, the toughest, hardest-working D-Girl in New York begins sobbing, full force.

"Oh," says Mike. "Is everything all right?"

"No, yes, I'm sorry," weeps Lizzie, jumping off the table and leaving her sheet behind. "That . . . that . . . wh-what you do," she hiccups through her tears and points at the massage table. "That is just great. It's the best thing that has happened to me in ages. How sad is that?"

"It's not sad at all. It happens sometimes that with the release of stored muscular tension comes the release of stored emotions. It's perfectly normal. You shouldn't be upset."

"I'm not upset," she says, obviously upset. "It's just that I . . . I hate my job and I hate my life and I broke up with this guy that I was in love with to pursue a career that never happened, and I haven't felt that way about anybody else since, and I don't think I ever will. I'm a sell-out and a fraud and . . . and an empty shell of a woman, and I think I have the Sandy Dennis syndrome. Do you know who Sandy Dennis was?"

"No," he says, handing her the sheet.

Lizzie blows her nose on it and tosses it to the floor. "Well, never mind," she says, now much more embarrassed by her tears than her nakedness and wishing that she had the kind of hair she could hide behind.

"I haven't cried in years and I don't know what's come over me. I'm so sorry. It's just that I feel like I'm turning into this hard, hopeless, pathetic person, and I'm not a hard, hopeless, pathetic person! Or at least I didn't start out that way. I came to New York so in love with the city and so inspired about movies and writing and so eager to write and meet new people and make an exciting life for myself. I used to have so much . . . love . . . inside me. Now look at me!"

Mike is in fact trying to maintain his professionalism and *not* look at her, but he finds Lizzie's emotional nakedness much too compelling to ignore.

"I don't know how to get out of this mess," she says. "And I think it's just . . . it's just . . ."

Suddenly, Lizzie realizes that Mike is crying, too.

"Oh. Oh, I'm so sorry," she says, wrapping herself up in the robe. "You see? I'm even depressing you."

"No, no," he sniffles. "I'm not depressed . . . I'm just moved. I know how hard it can be to change your life and find your way in the world. This is my seventeenth job."

"Wow," says Lizzie, drying her eyes.

"I've been a construction worker, a car mechanic, a day trader, a landscaper, but none of it satisfied me, so I started working as a paramedic, but I . . . I just couldn't handle all the suffering, y'know? I was so miserable until I started doing this, but I've finally found something that feels right, something that allows me to help people and connect with them, so the job satisfaction goes both ways.

"So many people live below their potential and we get stuck in these ruts and . . . you just want more out of life and out of your work."

"Thank you," says Lizzie, grateful for his understanding. "Thank you for getting it. And thank you for everything."

"It's okay," he says, turning a little shy. "You shouldn't feel bad."

"Well, it's very sweet of you," says Lizzie. "And it was very nice meeting you." She offers him a handshake, and they both laugh at the formality of it. They fall into an embrace instead and Mike hunkers over her, resting his head on her shoulder for a tender-hearted moment. It's a little boy's gesture, at once full of vulnerability, strength and unabashed tenderness, and the weight of his head feels uncommonly good to Lizzie.

They stay that way for several moments, holding on to each other tightly. As Mike releases his grip and pulls away, their cheeks brush against each other and they stop for an instant, nose to nose. Then, as if following some magnetic force, they kiss.

"Oh, I'm so sorry," Mike says, breaking the kiss. "I shouldn't have . . ."

"I know. Me too," says Lizzie, standing on her toes and stealing another kiss anyway, but Mike pulls away again.

"I just . . ."

"Shhhhh," she whispers, kissing him again and this time Mike doesn't resist.

Without breaking the kiss, he unties her robe and it spills to the floor like snowmelt. Lizzie pulls at the drawstring on his trousers, while he strips off his T-shirt. He lifts her up and carries her back to the table, neither one of them saying a word.

Somewhere in the back of her mind, Lizzie knows that what she is about to do is wrong, so she kicks the thought even further back, and listens to her body instead.

5

REPRISE THE DRIVING PERCUSSION OF LIZZIE'S NERVOUS heart and track with her as she makes her way up the center aisle of a drab basement function hall. The frame of her world trembles with hand-held shakiness as she passes by a blur of faces. The fluorescent lighting is much less overwhelming than the powerful beams of the Kodak Theatre's stage lights, though much less flattering, too. There are no dresses borrowed from the House of Cerutti, no orchestra, and no professional spokesmodels on this stage to greet Lizzie as she steps up to a cheap, office-supply podium. There is no internationally reknowned actress, either. Instead, Lizzie faces an audience of ordinary mortals, not at all the movie stars and moguls of her daydreams.

Pan the room to find Janie and Phil, looking proud and encouraging. Judy is there among the strangers, too, along with Stephanie, Ryan, Gil and even Jenna-5. Iago sits next to Daniel and his perfect country wife. Even Mike Fontana is there, oozing empathy, hunkiness and strength. Lizzie is especially surprised to see the Sandy Dennis character from across the hall. Lizzie has always assumed that her poor neighbor has no social life whatsoever, but there she sits, out on a weeknight, and twitching with expectation.

"Hello," Lizzie says tentatively into the microphone, and it squeals out a deafening complaint. Lizzie steps back, intimidated by it all.

"I can't do this," she says, turning away, but Mike is there to stop her. Gently, solicitously, he takes her by the shoulders and guides her back to the podium. He adjusts the microphone for her, and again Lizzie looks out over the crowd.

Whatever she is about to do, it is much more terrifying than winning any imaginary Oscars. She makes eye contact with Janie, who has summoned all her strength for this occasion and even ventured into the dark, dreaded city, and Phil gives Lizzie a nod of fatherly support.

"My name is Liz . . . Elizabeth . . . and . . ."

Lizzie's heart pounds louder and faster. Faster and louder. Much too loud, really, like the soundtrack of an Oliver Stone movie. She spots Judy, looking as calm and wise as ever, and Lizzie knows that what she is about to do must be the right thing to do.

"My name is Lizzie and I . . . I . . . Iamasexaddict!"

The heartbeat stops and the world goes silent.

Pan the room full of blank stares, past Janie and Phil and Judy and Stephanie and Ryan and Gil, and hold on Jenna-5, looking as stiff and icy as ever. Suddenly, she lets loose with a cackle full of heartless glee, like a poorly dubbed Roman extra in a vintage sword-and-sandal movie. Some of the strangers follow suit, and even Daniel can't resist a laugh. Iago and Mike give in, and soon the whole room is rocking and roaring with great peals of sadistic, mocking laughter.

"No! Wait!" Lizzie protests. "This isn't fair! Stop it!"

But the laughter only intensifies. It is insane laughter, replete with whoops and hollers and gasping oh-oh-ohs that beg for breath and mercy. Lizzie turns to Judy for help, but she finds her friend so racked with mirth that she is actually slapping her thigh. Lizzie searches out her parents, and finds Janie dabbing at her eyes, crying from the hilarity of it all, while Phil Hubbard is fighting a stitch of sweet, delirious pain.

"This isn't one of the damned Twelve Steps," Lizzie yells. "Knock it off! Stop it! Stop it, you insensitive bastards! I have a problem here!"

But the crowd only laughs harder.

"I said stop it! Stop!"

Smash cut to Lizzie, wild-haired and wild-eyed, screaming at the face of her alarm clock, which is screaming right back at her.

Travel with Lizzie as she arrives at work over two hours late. Full of white-hot determination, she storms into the reception area, startling Nick, who has been waiting for her.

"Oh, hi," he says, as he clumsily stands to greet her.

"Hello," says Lizzie, barely even looking at him. She charges down the hall, past her own office and straight into Gil's, right up to the edge of his desk.

"Hubbard, it's almost noon. Where the hell have you been?"

"Thinking."

"You've been thinking? Well, the phone has been ringing off the hook," he exaggerates. "And Nick has been waiting for you for an hour. I've been trying to reach you at home and on the cell phone, and let me remind you that I'm a busy man. Very busy. What, may I ask, have you been thinking about?"

"About my life and the mess that it has become."

"Well, Hubbard, it's not like it's hard to find a psychiatrist in this town."

"I don't need a psychiatrist, Gil. I need out. I'm giving my two-weeks' notice, as of today."

Suddenly thrown, Gil takes this in with a deep breath. It isn't like him to pause for thought, and now it's Lizzie who's thrown off a bit, but only for a moment.

"I'm running on fumes here, Gil, and I have been for years. This job is just eating me up and I don't like the person I'm becoming. To be honest with you, I never really wanted the job in the first place and I've been waiting for the company to fall apart just so I can collect some severance benefits. That's no reason to hold on to a job like this, Gil. You know it just as well as I do."

In full confession mode, Lizzie can't stop herself. She veers from the speech she has been practicing all morning and tells Gil that she is afraid of ending up on a daytime talk show panel about sex addicts, or even worse, like some lonely, nondescript Sandy Dennis character.

"Hubbard, what have sex addicts or Sandy Dennis got to do—"

"Let me finish!" Lizzie says, for once cutting him off. "Frankly, I think I still deserve a severance package, given my years of service, but of course that's entirely up to you, and your sense of fairness and decency. I do think that I have applied myself to the position professionally, for the most part, and I would at least expect a letter of recommendation before I go. If you want, I'll write it myself. I'll even return all of the office supplies."

"What office supplies?"

"Never mind."

Gil leans back in his chair and takes a long, hard look at her. Lizzie has nothing left to say and to her it feels like an ice age, or two, before he finally responds.

"Well, I appreciate your honesty, Hubbard, but I think you're being rash. Things are starting to pick up around here and I've presented you with a golden opportunity with Nick Inkersham's script."

Lizzie catches herself mid–eye roll. "You presented me with a diversionary tactic that is only going to end in disappointment for everyone involved, Gil. You know it. I know it. Let's not kid each other."

Gil studies her some more. "How did you get so cynical, Hubbard?"

"Working for you for six years?"

"Hmpf! I am many things, Hubbard, but I am not a cynic. I'm a believer. A true believer. I believe in the talent, I believe in the audience, I believe in the business."

This time Lizzie can't control herself, and she rolls her eyes with Gil's every thump of his flabby chest.

"I give everyone a chance, Hubbard. I gave you a chance, didn't I? Don't you know more about the movie business than when you walked in here with your smartypants coverage five years ago?"

"Six," she corrects him.

"Don't you see a whole lot more of what's up there on the screen? And what's behind the screen? Hmm? Didn't I teach you about the politics of the business, about taking a position and defending it? Didn't I teach you about prioritizing your contacts, about picking your fights carefully? You didn't learn that at NYU, kid. I gave you a chance when you were raw, and you've come a long way, Hubbard. I'll admit it. But the problem is you've become a snob."

"Oh, you flatter."

"And you're snide, too."

Lizzie bites her snide tongue.

"I know the company isn't doing as well as it was when you signed on," Gil understates shamelessly. "But if you'd lose some of that snobbery and that cynicism and that snide attitude and work with me a little harder, I think we could score a hit. That's all it takes, Hubbard, just one hit."

"You've been saying that for years, Gil, and you know just as well as I do that this script is going nowhere."

"Not true. While you were *thinking,* Van Allen's assistant called to set up a meeting. He wants to hear Nick's pitch. In person. In L.A. And I've got a meeting with Killian Louth set up, too. He wants to talk about *Split Second. Killian Louth,* Hubbard. We've still got a chance with both projects."

"Well," says Lizzie, kicking herself for not anticipating this turn of events. "It all sounds very promising and I'm very happy for you. I appreciate the offer, and I'm sorry that I can't stick around to take advantage of the opportunity but—"

"You've been on board this long, Hubbard, why not have something to show for it. If you go in there, give Nick your notes, and work with him on the pitch and the studio buys this script, I'll guarantee you a bonus—ten percent of my gross from the project."

"You're kidding. He's impossible and his script isn't going anywhere and you know it."

"Fifteen," says Gil.

"Oh, please. I wasn't born yester—"

"Think about it, Hubbard. That's all I'm saying. The pitch is due next week."

Lizzie does think about it, and suddenly, she sees an opening and a way to guarantee her severance terms.

"Twenty," she blurts. "And if it doesn't go forward, I want to be released with six months' severance and a one-year extension on my health insurance."

"Fine, Hubbard, but you won't need it. That's how confident I am of this project."

Lizzie is much less confident. When Van Allen passes on the project, as surely he will, Gil's housekeeping deal will expire along with it. If Lizzie can hang on for just two more weeks, she stands to enjoy a much more comfortable transition to freedom.

"And I want it in writing," she demands.

This catches Gil off-guard. "Don't you trust me, Hubbard? After all these years?"

Lizzie squares her shoulders and gives him a stony look, Faye Dunaway playing Joan Crawford standing up to the suits on the Pepsi-Cola board. She is many divas strong, and none of them trust him.

"Okay," Gil says. "I'll talk to my attorney right now."

Lizzie picks up the phone and begins dialing the number for him. It occurs to her that she has seen movies made from ancient sacred texts, long-canceled TV shows, amusement park rides, psychology case studies and some of the world's least favorite board games. She wouldn't be surprised if someone forced a movie out of a matchbook cover, a piece of bathroom graffitti, or Nick Inkersham's script, so she stops dialing.

"And I want a screen credit," she adds, just in case.

"Fine. You're my associate producer."

"Co-producer," she says, punching the final digit and handing him the receiver.

"Sharp, Hubbard. Very sharp."

"Sorry if I smell a little . . . European backpacker," says Nick, who is sitting on the sofa in Lizzie's office.

"Hm?" says a distracted Lizzie, wondering how she ended up here, at her desk, half-listening to this desperate no-talent defend the most outlandish points of his doomed screenplay when just this morning she was more determined than ever to free herself of exactly this kind of punishing absurdity.

"I've been sleeping in the park and showering at the Y, but I haven't had a chance to get there today," Nick explains. "So I'm probably a little ripe."

"Oh," says Lizzie, not knowing what else to say to this peculiar revelation. She reminds herself that there are only two more weeks until this farce plays itself out, Nick's script hits the wall of studio disapproval and she can finally collect all of the severance benefits she has been longing for. In the meantime, she is obliged to whip his story into some sort of presentable shape, surely the most challenging editorial task she has ever faced.

The day is almost done now, down to just a few more minutes, and she has overwhelmed Nick with notes. He has resisted every one of them, and Lizzie is thoroughly depleted. Nick, however, seems to have a limitless amount of energy when it comes to his own messy plot.

"So I was thinking, instead of using subtitles, maybe I should have Zontoc translate the Eruditians' dialogue," says Nick. "I can make him the interpreter."

Lizzie removes her eyeglasses, and methodically folds the arms, first the left, then the right, as Nick awaits her reply to his latest "fix." She sets the glasses carefully on her desk and looks straight into his eyes. She means this gesture to be intimidating, and it is.

"That would lead to an awful lot of exposition," she says gravely. "In general, movie audiences don't like to be talked to. They like to *watch* movie stars, preferably good-looking ones, talking to *each other*. But not too much. Why don't we think about eliminating Zontoc and the Eruditians altogether?"

"But Zontoc's key to the story. He's like Obi-Wan Kenobi."

"I thought we agreed an hour ago that realism was the

best of the many approaches you seem to have chosen," she says, her voice fraying with impatience. "Having a society of mole people with alien superpowers living underneath New York detracts from the reality of the story."

"Okay. I'll think about changing it, but it would involve some serious rewriting."

"Well, you know the old saying: 'Writing is rewriting.' Especially in the movie business."

"Noted," he bristles. "So, could you walk me through your notes on the second act one more time."

"It's nine o'clock and it seems to me that you've got plenty to keep you busy on act one," Lizzie says, as she begins to clear her desk. "I'm beat."

"Yeah, so am I," says Nick, tugging a fleece blanket out of his backpack.

Lizzie watches as he spreads it over her sofa, taking great pains to tuck the blanket under the cushions.

"Um, what are you doing?" she asks.

"Oh, I like my blanket to be tucked in nice and tight so when I go to bed it's like slipping myself into an envelope."

"Do you?" she says, watching as he plucks one of her zigzaggy hairs from the pillow before he gives it a good fluffing. "You aren't really intending to spend the night in my office, are you? I don't think Gil would approve."

"Oh, it was his idea," Nick says, unlacing his sneakers. Since I don't have anywhere to stay and we're going to be working together anyway, he thought it would be best for me to crash here. He's such a cool guy."

Lizzie rolls her eyes.

* * *

Three hours later, Nick is swaddled in his "envelope," listening to the nighttime traffic swish by and admiring the after-hours film noir shadows the streetlights are casting on the walls. It is the first time in days that he has had a properly cushioned surface to call his bed and he should be exhausted after that ego-bruising note session, but still, he can't get to sleep.

He keeps replaying the events of the past week over and over in his head, and it all amazes him. He jumps up and makes a note reminding himself to thank Tad again for passing his material on to that lawyer. Maybe he'll send Tad a gift from L.A. That ought to surprise him and let him know that there are no hard feelings about Didi.

This entire experience would seem like a dream to Nick, if only Lizzie weren't so difficult and condescending. *What a tough little nutcracker she is,* he thinks, crawling back into bed. *And yet, she must know something. Why else would someone as smart and successful as Gil Gorman be working with her?* Nick is determined to win her over, and he springs up again from the sofa and turns on the light.

Angle on Nick's notepad, an abstract study of chaos itself in runny blue ink. He looks over the notes he made during the afternoon's inquisition. Above the doodled renderings of the aliens Lizzie killed off so heartlessly are the words *Captains Courageous,* followed by a parade of question marks.

"Ohhhh," Nick says, suddenly enlightened and scratching his new whiskers. Wearing just his underpants and a threadbare T-shirt, he cracks his knuckles and sits down at Lizzie's desk.

Meanwhile, on the other side of the East River, Lizzie lies in bed counting the subway trains rumbling beneath her building. She should also be exhausted after that interminable note session today, but still she can't sleep.

Greatly relieved that she has finally told Gil how unhappy she is in her job, she's proud of the way she handled herself in negotiating her exit. There is finally daylight at the end of this long, dark night. Even Judy thinks she's doing the right thing. Lizzie should be happy, and she would be, if only she didn't have to spend her final days with that stubborn amateur, Nick Inkersham. She wonders how she's ever going to get through it.

She jumps up and rifles through her purse, relieved to find the phone number for The Floating World in her address book, and she suddenly remembers to breathe, deeply.

The next morning, Lizzie arrives at her office to find Nick parked at her desk. He is still in his underwear, maniacally tapping away at his laptop.

"Don't get up for me," she says.

"Oh, sorry sorry sorry," he says, jiggling immodestly over to his backpack, its entrails spilling out across the floor.

"I've been working all night on a new outline. That *Captains Courageous* note you gave me opened the floodgates! I've decided to make the hero a younger kid," he raves, pulling a pair of baggy cargo pants on over his boxer shorts. "Like a . . . a . . . prep school gangsta, y'know? And instead of making

Zontoc an alien, I'm going to have him be a junkie, but like a junkie who has gone underground. Literally. He'll go to any lengths to stay away from the stuff; that's how bad his addiction is. So the movie can have an anti-drug message. And the alien—I mean the ex-junkie—is the leader of this whole society of clean-living former addicts who live underground with the rats and the garbage and stuff. I like the irony of that, don't you? And this spoiled, snotty Upper East Side kid, who affects this whole tough urban pose, 'knowwhatimsayin'? Well, he'll have to grow up, learn some tough life lessons, as the junkie leads him on this adventure through the secret world under the city. So it's still sort of a fantastic world, but it's one that's not entirely impossible. No aliens, or anything. Oh, and I'm gonna change Zontoc's name, too. Maybe you can help me with that," he says, finally running out of air.

"How about Chad," she deadpans.

"I was thinking of something more classically heroic," he says, sniffing yesterday's shirt.

"Hercules."

"Hercules. I like it," Nick says cheerfully, buttoning up the shirt. "I'm going to the Y to grab a shower. Can I get you anything while I'm out?"

"Just some of that heroin that Chad—I mean Hercules—isn't using."

Nick laughs; Lizzie doesn't.

He hoists his backpack and heads out, as she kicks one of his dirty socks out of the way and curses herself for giving him any good ideas. *That has got to stop,* she tells herself, as she goes about putting her desk back in order.

Moments later, Gil is standing in her doorway wearing his deranged morning look. "Where's Nick?" he demands.

"You mean my new roommate? You just missed him."

"Don't give me that, Hubbard. He's not in your way; he's only sleeping here at night."

"Funny you didn't offer your sofa."

"Well I thought yours must be more comfortable, since you spend so much time sleeping on it."

"He has gone to the Y to clean up," says Lizzie. "And where's that contract laying out my severance terms?"

"My attorney is faxing it over today. But you're not going to need it, Hubbard. This story's a winner. Next week you're going to be my new co-producer. How's it coming?" he asks nervously.

"As well as can be expected."

"I want updates daily," he booms, while blowing into his office.

"Masochist," Lizzie mutters.

"I heard that, Hubbard!"

Nick returns later looking as fresh and as hopeful as a crocus in the frost. Lizzie has looked over his new outline and she grudgingly admits that he has done a fairly commendable job rethinking his premise and focusing his first act. He actually paid some attention and applied her notes. She is almost discouraged by the improvements, but she knows that a writer as raw as Nick won't have such an easy time of it in the dreaded second act. After all, some of the most crafty screenwriters in the business have lost their second homes, their first wives, and even their minds to their bedeviling and notoriously untamable second acts.

Of course, Lizzie knows that she could merely sabotage the project altogether just to get it off her desk. Despite her situation and her sincere desire to see this deal fail, and fail fast, a deeply ingrained work ethic and a good faith clause she has just signed her name to won't allow her merely to phone it in.

Instead, she throws everything she's got at Nick and his story, challenging him on every plot hole, character inconsistency and cliché she can find. As the week wears on, she grinds down his enthusiasm with her persnickety dramaturgy and he wears down her patience with his boundless energy and stubbornness. Just to get the most elementary points across, Lizzie has to get tough with him, not her normal tough, but Ida-Lupino-as-a-prison-warden tough.

For his part, Nick has to endure the tough love speeches that he supposes are meant to wise him up, but as he sees them, really just belie Lizzie's arrogant and jaded view of the world. It seems that there's nothing he can do to please her impossibly high standards, yet the more she challenges him, the harder he tries.

But even Nick has his breaking point. "Well, why don't you just write it yourself," he finally snaps, after three days of Lizzie's abuse.

She reminds him that she is not being paid like a screenwriter.

"Well, neither am I!"

"Not yet," says Lizzie sharply.

By Thursday, Nick and Lizzie have thoroughly exhausted each other, like a pair of perfectly matched prize fighters. Nick's enthusiasm, confidence and inspiration has been drained away, and for Lizzie, the dissonance of having to develop a story she knows is doomed and wants to see fail has become too much for her to bear.

Lizzie is enormously relieved when the increasingly antsy Gil sends Nick out to buy some presentable clothes to wear for the impending pitch. Finally getting the office to herself and not caring whether she is or isn't a sex addict, Lizzie pages Iago and sets up an afternoon tryst in the script library. She blesses the age of telecommunications, then heads out for a lunch meeting with an intense up-and-coming agent, a young woman fresh from a tour of duty in the Israeli army. Perfect training for the movie business, thinks lame duck Lizzie, who is still Gil's representative and must at least pretend to be interested in the young agent's bottom-of-the-barrel, over-hyped pitches.

While Lizzie suffers through a salty lunch and the agent's hard sell, Nick returns to the office, eager to impress her with his new suit. When the door buzzer rings, he hits the button.

"Sorry to be late," says Iago, who stops short in the doorway and wonders why there's a strange, half-naked man buckling up his pants in Lizzie's office.

"Oh, you can just leave the package on her desk," says Nick. "Do I have to sign for something somewhere?"

Cut to Lizzie as she breezes out of the elevator with all the grace, elegance and bad timing of Miriam Hopkins in *Trouble in Paradise.* More in need of Iago than ever, she enters the office just in time to find him rushing past the reception desk.

"Oh, Iago! Thank! God!" she gushes. "I'm so sorry to keep you waiting."

"No problem," he says discreetly, then hurries past her as if he were a bicycle messenger with actual packages to deliver.

"But where—"

"Hey, whaddaya think?" hollers Nick, strutting out of Lizzie's office in his new suit. It's an odd shade of green. The crotch is halfway to his knees and the triple pleats are suspiciously pouchy, making him look like an unprofessional smuggler. He does a proud little twirl. The jacket features two vents cut so high that it flares straight out on both sides like a set of propellers threatening to carry him away. "I got a great deal on it!"

Lizzie sighs, and rolls her eyes. "Did you keep the receipt?"

While Nick returns the suit, Lizzie calls The Floating World and books another appointment with Mike Fontana.

"Back so soon?" the receptionist purrs when Lizzie checks in later, and Lizzie wonders just how much she knows.

Mike gives nothing away, however, when he comes to meet her in the waiting room, but as soon as they're in the massage room, he locks the door behind him.

"Look," he whispers. "I'm sorry about the last time. It was totally unprofessional. I don't know what came over me. I swear I've never done it before."

"I've never done it before either," says Lizzie, kicking off her flip-flops. "But I need to do it again."

"What? I'm not a prostitute, you know."

"Good," she says, untying her robe. "Because that would make me just another cheap trick."

"Oh, no, you're not . . . I didn't mean . . . But I could get fired."

"Not if we're very, very quiet," she says, finding his drawstring and leading him toward the massage table.

Lizzie finds that having to be totally quiet during sex only intensifies her enjoyment of it. Even though Mike seems to have enjoyed it too, he apologizes again while getting dressed.

"Don't speak," Lizzie half-jokes, doing Dianne Wiest in *Bullets Over Broadway,* but Mike obviously didn't see the movie.

"I would really appreciate it if you'd call me personally, next time," he says, scribbling his number on the back of his business card. "If there's going to be a next time. No pressure."

"Good," she says, tucking the card into her robe pocket. "I just don't think I could stand any more pressure this week."

"So, don't I get a tip?" Mike asks, moving in for a good-bye kiss.

"I thought you said you weren't a prostitute," Lizzie says, kissing his naughty grin away.

"Mmm," he says, kissing her again. "Yeah, I guess I'm just a slut."

"Then there's a pair of us," she says, returning his kiss.

"You are something else," says Mike, tearing himself away from her.

"Hey," says Lizzie. "You want a tip?"

Mike stops at the door.

"Tuck your shirt in."

After a long hot shower, Lizzie feels contented, powerful, and just a bit wicked, like Patricia Neal in *Breakfast at Tiffany's*. Sandy Dennis never played *this* scene, she thinks later as she pays the receptionist, who suggests a punch card for frequent visitors.

"Ten massages in a year earns you a free one," says the receptionist, helpfully.

"Fancy that," says Lizzie, still a little high as she sashays off to the elevator.

On the ride down, she looks at the card Mike gave her. She doesn't know if she'll ever call him again, as this will surely be her last week on the job and her budget is about to shrink considerably. Besides, getting personal might ruin the thrill. Still, it's a powerful therapy he offers and Lizzie is not taking any chances. She tucks his card into her wallet, in case of emergency.

"Yup, I'm a sex addict," she says to herself as she glides past the seasoned Manhattan doorman, who has, finally, heard it all.

Lizzie drifts into work the next morning feeling calm, limber, and refreshed, until she finds Nick still in his underwear and a diorama of papers, coffee cups and take-out containers spread across her desk.

"Well," she says. "I guess we know who wears the pants around here."

"Oh, sorry," Nick grumbles, grabbing his trusty, ink-stained cargo pants off the floor and climbing into them. "And don't worry. This'll all be over as soon as Gil hears the pitch. I was up all night trying to rework the second act. I'm just going around in circles."

Lizzie knows this is very likely true, and for a moment she feels a stab of sympathy for poor Nick. Then she remembers how much she has riding on his script's failure. "Well, you just go in there today and give him what you've got," she says.

"But there's no love angle, no climax, and the second act is a blob, just like you said it was yesterday."

"I said it was a blob?"

"You said it was 'blobby.' "

"Good morning!" Gil trumpets, stampeding past Lizzie's office. "Is that pitch ready? I can't wait to hear it!"

Nick groans and sinks onto the sofa. He grabs a pillow and curls himself around it.

"Oh now, Nick, it's not that bad," Lizzie says unconvincingly. "You'll do fine."

"When can I hear that pitch, Hubbard?" Gil badgers. "I'm waiting! I've got a meeting at noon!"

Lizzie bounds into his office, closing the door behind her. Nick can hear her and Gil bickering like an unhappily married couple. It builds to an alarming pitch and there's some dull thumping, followed by a crashing sound. Nick jumps up, ready to intervene, but Lizzie enters looking unfazed and in her most professional voice says, "Gil is ready for your pitch now."

Slouching into Gil's office, Nick apologizes for the pitch before he has even started. He stammers and stutters and sweats his way through the plot, circling back here and there, patching up forgotten pieces and even improvising a few new sequences that only add to the confusion. This goes on for an hour, as Gil leans back in his chair and studies a nonspecific spot on the wall.

Lizzie feels sorry for poor Nick, who really has worked terribly hard on his story. After all, it's not his fault if his talent is limited and he has been used so badly by Gil to buy himself some time. Occasionally, she jumps in to keep Nick on track, but it doesn't help. The pitch is still a rambling mess, and Nick is a bad storyteller off the page, as well as on. He doesn't really finish his story; he merely trails off, offering several possible endings to his dark, subterranean, coming-of-age, urban adventure, none of them very satisfying.

After an awkward, stomach-turning pause, Gil says "Is that it?"

Nick nods, full of shame.

Gil rights his chair and looks at Nick, holding his gaze for an unnaturally long beat. Nick shrugs a little.

"Good job," Gil says flatly. "Excellent job."

Nick is stunned, and Lizzie is suspicious.

"However, I'd like to see a love interest. No one's going to make a movie without a love interest," Gil continues. "And I don't like any of your endings. I'd like to see the young hero battle—and conquer—his nemesis in the end. Who wants to see a story where some cops we don't even know suddenly come in at the end and save the day? Let's see a genuine mano a mano conflict. Audiences love that sort of thing. And let's work on tightening that second act."

Nick turns to Lizzie, who is too busy trying to figure out Gil's position to gloat, even though she has been making these exact points all week long.

"That's what Lizzie said, but—"

"And she's right, dammit!" Gil roars, startling Nick. "Now go back in there and do it!"

Nick hops to and scrambles out, with Lizzie following.

"Not you, Hubbard!"

She does an about face, and Gil motions for her to close the door and approach his desk. Go to a tight two-shot as Lizzie leans in close to his large, round head.

"That was the worst pitch I've ever heard," he whispers, pressing at a knot in his fleshy brow.

"That's what I've been telling you."

"Make him change it, Hubbard. Make it work. You signed a contract saying you would do so. *In good faith.*"

"There's nothing in that contract about performing miracles," she whispers back through her teeth.

"Hmpf! Don't be funny, Hubbard. I don't care if Van Allen passes on Monday, but I need you to make the damn thing presentable at least. I can't afford to look like an ass in front of Van Allen, and neither can you."

"I'm not so worried about it since I'm not going to be in front of Van Allen."

"Yes, you are. I want you to book a seat on Nick's flight and join us in L.A."

"L.A.?" she protests, as if it were the outer reaches of Kamchatka.

"That's right. Book a room for yourself at his hotel. No, don't book a separate room. I want you to stick to him like a birthmark. Maybe the hotel will provide a cot."

"Oh, do you think?" says Lizzie, batting her eyes sweetly, like Mary Pickford in *Sunshine Sue*.

"I want you to work with him all weekend on that story, Hubbard, and make him slow down and organize the damn thing. And forgodsake make him put in a love interest! What the hell have you been doing all week?"

Lizzie rolls her eyes and marches out.

While Lizzie makes her hotel and flight arrangements from the reception desk, Nick attacks the rewrite in her office. When she returns, she's surprised to find him on all fours laying out a whole new second act with index cards spread across the floor. It's as if his ego had not taken a battering at all. Indeed, Nick has been thoroughly re-energized by Gil's comments. Lizzie watches as he mutters to himself, moving the pieces of his plot around here and there, like a puzzle. Nick is like that amazingly resilient guy at the high school dance who always gets rejected, yet never stops asking. Lizzie marvels at this spirit, this enthusiasm, this willfulness, this unstoppable sense of dedication; it's something she hasn't felt in ages.

"Oh," he says, finally noticing her standing there. "Whaddaya think if I introduce, like, some sort of orphan who grew up underground as a love interest for the kid? She can be his guide, sort of like . . . like a Sacajawea of the subway tunnels."

"I think it's a good idea," says Lizzie. "But she should be an unreliable guide and lead him astray, like the kid in *Alice in the Cities*. In the final act, you can reveal that she has known the way out all along, but she hasn't told him."

"Early Wim Wenders! Excellent idea!" says Nick, writing "Sacajawea" and *"Alice in the Cities"* in red marker on a single sheet of paper. "But why would she do that?" he asks, taping the sign up on the wall.

Lizzie considers this for a moment. "Because she's lived underground all her life and she's never had a playmate her own age, and she likes toying with him. She needs a friend."

Nick looks at her as if she were a cinematic genius on the order of Eisenstein.

"Man you're good," he says, throwing himself on the sofa. "I'm so sorry I didn't listen to you and take your notes this week. I guess I can be a little precious about my ideas."

"You're not the first writer guilty of that crime," says Lizzie, granting absolution. "But you might be the first one who ever admitted it to a development executive."

Nick laughs. "I promise to be more cooperative," he says, crossing his heart on the wrong side of his chest.

"I don't," she says. "Now let's get to work. We have a long weekend ahead of us."

Nick works the rest of the day, incorporating the new character into his plot, while Lizzie ties up the week's loose ends, which include Iago. He is understanding, and tells her that he doesn't need to know anything about her relationships with other men.

"We don't own each other, Lizzie. We are neighboring solitudes," he says, quoting the book that is always in his messenger bag, Rilke's *Letters to a Young Poet*.

"Well, I'll let you know when the coast is clear, neighbor," flirts Lizzie.

"I can borrow from you, too, some sugar, my neighbor," he flirts back.

"My, my," says Lizzie. "Don't you just put the sin in syntax?"

Iago takes this as a compliment and slings his bag over his shoulder cockily. Lizzie admires the rear view of him as he struts out the door, then she goes about shutting down the office for the weekend.

When she checks in on Nick, Lizzie finds him dozing on her sofa and cuddling the pillow she once thought of as hers. Weeks of sporadic, restless sleep have finally caught up with him. He looks peaceful, with a childlike innocence that even Lizzie has to admit is sort of sweet. She feels sorry, knowing that he has invested so much energy in this futile exercise that Gil is putting them through and, for the first time, Lizzie feels guilty for her role in it. She moves to wake him up, but she can't bring herself to disturb his slumber. The least she can do is let him enjoy some well-earned rest.

Lizzie picks his blanket up off the floor and spreads it over him, then she tucks him into his "envelope" tightly, just the way he likes it. She dims the lights and tiptoes out, without catching Nick's contented little smile.

6

ESTABLISH A SILVER JET STREAKING RIGHT TO LEFT across the cold blue sky. Twin banners of vapor wave farewell to the east as the plane passes ghostlike through the clouds.

Inside, and much less poetically, Lizzie is crammed between Nick and the window and already missing New York. She has never really noticed how long Nick's frame is until now, as he shifts from one hip to another, extending his legs into the aisle then reeling them back in every time someone tries to pass. They seem like brand-new appendages he is trying out for the very first time.

The seat in front of Lizzie suddenly closes in just inches from her nose. The reclining passenger throws all of her weight into it, trying to steal an extra millimeter or two.

"Why can't people just sit up straight?" Lizzie carps. "What is she, an invertebrate?"

The passenger cranes her neck and shoots Lizzie a tough-luck look.

"Do you think I should name the girl Alice? Or is it giving too much away?" Nick asks, spreading his legs in an attempt to colonize some of Lizzie's precious leg room.

"Hey," she says, arching an eyebrow over her glasses. "This is how air rage starts."

"Sorry," he says, refolding his legs and twisting away from her, his bony hip digging into her right thigh.

None of this would bother Lizzie quite so much if she didn't know that Gil was up front in Business Class. The last time she saw him he was pinching a flute of bubbly between his pudgy fingers, a warm, scented hand towel still steaming on the little console at his side. "Updates. Updates," he squawked like a demented parrot, as Lizzie and Nick struggled past with their carry-ons.

Nick works on his pitch for the entire flight, and heedless of the seat belt prompts, Gil barges back to the cheap seats every ten minutes for progress reports. "How is everything?" he asks on his third run.

"I found the chicken less than inspired, the salad limp and let's face it, 2003 just wasn't a standout year for the Cabernet grape," says Lizzie, returning to her magazine.

"I wasn't talking to you, Hubbard."

The flight attendant comes along, gently reminding Gil that the captain has turned on the seat belt sign, but Gil ignores her.

"Well, Lizzie's had some great ideas," says Nick, trying to cut the tension. "And I'm incorporating the love interest and we're going to go over the entire thing word by word—"

"Sir!" shouts the flight attendant, not so gently this time. With her chest puffed out and with all the power vested in her by the FAA, she begins marching Gil back down the aisle.

"Hmpf!" he says over his shoulder.

"I *love* her," says Lizzie, slipping on a sleeping mask.

Two hours later, Nick is in awe at the endless sprawl of L.A. glittering below them. "Wow," he says, leaning over Lizzie to take in the view.

Lizzie peeks out from her mask. "The most impressive thing about it?" she says. "Every single one of those lights represents a hair salon."

After scoring a sporty red Miata from the car rental desk, Lizzie and Nick check into their "junior suite" at a mid-range West Hollywood hotel where they do, thoughtfully, supply a rollaway cot. Lizzie calls dibs on the queen-size bed, but Nick suggests they should alternate. After all, he argues, it is his script they're pitching.

"If the pitch goes well, you can have the bed tomorrow night," she says, secure in the knowledge that the bed is now hers, and hers alone.

When Lizzie wakes up the next day, Nick is more riled than ever and already practicing his pitch. He launches into it without even a "good morning."

"Oh, please," says Lizzie, scuffling into the bathroom. "Let's at least order room service."

Over breakfast, he tells Lizzie the story for the hundreth time. She can no longer tell if it's good or bad, and if it is bad, where it needs work. Instead, she orders him into the shower, where he actually pitches an alternate version of the second act through the curtain while Lizzie yawns and rolls her eyes.

Gil calls several times inquiring about the pitch, and Nick gives him an earful of it over the phone. On Gil's third call, he decides that he prefers the second version, so that's the one they're going with, and Nick hands the phone over to Lizzie.

"What is he wearing, Hubbard?"

Lizzie peeks into the bathroom, where Nick is shaving and pitching to his reflection.

"A towel."

"A towel! Well, get some clothes on him! He can't wear a towel to a meeting with Garth Van Allen!"

Gil is chattering away like a cartoon chipmunk as Lizzie hangs up the phone. She grabs Nick's cargo pants and tosses them at him.

"Let's go!" she says. "Fast!"

While Nick fumbles into his clothes, she calls the valet for their rental car.

"Where are we going?" Nick asks later in Beverly Hills, where Lizzie scores some plum on-street parking.

"Follow me," she commands, leading him into one of those hair salons they saw from the sky.

"Shouldn't we be working on the pitch?"

"We are," she says, as she approaches a rocker-slinky hairdresser in painfully pegged pants. "Are you available for a walk-in appointment?"

"Oh, yeah," he says, marveling at Lizzie's wondrous mop.

"Not for me. For him," she says, indicating a sheepish-looking Nick.

"Too bad," says the hairdresser. "I love a challenge. What are we doing?"

"He has a pitch meeting with a VP this afternoon," says Lizzie.

"TV, movies or music?"

"Movies."

"Indie or major?"

"Major."

"Oo-oo-oo-oo," the hairdresser says with a shiver. "So, stylish and effortless, but not too slick or outrageous? And we want to accentuate youth, right?"

"Exactly," says Lizzie, sitting down with a fashion magazine as heavy as a cinder block.

As the stylist fusses over him, Nick continuously mutters his pitch, trying out new phrases, toying with synonyms and shuffling scenes about. The stylist works around him expertly, and even offers a note, here and there. He totally ignores Nick's protests when he uses a big "girly" clip on him and later, as hanks of hair fall to the floor. He rearranges Nick's ordinary, tousled, dirty hair into an extraordinary version of tousled, dirty hair.

When the stylist is finally finished, for the first time all day, Nick is thrown from his pitch by the shock of his own reflection.

Looking over Nick's shoulder, the hairdresser says, "Hey, playah." He spins Nick around in his chair to show him off to Lizzie.

"I call it 'Finger on the Pulse,'" he says proudly. "What do you think?"

"You're a genius," says Lizzie, whipping out the company credit card.

* * *

Later, with Nick still pitching in her ear, Lizzie races back toward West Hollywood, just clearing a couple of red lights. Although she looks down on L.A. with typical New York chauvinism, Lizzie secretly enjoys navigating its clean, orderly streets and its peculiar folkways.

"Where are we going now?" Nick asks.

"We're going to get you some new clothes."

"I don't want new clothes. What's wrong with these?"

"Oh, look," dodges Lizzie. "There's the Academy. Pay attention."

"First we have to upgrade the car, then we have to upgrade my hair, now we have to upgrade my pants?"

"In Hollywood, image is everything."

"I'm a writer, not an actor, and who's even going to see the car?"

"Everyone's an actor in this town, and you never know who's going to see your car. That is exactly why you don't want to be caught dead in a Kia Rio by anybody. Not even the coroner."

"If that's the case, then why didn't we take the SUV the agent was pushing?"

"Because the codes here are very strict, like in high school. SUVs are for recording execs, pimps, nannies, trophy wives, young mothers and over-privileged teenagers. Unless you are a member of one of those groups, you have no business bombing around in an SUV," she lectures. "You upset the social order and it confuses everyone."

She turns into the parking lot at Fred Segal.

"I hate this place," Nick says, unbuckling his seat belt.

"Well you'd better learn to love it if you're going to be a screenwriter, Nick."

"If it's so essential, why don't you live here?"

"Acute ambivalence," she says, getting out of the car and handing the keys over to the valet.

"Can we trust that guy?" asks Nick.

"Of course not."

In Fred Segal, Lizzie entertains herself at Nick's expense, forcing him to try on some of the more outlandish ready-to-wear outfits she can pull off the rack.

"This is so much fun," she says to the clerk. "I feel just like Norma Desmond."

"Who's that?" asks the clueless, twenty-something saleswoman.

"You don't know?" says Lizzie. "You should go work in development for the studios."

"I have an interview on Wednesday," says the clerk, hopefully.

Nick looks ridiculous, and impatient, in a Versace party-boy get-up.

"Okay, okay," Lizzie says, and she finally gets serious with a smartly tailored pinstriped suit by Jil Sander.

When Nick emerges from the dressing room this time, Lizzie makes him turn. "Why, Nick Inkersham," she says, as lecherously as Anne Bancroft in *The Graduate*. "You have a profile."

Even Nick can't believe how good the suit looks and feels.

He squirms and wiggles a bit. "Yeah, but I don't think these pants are agreeing with my boxers," he says, and at a signal from Lizzie, the clerk runs to get a pair of proper European briefs.

Lizzie also orders up a pair of futuristic-looking Prada walking shoes, but decides that Nick's own beat-up All-Stars add just the soupçon of writerly rebellion the outfit demands and the local culture expects. When the clerk suggest a trendy trucker's cap to complete the look, Lizzie passes with a simple "Ugh."

While Nick panics about the dwindling time, Lizzie and the clerk strain to figure out why the Paul Smith shirt that looked so striking on the rack just isn't clicking. Angle on another clerk passing by with a batch of T-shirts on hangers.

"Wait. What's that? Stop," Lizzie commands.

She takes a French cut T-shirt from the top of the pile. It's a deep olive green and in the middle of the chest is the outline of the Buddha traced in hot pink. It's the sort of "authentic" street wear some young designer worked very hard at knocking off.

"We'll take two of these," says Lizzie.

"These tees ride a little high," warns the clerk.

"So do we," says Lizzie, snapping the company credit card down on the counter. "So do we."

To complete Nick's ensemble, Lizzie also selects a pair of retro D&G sunglasses that recall Marcello Mastroianni, circa 1964. They are so dark that when she treats Nick to lunch and some classic Hollywood atmosphere at Musso & Frank later, he has to feel his way to their booth. When the food comes, however, Nick is much too nervous to eat.

"Listen," says Lizzie, digging into her Caesar salad. "I know this is exciting for you, and you have a lot at stake, but don't sweat it too much. Take some pressure off. The truth is, every year millions of screenplays get written, and only a fraction get bought. Even fewer get made. The odds are against you. They're against all screenwriters. I don't want to set up false hopes, and I think you should try to relax a bit."

"Great, that's really helping me to relax."

"Nick, the important thing is, they'll know who you are, which is a huge advantage for you over the other ten million screenwriters scribbling away in the flyover states."

"I'll try to remember that, too. Can we go over the second act again?"

"Only if we do it over dessert."

When Lizzie and Nick blow into the studio lobby later, Gil is already waiting for them and agitated as usual.

"Where have you been, Hubbard? I've been calling you all day."

"Working. Doesn't Nick look great?"

Gil gives him the once-over. Nick does indeed looks stylish, handsome and very hip, and Gil decides to worry about the cost of this makeover later. "We were supposed to go over the pitch one more time, Hubbard."

"We did. And a lot more than once. You should have been there," says Lizzie, making straight for the receptionist. She rings for Andrea, the assistant's assistant, who in turn takes them back to meet Carol, Van Allen's actual assistant.

Carol is a career studio administrator, the rare employee who has no designs on moving vertically or laterally within the industry. Loyalty and stasis are her defining traits, along with a stiff ash blonde hairdo and an unflappable, easygoing manner. Given her position, she obviously has at least ten things she should be doing right this second, but she gives none of it away. Her entire professional career is a perfect Oscar performance.

"Hi guys," says Carol, like a folksy diner waitress. "Garth is just tying up a conference call. Can I get you something? Coffee, mineral water, green tea?"

"Green tea would be great," Gil blurts like a brown-nosing student with the right answer.

"Okay, feel free to play, or meditate," she says, indicating a Zen sand garden built into the center of the coffee table.

While Carol goes to prepare the tea, Lizzie and Gil snarl at each other and Nick trembles in a private little hell of his own flailing nerves. He picks up the little rake in the sand garden and realizes that he has no idea what to do with it. Despite Lizzie's advice, he can't help feeling that his entire future rides on his performance today. If he fails, it is straight from here to a life of caramel chai lattes and double decaf macchiatos.

"Okay, let's go in," says Carol, and she shows them through a set of grand doors.

Garth Van Allen's office is done up like a minimalist Zen temple, with much of the furniture "rescued" from an actual

Zen temple. The emptiness, however, is more intimidating than soothing.

Van Allen is an elegant, impeccably dressed man with steel blue eyes and close-cropped silver hair. He stands at a rough hewn wooden slab that used to be the temple door, now put to work as his desk. It holds nothing but a telephone and a Palm Pilot, and Lizzie looks around wondering where he keeps his Post-its and paper clips.

"Gil, so good to see you," Van Allen says too softly while shaking Gil's hand.

"You remember my associate, Elizabeth Hubbard," says Gil.

"Of course," Van Allen lies, grasping Lizzie's hand and looking directly into her eyes. He is obviously trying to "read her energy" or "transfer" some of his own, but all Lizzie gets in an ice cold chill.

"And this is the brilliant young Nick Inkersham," says Gil.

Van Allen switches his soulful beam to Nick, who freezes like a deer staring down a runaway truck. Lizzie regrets neglecting to warn him about Van Allen's "spiritual" side, but Van Allen catches the pink Buddha peeking out from Nick's jacket and smiles a smile full of counterfeit serenity.

"Interesting shirt," he says, testing to see if Nick is a fellow traveler.

"Oh, thanks," says Nick.

"Are you a Buddhist?" Van Allen asks, still holding Nick's gaze.

"Uh . . . well, I was raised Lutheran, but I like to think of myself as a pantheist, really."

"Mmmm," says Van Allen, savoring this profound information with a slow, mechanical nod. "I'm very eager to hear your pitch, Nick."

Suddenly, Carol draws a shoji screen that opens onto a large platfrom. In the center is the other door from the looted temple, balanced on three smooth rocks and set for tea. There are cushions scattered artfully on the tatami mat and a curtain of water flowing down a slate wall and shimmering like a sheet of cellophane.

"Come," Van Allen says, leading the way in stockinged feet.

Carol indicates that the others should also leave their shoes behind, and the three set to the tricky task of unlacing and unbuckling and unstrapping their footwear without falling down.

As they step up to the platform, Nick feels especially vulnerable with his big toe poking out of his left sock, the only item that wasn't part of his makeover. Gil's face goes crimson as he strains to lower himself onto a cushion. Lizzie has an easier time taking her seat next to Nick, but she wishes she'd worn pants and, once again, Nick's fidgeting, gangly legs seem to be trying to get away from him, fast.

"I'm sensing a little negative energy in the room, which can happen," Van Allen allows. "Let's all take a moment to clear it away together."

Van Allen closes his eyes and seizes three deep breaths. Gil, who knows the drill, follows suit. Nick looks to Lizzie, who just rolls her eyes. When everyone is sufficiently aerated and the bad energy has been vanquished, Van Allen pours the tea into four tiny cups.

"It's from the eighteenth century," he brags.

"The tea?" asks Nick.

"No, the pot," says Van Allen humorlessly.

Everyone sips, and with a little bow, Van Allen says, "Please, Nick."

Nick's pitch comes in a torrent of words, and Gil has to remind him to take his time. Van Allen suggests more deep breathing for Nick, who feels absurd and self-conscious doing it, but finds that it actually helps.

Nick starts over at a more reasonable pace, and soon Van Allen's eyelids begin to flutter with heaviness. By the the second act, he has lapsed into a trance and his eyes have closed altogether. Nick, however, has found the rhythm he has been rehearsing all day and he isn't stopping for anything. He has blocked out the distracting piddle of the indoor waterfall, the unyielding cushion beneath his ass, his implacable legs, the glare of his big toe, and even the weird studio honcho across from him. Giving up on Van Allen altogether, Nick pitches the story directly to Lizzie and Gil, instead.

Pan to Gil, who has one eye on Nick and the other on Van Allen. *This isn't so bad,* Gil thinks. *There's not much of a hook to sell, but the world of the story is really quite vivid. Two young up-and-comers might keep costs down and bring in the kids. The adult roles are colorful, too. They could attract some talented name actors to broaden the audience. Hackman would be good as the leader. Michael Caine loves to work, and he's such a pro. The sets are expensive, but not prohibitive, and there aren't too many special effects. I wonder what the hell Van Allen thinks . . .*

Pan to Van Allen, and hold on the whispering wind of

nothingness. Nick's pitch echoes unintelligibly somewhere in a distant void.

Now pan to Lizzie, who is hearing the reworked pitch in sequence for the first time. *Huh,* she thinks. *Is it me, or does this actually make sense? I can't tell anymore. I've got to get out of this business. He sure is dedicated; I'll give him that. But look at that toe! It's like a searchlight! Why didn't I think to buy him some new socks? Stupid, stupid, stupid, stupid . . .*

When Nick gets to the end, where the young lovers part, he suddenly improvises a coda, and for a moment Lizzie is worried.

Oh no. What's he doing? Here we go . . .

Nick pitches a flash-forward in which the underground orphan girl, now grown up, secretly watches over the former prep school gangsta as he goes about his happily-ever-after life playing with his kids in the park. It lends the plot's downbeat ending a poignant grace note.

Lizzie finds it smart and genuinely affecting. Van Allen, however, has either fallen into a deep slumber or achieved nirvana, and his eyes stay closed for an endless minute. Lizzie motions to Gil, who shrugs helplessly. She fakes a little cough, but Van Allen still doesn't respond, and Nick is crestfallen. For all of his hard work, his big opportunity finally comes along, and the studio executive falls asleep!

Slowly, Van Allen comes back from wherever he has been, until his eyes are fully open. He looks at Nick—or rather, into Nick's soul—as everyone waits for some reaction, some relief from the unbearable discomfort that follows even the best of pitches.

"Mmmm. Thank you for coming here today, Nick, and sharing your story," he says, like some touchy-feely daytime talk show host. "There's something there."

"My pleasure," says Nick, not knowing what to make of this cryptic comment. "I missed a bit of the subplot involving the social worker in the second act . . ."

Carol's shadow passes by the shoji screen, a subtle cue to her boss. Abruptly, Van Allen apologizes for having to run to his next meeting, but offers to let his guests stay and finish their tea. They decline graciously and Lizzie and Nick help Gil up from his cushion.

While they fumble into their shoes, Van Allen slinks out and Carol covers for him with breezy, efficient small talk. No mention is made of the pitch whatsoever. They merely exchange a round of standard, superficial good-byes with the assistants, in descending order, then head to the lobby with remnants of their Hollywood smiles still aching on their faces.

Nick is crushed as he slouches past the receptionist, feeling foolish and fraudulent in this slick, expensive suit and this hipster's haircut. A beacon of late afternoon sunlight blinds him as he exits the building and suddenly he finds himself locked in a tight embrace.

"Great job, Nick!" says Lizzie.

"Very well done, Nick! A bang-up job!" says Gil, grabbing him by the ears and kissing him straight on the lips.

Nick is staggered. "But he fell asleep!"

"He wasn't sleeping," says Gil. "That's just the way he listens. He always does that during a pitch. Never underestimate

Van Allen. He just seems like a flake. Sometimes I wonder if it's just an act he puts on to undermine the competition. I wouldn't put it past him, the shrewd bastard."

"But he didn't even say anything," whines Nick.

"He said 'There's something there,'" Gil boasts. "Did you hear that, Hubbard?"

"I heard it," she says, ringing her car keys merrily.

"I've never heard Van Allen say something like that after a pitch before," Gil marvels. "After we pitched *Night Equals Day,* he just drifted out of the room like a zombie."

"We were sitting there for forty-five minutes before Carol came back to tell us he'd left for a weekend retreat," Lizzie explains.

"But he made the movie anyway," says Gil. "And he got behind it one hundred percent. That's his M.O. He likes to play it close to the vest and think it over. No talk about the product. It might be some kind of Buddhist superstition, or something."

"So that went well?" asks Nick, still flummoxed.

"Swimmingly," says Gil. "And I liked that pantheist bit, Nick. That's thinking on your feet. Hubbard, call Carol and find out Van Allen's shirt size. Get him one of those T-shirts, but send it from Nick, not me."

"He's a large, and I already bought it."

"You're an ace, Hubbard," he says sincerely. "I bet you're glad you didn't quit now."

"You were going to quit?" asks Nick.

"The thought crossed my mind," says Lizzie, getting into the car.

"But she liked your script so much, she saw its promise and decided to stay on," says Gil, giving Lizzie a sly, smug smile.

"But she passed on my script."

"Before she reconsidered," Gil gloats. "The nice thing about Hubbard is that she's always willing to admit when she's wrong. Aren't you, Hubbard?"

Lizzie smirks at him.

"Wow, so just when you think you're out, they pull you back in," observes Nick, by way of Michael Corleone.

"Yes, and let it be a lesson to you," Lizzie says, finding Nick in her rearview mirror. "The only thing trickier than breaking into the movie business, is breaking out of it."

For the rest of the day, Nick is surprised as Lizzie and Gil continue to get along like an unhappily married couple, but an unhappily married couple who have suddenly remembered why they fell in love in the first place. Over dinner at Mr. Chow they entertain Nick, and each other, with their reminiscences, goading each other on, finishing each other's sentences, and filling in the overlooked—but vital—details.

There was the time that writer showed up for a pitch wearing just a bikini, her thigh still breaded with sand. There was the all-star *King Lear* adaptation that was nearly derailed by an "early costume malfunction" when the august—and freshly deceased—Shakespearean actor's left testicle made a surprise cameo appearance in the rushes. And there was that pitch about a team of young spelunkers who must save the president and the world by venturing into his urinary tract to destroy "the mother of all kidney stones."

"That actually sounds sort of cool," Nick says, and when they laugh at him, he laughs, too. He still doesn't know why they're so chummy all of a sudden, but it's a welcome change from their usual bickering.

"So, why was today's pitch good again?" Nick asks, biting into a fancy egg roll.

"Because Van Allen is a tough audience," says Gil, before turning to the waiter to order a bottle of champagne.

"Okay, but what's next?" asks Nick.

"We celebrate," says Gil, who has learned to savor even his smallest victories. He knows that there'll be plenty of time for moaning and groaning over the inevitable setbacks and defeats to come. "We've earned it."

"Hey," Nick says, looking past Lizzie's shoulder. "Isn't that Nicole Kidman? And George Clooney?"

Unfazed by celebrity, Lizzie opens her menu instead. "My favorite thing to read," she says, putting on her glasses.

Gil, on the other hand, is seriously fazed by celebrity and he gives the stars a hard-to-miss wave. When the room suddenly erupts in a disruptive crescendo, however, even Lizzie is forced to pay attention to the hubub.

"Hey, I think that's Killian Louth," says Nick.

"What? Where?" says Gil, waving before he has even spotted the Irish megastar.

Switch to slow motion and quote the theme from *The Good, the Bad, and the Ugly,* as Killian Louth, or "Special K" as he prefers it, makes his entrance. The sports-car-crashing, photographer-bashing, hotel-room-smashing, box office bad boy saunters past the maître d' as if to say, "who needs you."

He is flanked by his ever-present posse, or the "K-Lads," as the gossip columnists have dubbed them. Officially they're his bodyguards, but they're really just the childhood friends from the council flats that Killian has brought along for his wild ride with Hollywood fame. Indeed, the K-Lads tend to get their leader into much more trouble than he could ever find on his own. As usual, they're all got up like African-American gangstas, and they're traveling with one genuine African American, an actual professional bodyguard and ex-Marine named Dwayne who also dresses like a gangsta to lend them some "cred." It is all part of his contract, gleefully featured on the The Smoking Gun website.

They strut through the dining room, Killian peering over his sunglasses and casing out the other tables. He waves to Nicole Kidman and shoots George Clooney with an imaginary gun. They wave back, smile politely, and hope to God he doesn't join them.

"Killian!" Gil says, waving too enthusiastically and breaking the spaghetti western spell.

"Yo!" shouts Killian. "Double-G! 'Sup?"

"Wow, I thought he was taller," says Nick.

"Sh-sh-sh!" shoots Gil, as Killian bobs toward the table with well-rehearsed jive.

"Gil Gorman, these are my bloods," he says, indicating the K-Lads with a hip-hop gesture. Gil is forced to fumble his way through their elaborate and confusing signature handshake four times over.

"And these are my . . . bloods," Gil says, introducing Lizzie and Nick.

"Nice to meet you. Mind if I sit, lass," Killian says to Lizzie without waiting for her permission. The K-Lads surround the table, forming a human screen of denim and nylon, with 24k gold details. They take turns scoping the room like fidgety sentinals.

"These are the only lads in the world I can really trust," says Killian, his pretty, lilting brogue clashing with his American hoodlum masquerade. "You'll find no better. Loyalty and the old neighborhood, and all that."

The K-Lads let the waiter through with the champagne and eye him as he pours.

"Champagne, is it?" says Killian. "Garçon, let's have another go-round with the bubbly? On my bill. And some glasses for the lads, too."

"So, Killian, to what do we owe the honor?" Gil fawns.

"I need some diverson. A busy day of dubbing on *Manifest Destiny,*" says Killian, referring to his latest long-in-the-making action picture about a pioneer who must protect his family from a lost tribe of marooned alien explorers who feed on human flesh. When it made the rounds four years ago, the script was hyped as a "tribrid," part science fiction, part horror movie and part classic Western. The skyrocketing budget and trouble-plagued production have been rich fodder for the entertainment press.

"I can't wait to see it," says Gil, and Lizzie rolls her eyes behind her menu. "Did you get a chance to look at *Split Second*?"

"No, I'm a bit of a slow reader, m'afraid. It's the dyslexia," says Killian, fishing for pity.

"And yet you're writing a children's book," says Lizzie.

" 'Mazing, isn't it? That was all my manager's idea, really. He thought it would be a good P.R. move after the unpleasantness," says Killian, in an understated reference to a spate of public brawls he and the K-Lads have enjoyed much more than their victims.

"And how did you get tangled up with this lot, shorty?" Killian asks Lizzie's breasts.

"She's my development person," Gil says, before Lizzie can get snappy.

"And she's developed nicely, too," Killian says with a leer.

"And Nick is a talented young screenwriter," Gil interjects, preempting Lizzie again. "He just made a terrific pitch to Garth Van Allen."

"Well done, dawg," says Killian, sizing up Nick. "Is there a role for me in it?"

"Not really," says Nick.

"Of course there is," Gil corrects him. "Killian would be great for Hercules."

"But he's supposed to be an old man," Nick protests.

Gil kicks him under the table as Finbar, the most bored-looking K-Lad of all, leans in to murmur something in Killian's ear.

"Look, I'd love to hear more about it," Killian says. "But the lads don't trust the room tonight. Security risk. We're movin' on. Why don't you join us, Double-G, and tell me all about it."

"Of course! Yes, I'd be glad to," says Gil, obviously put out but feeling duty-bound to the opportunity and to the Hollywood rule that one never says "no" to a movie star.

The next thing Gil knows he is being squired out of the

room by three thugs posing as bodyguards, and one actual bodyguard posing as a thug, while one grossly overpaid and utterly corrupted actor turned movie star holds onto him in a physical expression of male affection most would call a head-lock.

"Goody," says Lizzie, yanking the champagne bottle from the ice bucket. "More for us."

"Wow," says Nick, watching them go.

"Wow," says Nick again, staring over the lights of the city from Mulholland Drive.

"Hooray for Hollywood," slurs Lizzie, who has had more than her share of the champagne. She joins him at the edge of a sharp drop-off. "Just think, kid. Someday this could all be yours."

"I don't think I could afford the electric bill."

"Don't worry. In California no one can afford the electric bill, and yet, the lights blaze on."

"Do you think Gil's going to be all right with those guys?"

"You mean 'Double G'? Don't let the doughy exterior fool you. The man is a piranha."

"Why do you work for Gil if you dislike him so much?"

"Who says I dislike him? He's like the overweight, over-bearing, impossible, irrational, violent gay uncle I never had."

"Gil is gay?"

"Gayer than the turn of the century."

"Does he have a lover?"

"Gil? Never."

"Hm. I wonder why."

"You do?" says Lizzie, amazed.

It has never occurred to her that anyone would wonder at the perpetually barren love life of an abrasive cur like Gil.

"God, you're good," she says, genuinely impressed. "You're a truly good person."

"Thanks," says Nick, genuinely flattered.

They stand there taking in the sweeping, sparkling view.

"It really can be a lovely place," says Lizzie. "From far away. In the dark. If you squint."

"So. You were wrong about me, weren't you?" says Nick, daring to feel triumphant.

"I *was* wrong, and I apologize for not seeing your utter goodness through your glaring flaws sooner," Lizzie backhands. "I'm disappointed in myself, frankly."

Nick smiles and shakes his head, knowing by now that there's no winning with Lizzie.

Suddenly Lizzie stumbles, and Nick grabs her around the waist. "Whoa, are you okay?"

"Of course I'm okay," says Lizzie, noticing the little flecks of gold in his green eyes for the first time and thinking that they're awfully pretty.

A Humvee full of teenage girls joyrides past and their headlights catch Lizzie and Nick in their apparent clinch.

"Whore!" shouts one of the blondes inside.

"Cheerleader!" Lizzie shouts after them, cracking herself up. She is having the most fun she's had in ages. "I guess I told her, didn't I?" she says, turning back to Nick.

"Yeah, but maybe we should go before they come back. I don't want to get beat up by a gang of girls."

"Ah, we can take them," Lizzie says, walking back to the edge. From Lizzie's privileged point of view the cityscape wavers and warps.

"Wait, what was that?" she says, grabbing hold of Nick's arm. "Did you see that?"

"What?"

"You didn't feel an earthquake, or anything?" she asks, looking a bit blanched.

"I didn't feel a thing."

"Nothing?" Lizzie peers at the city distrustfully and sways a bit, but Nick holds her steady again and she has to clutch onto his jacket just to keep the world still. She pats his pinstriped lapel gratefully.

"Now, my good man," she says, Maggie Smith mustering her bruised dignity in every movie in which her dignity suffers a bruise. "If you would be kind enough to drive me back to my hotel. If I can't throw up in style, I would at least like to do it in mid-range comfort."

7

CLOSE UP ON LIZZIE AS SHE GREETS THE NEXT MORNING with a pained grimace. She scowls at the stripes of California sun seeping in through the blinds. She tries to pull the blanket over her head, but she can't move her arm because she is restrained in a tight straightjacket. She wriggles and struggles against it, this way and that, like Olivia de Havilland in *The Snake Pit,* but the more she fights it, the tighter it seems to become.

This is not a good dream at all, she tells herself. *Must wake up.*

But Lizzie isn't dreaming at all. Nor is she trapped in a straightjacket. She is merely entangled in the long, viney limbs of Nick Inkersham, who is breathing softly into her curls. She feels his smooth belly moving in and out, in and out, in and out, against her naked back.

Oh, no! What have I done? I slept with a screenwriter? He doesn't even have any credits! I really am a sex addict!

She tries to extricate herself again, but Nick cozies up to her, making a nuzzling motion with his hips that shocks the heretofore unshockable Lizzie. Not sure what to do and filled with dread, Lizzie just lies there, trying to recover the queasy from the night before.

Flashback as Nick escorts an inebriated and rubber-legged Lizzie through the hotel lobby and onto the elevator. . . . Jumpcut to the bathroom, where Nick is offering her a tall glass of water and force-feeding her aspirin, while Lizzie insists on a shower. He tries to stop her, and she stumbles into his arms. Their faces are close, very close, just-inches-from-a-drunken-kiss close. . . . Jumpcut again to a sudsy Lizzie washing off a long, difficult day in the warm steam. The shower curtain opens with a bodice-ripping sweep, and Nick stands there, bare-chested and smouldering. . . .

"Oh, crap," Lizzie groans from the present discomfort of his arms.

Nick stirs and loosens his grip. He goes into a long, trembling stretch and growls out a yawn, then grins at Lizzie.

"Hi," he says softly, languorously, a greeting dripping with intimacy gained.

"When you speak of this," says a mortified Lizzie. "And you will someday, please be kind."

"Huh?" says Nick, still too sleepy to place the quote from *Tea and Sympathy*.

She gathers up her hotel-issue robe and scurries to the bathroom. Nick looks after her, lets out a grunt, and rolls over for another round of sleep.

"Mmmm," he murmurs, snuggling up to her still warm pillow.

Lizzie stays in the bathroom long after her shower is finished, her hair brushed and her skin moisturized, trying again to put together the missing pieces from last night, then trying not to. An hour later, Nick raps on the door and Lizzie opens up to find him patting his belly the way men do when they're feeling self-satisfied.

"Breakfast is here," he says.

Already the dynamic between them has changed. Nick is suddenly solicitous, confident, a little cocky even, and it seems to Lizzie that he's speaking louder and more forcefully than before. He has even made Lizzie's breakfast selection for her, something she deeply resents.

Typical pelt pirate, she thinks as she sits down to eat. *Now that he has conquered me, he's all alpha-male and arrogant. Boy, did I read him wrong.*

"I don't like bacon," she lies.

Nick reaches over and grabs the bacon off her plate. "I do," he says, stuffing it into his mouth.

Look at him. All of a sudden he's Stanley Freakin' Kowalski!

"I want to apologize for last night," Lizzie says after a few uncomfortable minutes of silence.

"No apology needed. You rocked."

"No, I didn't rock, or I didn't mean to anyway. It was really unprofessional of both of us."

"It was? We were just having a little fun."

"No, it wasn't fun. I have never done that . . . I have never . . . slept with . . . a writer before, and I really regret it. I let the alcohol cloud my judgment. I'm sorry that it happened, and I hope that it doesn't affect our working relationship."

Looking wounded, Nick stops eating. "Are you saying that it wasn't good for you?"

"No, no. That's beside the point. I'm saying that we have to put it behind us, pretend like it never happened, and move on."

"I don't know if I can do that," he says heavily.

"Well you have to if we're going to keep working together, Nick. And it looks like we're going to keep working together."

"But I can't just forget it. There's a point that a man reaches when he can't turn back and he can't hold back anymore."

"I understand. Believe me, I do. But we're going to have to make the extra effort, Nick."

Suddenly, Nick cracks up laughing.

"What's so funny?"

"You! You're so funny, Lizzie."

"Why?"

"Because nothing happened!" he says, still laughing.

Lizzie looks at him suspiciously. "Then why were you in the shower with me?"

"I was in the shower because you wouldn't get out! You were in there for an hour singing 'L.A. Is My Lady' at the top of your lungs and the front desk called to complain. You had to be stopped."

Flashback to Lizzie, belting out 'L.A. Is My Lady' into a back-scrubber. Nick sweeps the shower curtain aside, as

Lizzie screams and splashes water at him. That smouldering expression looks much more like impatience now. Despite the dousing, he takes great care to look away from her as he turns off the water.

"I was a total gentleman about it," he says, not admitting to the one-eyed peek in the mirror he stole as he passed her a bathrobe.

"Okay," she says warily. "But why were you in my bed this morning?"

"Oh, are we going to start that again?"

Flashback again to the tipsy Lizzie all wrapped up in the robe as Nick marches her out of the bathroom. She heads for the bed that he has already been trying to sleep in.

"Nuh-uh," he says, steering her toward the cot. "It's my turn for the queen. Remember? Our deal?"

"I do remember our deal," says Lizzie, weaving back toward the bed as he towels himself dry. She plops herself down.

"If Van Allen had accepted your script flat out, that would earn you the queen," she says, not too drunk to miss a loophole. "He merely indicated strong interest."

"Strong interest? The queen is mine," Nick insists. "You said so last night."

"No, no, no, no, no. When the ink is dry, that's when you get the queen," Lizzie says, attempting to point at him. "Now, g'night," and with that, she plummets into a deep slumber.

"Hey. *Hey!*" calls Nick, but Lizzie isn't taking any calls from anyone at the moment.

"Fine," he says, crawling under the covers on the other side of the bed. . . .

Back at the breakfast table, Lizzie is almost buying this version of her missing scenes, but it still doesn't quite add up.

"So why were you clutching onto me wearing only your, your, your . . . slingshot when I woke up this morning?"

"Sorry about that, but you're the one who bought the underwear, and I must have thought you were my huggie," says Nick, guzzling down some orange juice.

"What the hell is your huggie?"

"I like to sleep with two pillows, one under my head, and one to hug. My mom always called it my huggie."

"Isn't that sweet," deadpans Lizzie.

"It's part of my sleep hygiene," Nick says with a shrug as he bites into his toast.

"So, nothing happened between us?"

"Well, yeah. You kept me up with your singing and then you bogarted the bed."

"Well, I'm sorry," she says grudgingly.

"No problem. You have egg on your face."

"Yes, I guess I do."

"No," says Nick, reaching across the table with his napkin. "You really do have egg on your face."

When Nick and Lizzie squeeze past Gil on the plane later, he looks wan and slack, as if he has somehow developed a slow leak.

"Good news," he says hoarsely. "Killian loved the pitch."

"What happened to your voice?" asks Lizzie.

"We went to some loud nightclubs."

In fact, Gil has survived no less than five of Los Angeles's hottest, trendiest night spots. He is not sure if his throbbing headache is from the endless flow of Irish whiskey, or the tuneless music still thumping and hammering inside his temples.

"Party animal," teases Lizzie.

"It was all worth it," Gil croaks. "Imagine if we can get him attached to both projects, Hubbard."

Lizzie imagines it and rolls her eyes behind the darkest pair of sunglasses she owns.

"That means you have to get to work, Nick. Work, work, work," Gil hectors, as Lizzie and Nick scootch onward to the cheap seats. "And don't forget to make Hercules younger. And Irish!"

The flight attendant steps up to Gil's row. "Sir, would you care for a complimentary cocktail?" she asks.

Gil lunges for his vomit bag.

A silver jet makes it way left to right somewhere over the Great Plains. Inside, Lizzie is staring down at the modernist arrangement of rectangles below, while Nick is busy at his laptop. His fidgeting leg sidles up to her of its own accord.

"Sorry," says Nick.

"It's okay," says Lizzie, staying his leg. "It's these damn planes."

Lizzie is getting used to having Nick so close, so much that she is once again beginning to worry about her overactive libido. "So, can I ask you something about last night?"

"I thought we weren't going to mention it ever again."

"Well, just this once. I didn't do anything . . . inappropriate, did I?"

"I'd say just about everything you did last night was inappropriate."

"I mean anything . . . untoward?"

"Untoward? Who even says that anymore?"

"Okay, anything improper and aggressive . . . of a sexual nature?"

"You mean, did you make a pass at me?"

"Yes."

"No, that I would remember."

"Okay, thank you. And thank you for being such a gentleman about it."

"You made it pretty easy."

"Oh, well, thanks a lot."

"No, I don't mean it that way. I mean, I wasn't going to take advantage of a drunk."

"Oh," says Lizzie, almost flattered. "Well, what if I hadn't been drunk?"

"Ohhhh, I get it," says Nick, wagging a long finger at her. "You want to be sure that I didn't take advantage of you, but you also want to be sure that I *wanted* to take advantage of you."

"I do not," says Lizzie with more pride than conviction. Much more.

"Chicks," says Nick to no one, as he turns back to his computer screen.

"The leg," says Lizzie, suddenly not feeling so generous with her personal space.

* * *

"Okay, good news/bad news," says Judy Tolliver, who has called a special meeting of the D-Girls to send Ryan off into full-time stay-at-home fatherhood. "First, the guest of honor."

"Well," says Ryan. "The good news is that the baby said his first word last week, and it was 'daddy.'"

"Awww," say the D-Girls, as they raise their glasses and drink to this landmark event.

"And the bad news is that I'm not going to be seeing as much of you, and you have all been such great friends."

"Awww," they say again, drinking to that, too.

"Okay, Lizzie," Ryan says. "You're up."

"Well, the good news is that the pitch I was complaining about the last time actually seems to be moving forward."

"Wait," says Stephanie. "That's the good news?"

"Yes. We completely reworked it from the premise up. Garth Van Allen loved it and the writer has really come a long way. He's been such a quick study, I'm in awe of him."

They're all happy to hear genuine good news from Lizzie, for once, and they all congratulate her as they drink.

"And the bad news is . . ."

Freeze the frame and hold on Lizzie as the D-Girls wait for their next sip. In the past week she has experienced more job satisfaction than she has in her entire six-year tour of duty with Gil Gorman Productions. Preoccupied with snaring Killian Louth for both projects and hammering out Nick's contract with Laszlo, Gil has left the development to Lizzie. Remarkably, since returning from L.A., Nick has been much less resistant and stubborn, and when they do tangle or disagree, it is more as equals than as student and teacher. Even Lizzie has come around to see the project's potential, and for the first time in years, her job doesn't feel like a futile exercise undertaken for subsistence and insurance benefits. It is more like a collaboration and one that she is seriously invested in, as she stands to turn a real profit if it succeeds. It has also given her more creative satisfaction than she has enjoyed in years, and for the first time ever, her dream job feels almost like a dream.

"I'm stumped," says Lizzie, and the D-Girls all look around at each other, stumped as well.

"Can we drink anyway?" asks Stephanie.

"Of course," says Lizzie, and they all drink to her good news, except for Jenna-5.

"And what's that writer's name again?" she asks.

"Nick Inkersham," Lizzie says, reluctantly. "So enough about me. Steph—"

"Who represents him?" presses Jenna.

"He doesn't have an agent. Steph—"

"He's working without a deal?" says Jenna, full of suspicion.

"Laszlo Baranszky is handling his option."

"The criminal defense attorney?" asks Jenna, nearly clucking with disapproval.

"Yes," says Lizzie. "He's a friend of Gil's."

"Is he part of the gay mafia, too?"

"No, because there is no gay mafia," says Lizzie, now clearly annoyed. "Stephanie!"

"Well, the bad news, as you all know, is that our latest cinematic mess opened in ninth place at the box office last week," Stephanie announces grimly. "I told Raul that just because you can remake Hitchcock doesn't mean that you should. And the good news is that he made a deal to design a line of affordable sportswear for Target. So, the company breathes on."

They all drink, and drink again to Stephanie's remarkable survival.

The next morning when she arrives at work unusually early, Lizzie is surprised to find a large bouquet of flowers on her desk.

"Where did these come from?" she asks Nick.

"From me," he says, turning her desk over to her. "I wanted to thank you for all your help, for the use of your office and all your patience and hard work on the script. I really appreciate it, Lizzie."

"Nick, that's so lovely."

It has been years since anyone has bought Lizzie flowers and she is so touched she nearly falls into her chair.

"And look," she says, recovering. "I brought you something, too." She presents him with a tin of cookies. "I made them myself."

"You did?" says Nick, biting into one. "Mmm. I didn't know you liked to cook."

"I don't. I just like to bake sometimes. Daniel was the cook."

"Who's Daniel?"

"Oh, my ex."

"Oh," says Nick, who has become so used to having Lizzie to himself he actually feels a pang of jealousy at the mention of another man in her life, even an ex. "That's like me and Didi, my ex."

Nick goes on to tell Lizzie about his relationship with Didi, and how she came to fall in love with his best friend.

"And you lived with them for three months?" says Lizzie incredulously. "You're a saint."

"More like a fool, and, believe me, it wasn't easy, even though it was already over between Didi and me. I was all tangled up and conflicted, because even though I was the odd man out, I still wanted them to be happy, the way that you still care about old friends even after you've outgrown them. Don't you want Daniel to be happy?"

Lizzie considers this for a moment. "Well, you know what Flaubert said about happiness. 'A person only needs two things to be happy: good health and stupidity.' "

"Lizzie! You aren't really that cynical. You can't be."

"Well, since you're holding a bouquet of flowers to my head, I guess I can admit that I do want Daniel to be healthy and . . . happy, for lack of a better word, but I would like to feel that I am just as happy."

"Aren't you?"

"Well, my life is better these days, but it could be better still."

"And what would it take to make you happy?" asks Nick, meaningfully.

"Me?" says Lizzie a little uncomfortably. "Another cookie?"

She reaches into the tin and finds his hand already there.

"Oh," she says, and they stay that way, holding each other's gaze.

Nick raises his eyebrows, challenging her for an answer, or a cookie, and Lizzie notices those bits of gold again.

"Hubbar-r-rd!" Gil thunders and rains on the moment.

"Quick," says Lizzie, closing up the tin. "We'd better hide these, or he'll eat them all."

Later, Lizzie shows up at The Floating World to keep a previously made appointment with Mike Fontana.

"Nice to see you, again," says Mike, playing it cool. "How are things going?"

"I can't complain," Lizzie says. "Literally. Ever since I got back from L.A., I seem to have lost the ability."

"That's good," he says, laying his hands on her naked back. "Isn't it?"

"It is," she says, yielding to the insistent pressure. "I mean I'm working hard, but I'm working well, and I'm enjoying it."

"No knots or kinks, either," says Mike, sounding a bit disappointed.

He proceeds to rub and tenderize her, carefully, expertly, and as lovingly as ever. When he has smoothed out her neck, her back, her legs, her arms, and her digits, he waits for some cue to go further, but Lizzie has drifted off like a lazy bird coasting on the thermals high above the ordinary lives of all the earthbound drudges.

Surrendering to the idea that sometimes a massage is just a massage, Mike finally says, "Take your time," and tiptoes out, just as he would with any other client.

* * *

While Gil and Laszlo negotiate the option on his script, Nick grows impatient to share the good news with someone. In anticipation of his meager payment, which seems huge to Nick, he buys a cell phone and calls Tad and Didi.

Intercut between Central Park, in the full flush of spring, and the one-bedroom apartment in Madison that Nick used to call home.

"Guys, you wouldn't believe it. I met Killian Louth."

"Get outta town," says Tad.

"No, really. He was with the K-Lads and everything. I even drank his champagne."

"What's he like?" asks Didi.

"Kind of a tool, but he's interested in my script."

"Sweet," says Tad.

"I'm learning so much, and I'm working with this great woman," Nick says. "She was a real pain at first, but she's smart and she's tough and she's funny and she's cute. She's just been great for the story."

"Wow," says Tad. "So, are you seeing her?"

"Dude, she's like my boss."

"Yeah, but that's what makes it so hot."

"Ta-ad," says Didi. "I'm right here."

"Oh. Sorry, babe."

"Anyway, the script has really come a long way," says Nick, steering the conversation away from his feelings for Lizzie. "I can't wait for you guys to read it."

"Oh, this is so exciting," says Didi. "I can't wait to see it in a theater."

"Congratulations, man. We're totally proud of you," says Tad. "And we've got some good news, too. Didi and I are engaged."

Didi rocket-launches a disapproving look from the kitchen to the bedroom, where Tad makes an I'm-in-control gesture.

"Engaged? Congratulations! That is so, so great," Nick gushes. "I am so happy for you both. Things really are looking up for all of us, guys. I really owe you for the Laszlo favor, Tad. And guess what? He told me that someone from Don Flynn's company has already called inquiring about me. Isn't that incredible?"

"Who's Don Flynn?" asks Didi.

"Y'know, *Combustible, Fire Hazard, At Your Own Risk, Slippery When Wet,*" Nick inventories.

"Gee," says Didi, fingering her diamond engagement ring, which suddenly seems smaller and less brilliant than it was just minutes ago.

Cut to a world-weary fax machine as it spits out page after page of legal-sized paper. Lizzie, glasses perched low on her nose, reads them over with great interest.

Enter Gil, wheezing from the effort of a morning commute that any typically sedentary, overweight American man might find tediously unchallenging.

"Hubbard," he hyperventilates. "Has Laszlo returned Nick's contract?"

"It's right here," says Lizzie, chewing on a bagel.

"Where? Give it," he says, snatching it from her hand.

"I wasn't finished!"

"Yes, you were."

"What are you up to?" she asks, tailing him into his office.

"Work, Hubbard. This is a place of business. Not a library."

"You could have fooled me. Besides, I was looking over a writer's contract, which is not exactly a beach read."

"Well, it's not your department."

"My department? I don't know if you've noticed," she says, lowering her voice to a sarcastic whisper. "But there are only two of us left here."

"Hmpf!"

"Look, I know that you're taking advantage of Nick; I wouldn't expect anything else. I'd just like to see how much. I'm taking an interest in the business, for a change. How else do you expect me to learn?"

"Taking advantage? How dare you!" Gil foghorns.

Lizzie has seen this histrionic shtick countless times, and she knows that behind it is certain guilt.

"Don't forget who's the boss around here, Hubbard."

"I wish I could," Lizzie mutters, heading into her office.

Even with a shark as fierce as Laszlo Baranszky signing off on his contract, Lizzie knows that Nick is vulnerable without a dedicated agent representing him, someone who is involved in the movie game on a daily basis. And no one deserves a fair chance more than Nick, she has decided. He's so sweet, after all, and so utterly decent, in a provincial, middle-American way. Why, he's downright Capraesque, thinks Lizzie, and even though she doesn't usually go for all that corny Capra sentiment on screen, she is surprised to find the qualities that defined his classic heroes so refreshing in real life.

Nick has worked so hard and come so far under her tutelage that she now feels a certain proprietary responsibility for him, as if he were her creation. It may be too late to help him land a better deal on *The Way,* but she'll be damned if she will let a conniving schemer like Gil Gorman hold him back in the long term. And so, like Donna Reed, like Jean Arthur, and like Barbara Stanwyck before her, Lizzie goes into action to support her own lanky, pure hearted, idealistic, and noble American everyman.

Lizzie taps into her address book and scrolls down a list of writers' agents. Although she has been avoiding some of them for months, and even years, she begins making calls. She feels silly tossing off hyped-up phrases like "hot new writer," "fresh new voice," and "the next big thing," but she knows that they'll get results. Lizzie also knows that no favor is done without something expected in return, and for her kindness, she will surely have to suffer through a cruel season of lunches she already can't digest and submissions she can't bear to read. This is how fond of Nick, and how protective over him, Lizzie has become in just the few short weeks they have been working together.

What Lizzie doesn't know is that Nick is already engaged in a meeting uptown, where he is seated in a timeless Le Corbusier chrome and leather armchair. Nick wouldn't dare slouch in a chair like this, for fear of disappointing it. It is so firm, so supple, so rich, he feels like a different man, one more powerful, more important and more worthy than the one who just a month ago was trying to make head barista at a second-rate coffeehouse.

On the walls, oversized movie posters of Don Flynn's greatest box-office hits loom down at him in French, Hebrew and Tagalog. Across from Nick, Jenna Wahl sits at her glass-top desk, a deep-focus view of the Manhattan skyline her impressive backdrop, while her impossibly handsome assistant is pouring some thick libation into a goblet, like her own personal Ganymede.

"Thank you, Theo," she says, monitoring the pour. "Protein shake?"

"No, thanks," says Nick. "Water's fine for me."

Jenna flexes her mouth in an officious smile and Theo drifts out on an imaginary runway. The door closes behind him without so much as a click.

"Well, Nick, thank you for coming up on such short notice. As I was telling your attorney, I couldn't wait to meet you when I heard about your story, and I didn't want to wait until I got back from Cannes."

"Cannes," says Nick, impressed, and Jenna makes a perturbed little face that says, "It's not all that."

"So, how did you hear about my script?" he asks.

"Oh, the New York development scene is so small, word travels fast. Everyone's talking about it."

"Really?"

"Of course. But can I ask you something, Nick? *Why* Laszlo Baranszky?"

"Well, my friend did some work for him and he passed my script on to Laszlo and Laszlo passed it on to Gil Gorman and . . ."

As he speaks, Jenna nods sympathetically, too sympathetically, like a bad actress who has taken up psychotherapy. "Well, good for you," she says, making a little "rah" gesture with her small white fist. "But is he doing right by you?"

"Well, I guess. I mean, I never actually met the guy, to tell you the truth, but Gil was in a hurry to get the deal done and . . ."

"Mmmm," Jenna says, all understanding and support. She leans toward him confidentially. "You do know that things aren't going very well for Gil these days."

"They aren't?"

"No. His deal is in trouble and no one else wants to get in bed with him."

Nick remembers Lizzie saying that Gil is "desperate," but Lizzie also tends to take a dark view of the world.

"It's too bad," says Jenna. "He made some decent pictures in his time, but bad behavior and poor choices like that are bound to catch up with you in a tight little business like this. I just wonder if Gil is giving you the best possible deal you can get."

"Well, I sure am doing better than I was two weeks ago. I'm just so grateful for the opportunity—"

"Oh, no, no, no, no, Nick. You musn't think that way."

"I mustn't?"

"No. You can't be grateful for crumbs when everyone else is gorging on cake. This is a critical point in your career, Nick. You want to make sure that you forge the right relationships. You want to work with people who can help you. You want to go with a company that can really run with your script."

"You don't think Gil can run with my script?" asks Nick, not even sure what this means exactly.

"Well, let's hope so," says Jenna, full of unmistakable doubt.

Nick looks just as doubtful when he shows up for his note session with Lizzie at the end of the day.

"Hi. Not like you to be late," Lizzie says. "I was getting worried."

"I had a meeting."

"Already?" says Lizzie, thinking that her phone calls have paid off. "Well, well, well, bigshot. With whom?"

"Jenna Wahl."

Cue the sound of screeching brakes as Lizzie flashes back to Ryan's retirement bash. *Me and my big mouth*, she thinks.

"Jenna-Five? Well she works fast, doesn't she? So, how did that go?"

"I thought she was nice."

"She's not actually nice, it's just some 'nice' chip her programmers implanted at the factory."

"She seemed to know a lot," says Nick, refusing to play along. "I was impressed by her."

"Yes, well, it is impressive the things they can do with latex these days. So, are you working on a project for Don Flynn now?"

"I might be," he says coyly. "Jenna wanted a writing sample, so I left a copy of my outline with her. She's going to read it on the plane to Cannes."

"She's going to Cannes?" says Lizzie, her face getting hot. "D-Girls don't go to Cannes."

"*She's* going. Something she developed is in competition."

"Well, if it wins, look for another French Revolution," predicts Lizzie.

"Did you get a chance to go over my new pages?" Nick asks, resting his right ankle on his left knee and already missing Jenna's glove leather chair.

The ungrateful rat bastard, thinks Lizzie, *swaggering in here an hour late after a meeting with Jenna-5 while I spent the afternoon schmoozing him up to half the agents in the business!*

"I did," she says coolly.

"What did you think?"

"I think the plot still needs work."

"How so?"

"Well, I think the first act is too sluggish. That's not the time or the place to be testing the audience's patience. And in the revised outline, the second act is still soft, and I don't think the climax you're proposing is going to be big enough."

"So that would be all three acts, wouldn't it?"

"More or less."

"And what did you think of the new dialogue?"

"Well, when Gil said to make Hercules Irish, I don't think that he meant for him to be a leprechaun."

"He's not a leprechaun."

"He reads like a leprechaun. Irish people don't actually talk that way. We have some Jim Sheridan and Neil Jordan movies in the video library. I suggest you watch them."

"I've already seen them."

"Well, maybe there are some you missed."

"I've seen them all," he insists.

"Well, maybe you should just listen to them."

"And maybe you should try a little diplomacy."

"Maybe you should try to be a little less thin-skinned. You're not going to get anywhere in this business being thin-skinned."

"Well, I seem to be doing okay, and Jenna Wahl didn't talk to me this way."

"Well, well, well, aren't you just full of Jenna today?"

"That's right, I am," says Nick. "Because I know what you're up to, and I know that you're trying to take advantage of me because I'm new at this. I'm happy to let you use my script to prop up your failing operation, but I can only take so much abuse."

"Abuse? Abuse? Prop up my failing what?"

"Jenna told me that the company hasn't been doing well, and that's why you and Gil were so elated all of a sudden in L.A. You're both hoping that my story will save your ass."

"I will remind you that you didn't have a story until you started working with me, so it is *I* who am saving *your* ass."

"And I will remind you that I can still take *my* story and *my* ass elsewhere."

"Then maybe you should do just that. Go work with . . . that evil fembot . . . and see how well that goes."

"I think I will!" Nick says, grabbing his knapsack and his duffel bag and stomping out.

Lizzie sits there staring at the empty sofa and wondering

what just happened as Nick ducks back in to snatch his new huggie.

"That's right," she calls after him. "And take your damned huggie, too!"

When Iago shows up later, Lizzie is still sitting at her desk, her head in her hand, her face drooping with dismay.

"Lizzie, your face wears a grim mask. What lurks behind it?"

"Well, let's see. There's one ungrateful screenwriter, one cutthroat former employee, one unreasonable boss and one jaded, chronically unhappy D-Girl who hoped against all reason and experience that she might be able to parlay one undeniable long shot into a winner."

Iago isn't following.

"That ingrate Nick Inkersham is taking his story over to that other ingrate, Jenna-Five!"

"Oh, Lizzie, you see the world through such a dark glass," he says, mangling the Bible and taking her hand in his.

"I can't believe I fell for that aw-shucks Jimmy Stewart routine," says Lizzie, rising from her chair. "I should know better, Iago. Ugh, I feel so dumb."

"Is there some way I can help?" Iago whispers, kissing her fingers tenderly, one by one, his breath tickling her knuckles.

"No, I'm afraid not. It's hopeless," she says, hooking her index finger into the waistband of his bicycle shorts and pulling him to her.

They collide in a kiss and tug at their clothes as they

tumble onto the sofa. Iago covers her with kisses, but Lizzie puts her hand to his face.

"No, no, no, not here," she says. The sofa reminds her too much of Nick.

Iago lifts her up and carries her over to the desk. He lays her down and pecks a trail of kisses all the way from her throat to her navel. With her right leg hooked over his shoulder, he sows another row of kisses inside her thigh, then buries his head beneath her skirt.

Lizzie, however, can't seem to feel a thing. "No, Iago," she says, reaching down to stop him.

He comes back up. "Perhaps you would prefer the script library?" he wonders, ankle-deep in a puddle of spandex and fully at the ready.

"No, I'm sorry," she says, pulling herself together. "I don't think that's a good idea either. I don't know what's wrong with me. I can't do this. I just feel so lousy."

"But you always feel lousy before we do it."

"I know," she admits. "But I think I just need to be alone right now."

"Maybe you would just like to talk," he says, now deeply concerned and pulling on his shorts. "You have been betrayed, by your writer friend and your own wild tongue. It stings like the scorpion, betrayal, but you know that I am constant, Lizzie. Like the sun."

"I know. You're a pal. But I can't."

"Okay. I understand. You can page me anytime you need me. It doesn't have to be during the business hours."

"Thank you," says Lizzie. "That makes me feel better."

He strokes her face tenderly and leaves Lizzie sitting there, wondering what's next, and not looking forward to it at all.

After a dinner of Special Double Happiness, a half bottle of wine and a telephone gripe session with Judy, Lizzie thrashes through a fitful night of anxiety dreams worse than any student film festival she has ever had to suffer through.

When she arrives at work the next morning, she finds Gil sweating and panting and cramming the contents of her desk into an old milk crate.

"Good morning," she says.

"Hmpf!" he pops.

He has obviously heard of her clash with Nick.

"It's very thoughtful of you," says Lizzie. "I've been meaning to clean my office for months, but I really don't want you to hurt yourself."

"It's not your office anymore, Hubbard. Is this yours or mine?" he asks, holding up a novelty coffee mug with the word "Queen" written in regal calligraphy across it.

"Mine," says Lizzie.

Gil places it in the box. Lizzie slams it back on the desk.

"Laszlo called me last night. He was very upset on Nick's behalf. Nick is refusing to sign the contract and he's withdrawing his submission. He said that he'd never work with you, or me, ever again. What did you do, Hubbard?"

"Nothing. I gave him some notes and he got defensive. You know how screenwriters are. One measly deal and it goes to their heads. It's his prima donna phase."

"And what do you expect me to tell Garth Van Allen and

Killian Louth? They were very interested in this project, Hubbard. Very interested. And now it's all over," he says fatalistically.

Lizzie rolls her eyes.

He finds the cookie tin stashed in her bottom drawer. "Where did these come from?" he asks.

"I made them."

He stuffs one into his mouth with a satsified grunt and goes about emptying the rest of the drawer.

"Okay, so it's over," says Lizzie, calling his bluff. "When can I expect my severance payment?"

"Your severance payment! You quit. Remember?"

"And you offered me an incentive to stay—which I fulfilled. Remember?"

"But you blew it before we closed on Nick's deal. Remember? So I owe you nothing, Hubbard. Nothing."

The door buzzer sounds and Lizzie, fired or not, reflexively jabs the button. Gil refuses to look at her and keeps loading up the box. Although Lizzie has been fired many times before, she has never seen Gil take his threats quite this far, or exert this much physical effort, and she is beginning to believe that he really means it.

"After six years of cleaning up your messes, and hiring your interns, and firing your writers, and pretending to be your receptionist, and doing your damage control and dodging your damned paperweights, I feel I deserve something! That's six years of my life, Gil. Count 'em!"

"Here," says Gil, handing over a stack of Post-its that Lizzie has squirreled away in the back of the drawer.

"You can't be serious," she says, just as a stranger in overalls appears at the door.

"Yeah," he says. "Somebody call for a locksmith?"

"I did," says Gil. "I want all the locks changed."

"Oh, puh-lease," says Lizzie, slamming her keys down on the desk. She shoves the cookie tin into the milk crate, then yanks it away from Gil. "I've been dying to get out of here for years! You can tear the doors off the hinges for all I care, 'cause I won't be coming back!"

Track with Lizzie, straining with the overloaded crate. She wobbles out of her office, down the hallway, past the script library and the reception desk, and out the front door of Gil Gorman Productions for the last time in her life.

She elbows the elevator call button and does not look back, even as the locksmith's drill sings *zzzee-ee-ee-ee-ee-ee-ee-ee-ee-ee-ee*.

8

"WELL, THE GOOD NEWS IS THAT I AM NO LONGER WORK-ing at Gil Gorman Productions," says Lizzie, who has called another special D-Girl meeting with Judy and Stephanie, who was only too eager to add another cocktail hour to her datebook.

"Oh, happy day!" shouts Judy, as they all take a celebratory swig of their drinks.

"And the bad news is that I have left with no benefits whatsoever, so I am now officially living off my meager savings."

"Well, that ain't no way to treat a lady," says Stephanie, before tossing back the rest of her martini.

Lizzie fills them in on the circumstances leading up to her dismissal, including Nick's traitorous meeting with Jenna-5 and Gil's hissy fit.

"Any abrasions or contusions?" asks Judy, inspecting Lizzie like a doctor.

"All injuries were sustained by my pride."

"When I got fired," Judy reminisces. "He lobbed a potted plant at me."

"Wow, did you get hurt?" asks Stephanie.

"Oh, no," says Judy. "He throws like a girl."

"A blind girl," adds Lizzie, as the waiter arrives with another round.

"So, what are you going to do for your next act?" asks Stephanie.

"I'm doing it," says Lizzie, licking the overflow of whiskey from her fingertips.

"Well, they throw you out of this place at two," says Judy.

"Three," says Stephanie, from experience.

"I really haven't had time to give it much thought," Lizzie admits. "I want to get back to writing again, but I'm not sure if I can remember how, or even if I can afford it. It's been so long. I just want to savor the feeling of freedom for a bit."

"Well, I don't want to insult you, and I don't even know if you'd consider it," says Judy, exercising some preemptive diplomacy. "But you could always do some freelance reading for me. I know you're way over-qualified and it doesn't pay much, but I could use your help and at least it can stanch the bleeding in your bank account until you find something else."

"Oh, thank you, Judy. That's so generous. And I'm not too proud; I just spent six years working for Gil Gorman. But can I have some time to think about it?"

"As much time as you need. The door is always open."

Lizzie's future has never felt like such a blank slate, and the uncertainty scares her much more than she is letting on even to her closest friends. She can't bear to talk about job search plans and money worries for now, as it will only exacerbate her anxieties and set off the little internalized Janie who wrings her hands somewhere deep within Lizzie's psyche.

"So, Stephanie, good news/bad news," says Lizzie, eager to change the subject.

"Well," says Stephanie, holding up her glass. "The good news is that the orders for Raul's ready-to-wear line are going gangbusters."

Lizzie and Judy mutter some congratulations and sip their drinks, then Stephanie delivers the rest of her news run-on fast: "And the bad news is that the company is still in trouble and just like Gil, Raul is blaming me for all of his crappy taste and his dumb decisions and he's letting me go at the end of the month."

"What? Oh no! This rotten business," say Lizzie and Judy, tripping over each other with indignation and shock, chased with hearty belts of booze, as they drink to the sad demise of yet another New York D-Girl.

Cut away from this glum klatch and return now to the depot of broken dreams otherwise known as The Port Authority Bus Terminal. Nick has rebooked his ticket home, and he is lined up with another batch of Midwestern returns, each one looking more dejected than the next. When a cell phone begins William Telling, everyone looks at Nick, impatiently, disapprovingly, until he finally gets the hint.

"Yeah," he answers, as the line inches up toward the bus.

"Hi," says an unfamiliar and very professional-sounding voice. "Kyle Flaherty calling from Bootsy Barron's office."

"Sorry, you must have the wrong number."

"Oh, I'm sorry. This isn't Nick Inkersham?"

"Yeah. It is."

"Hi Nick, I'm calling from CTA New York. In regards to your writing sample? Bootsy read your outline over the weekend and she really loved it."

"She did? How did she get it?"

"Oh, uh, let's see." Kyle clatters away on a keyboard. "It came as a confidential submission."

"But I wrote it. You can't tell me who sent you my outline?"

The silence informs Nick that Kyle cannot.

"Well, when did you get it?" Nick presses.

"Last week. On the sixteenth. Bootsy would like to know if you're still available for representation."

"Um . . . yeah," says Nick, trying to make sense of all this.

"Well, can you come in to meet with her next week?"

"Oh, no. 'Fraid not. I'm on my way out of town," Nick says as he steps up to the same baggage handler as before. The man grabs hold of one of the handles, but Nick keeps his grip on the other.

"Oh, that's okay," says Kyle. "We can make it later. When will you be back?"

"It's hard to say, really."

The baggage handler gives the duffel bag a tug, but Nick isn't letting go. Finally recognizing Nick, the man tugs even harder, and Nick gives up.

"Well, when you get some idea, give us a call so we can set

up an appointment. Bootsy is really eager to meet you . . ."

"She is?" asks Nick, as he steps up to the driver to hand over his ticket. "Is she really eager to meet me or is she just saying that she's eager to meet me?"

"Um, no, she's really eager," says Kyle, who is already wondering just what kind of needy, paranoid writer he is going to have to take care of now.

"Y'know what?" says Nick, yanking his ticket back from the driver. "I think I can come in next week after all."

He sidesteps over to the baggage compartment and grabs his duffel bag away from the handler again.

"Really? Great," pretends Kyle. "Does Tuesday at eleven work for you?"

"Yeah, it works fine," Nick says, fighting his way against the mob of passengers and ignoring the baggage handler's helpful suggestion that the next time, he consider going Amtrak.

On her tenth full day of freedom, Lizzie wakes up at seven-thirty out of stubborn habit, then steals two more hours of sleep, just as she has done on the previous nine days.

Lizzie has discovered that the best thing about unemployment—other than the leisurely sleep schedule it affords her—is the luxury of indulging even her mildest curiosities. At breakfast, she reads the newspaper cover to cover, free of Gil's annoying interruptions for a change. She finds herself absorbed in articles about new discoveries in the geological makeup of Mars, a pro basketball player's stunning early retirement, and one biologist's intriguing theories about the coelecanth's link in the evolutionary chain, among other topics for which she has no burning passion whatsoever. Lizzie takes particular interest in one article about the runaway success of a single mother who has made millions selling sex toys in the suburbs, Tupperware style. Although not ready to host any "Pandora Parties" herself, Lizzie is inspired by the woman's pluck and resourcefulness, and sometime around noon, she decides that it's time to move her own career forward.

Lizzie begins chiseling out her résumé, but with every draft, she finds herself reliving the extended nightmare of her tenure as Gil's D-Girl, and try as she might, she cannot put a positive spin on her professional experience.

Within the movie business, Lizzie is certain that she bears the stink of Gil's flops by association, and on this overcast, late-spring morning Lizzie finds herself face-to-face with the brutal reality that so many New York D-Girls have to come to terms with sooner or later. Her network of contacts is so limited and her skills are so rarified that they are almost totally useless outside of the movie business. In the practical, mortal world, there simply isn't a great demand for those who can evaluate a screenplay, analyze its dramatic and commercial potential, and perhaps see it through to production. Dodging paperweights, administering eye drops and imitating a breathy receptionist don't stand for much in the general marketplace either.

Luckily, unemployment in New York also comes with the opportunity to indulge in long, leisurely walks, so Lizzie takes her troubles and frustrations to the Brooklyn Bridge, her favorite place to clear her head and settle her bad moods. The view is a constant source of inspiration and it keeps Lizzie's relationship with the city ever fresh.

She takes a bench with a view toward the Manhattan skyline, and from here, Lizzie can see the building where Judy works. She wonders if she could really take Judy up on her offer of freelance reading work, a regressive move if ever there was one. She thinks back on her own days as a freelance reader, and as Lizzie remembers the isolation and anomie that are its peculiar occupational hazards, a leaden ball of dread sinks from her chest into her stomach.

Thinking it might be better to switch her view, Lizzie dodges some fast-moving cyclists in the bike lane, keeping an eye out for Iago. Lizzie has not seen him since she was fired and she wonders if he has heard the news yet.

She looks out over the harbor, where the Statue of Liberty stands with her torch upraised. To one side is Brooklyn Heights, Lizzie's own neighborhood, stately and staid, a refuge of civility in the city's relentless brashness. On the other side stand downtown's skyscrapers jostling each other with chesty self-importance, and in between, over the gray-green waters of the harbor, massive clouds are tumbling like old sheets in a giant clothes dryer. As grand as the view is, it still doesn't help to soothe Lizzie's disquiet. Indeed, the voices of doubt and despair only seem to be reverberating louder and louder in her head, drowning out the rush of the traffic rising up from the deck below her.

Could it be that we really are defined by our soul-deadening, dreary desk jobs? Lizzie wonders, nervously gnawing on the arm of her glasses. *What if that was my peak? Those six years at that meaningless farce of a job! I'll never work again, and the thing is, I don't want to work again. Not in the movie business, anyway. Movies bore me to death. But what else can I do?*

Oh, what has happened to me? I used to be so easily inspired, so passionate, so idealistic. Romantic even. I had a boyfriend, forgodsake! I wrote plays and poetry and I had notebooks full of dumb, ambitious, big ideas. Why can't I get that feeling back? Where did that person go? What is to become of me? Am I going to be alone forever? Am I really turning into a Sandy Dennis character? I think I really am.

Oh, and look, here come some rain clouds. Wouldn't it figure?

Looking cool in the suit that Lizzie bought him in L.A., Nick sits across from Bootsy Barron in her well-appointed office. It's as rich as Jenna's lair but it's also a little cluttered, with shelves crammed full of books and scripts, and Nick likes its lived-in feeling.

"You wouldn't happen to have a cigarette?" Bootsy asks, after the introductions have been made.

"Um, sorry, no," says Nick.

"God, I've been dying for a smoke ever since I quit."

"Oh, when did you quit?"

"Nineteen-ninety-one," she says, as she goes about searching her desk drawers.

A one-time East Side deb, Bootsy Barron was a notorious party girl in the 1980s but she snorted her trust fund away by the time she was twenty-five. After an extended stint in rehab and some corrective surgery to her septum, Bootsy suddenly had to find a way to afford the lifestyle she had been accustomed to since birth. Thanks to her over-privileged education, her over-privileged social connections and her over-privileged adrenal glands, she managed to turn her monstrous drug addiction into a monstrous work addiction and she has since become one of the most successful writers' agents in the business. She is so well respected that she has recently taken her clients to CTA, the most successful entertainment agency in L.A., and therefore, the world.

"What about Nicorette?" she asks in a panicked voice. "Do you have any Nicorette?"

"No, gee, I'm sorr—"

"Kyle!" she screeches, startling Nick.

Kyle, her efficient young assistant, is suddenly there. "What is it?" he says, like a concerned babysitter.

"Kyle, there's no fuckin' Nicorette! Are we out of fuckin' Nicorette?"

"Here you go," Kyle says reassuringly, producing a box from a file drawer stuffed full of the nicotine chewing gum.

"Jesus Christ on a Carnival cruise," she says, stuffing a piece of the gum in her mouth and chewing desperately. "Thanks, sweetie."

"No prob," Kyle says, giving his pen a sharpshooter's twirl as he heads back to his cubicle to await the next crisis.

"Nicorette?" says Bootsy, offering Nick a piece.

"I'm good, thanks."

"Good for you. You don't want to start. Let me tell you, Nick, I kicked cocaine, alcohol, tobacco, prescription pain-killers,

173

caffeine, and butter, and none of it was as addictive as this shit. I can't live without it."

"It sounds rough."

Bootsy shrugs. "But hey, I loved your story," she says, getting down to business. "It's really fun. I'm dying to read the script. I love that it's so dark and gritty on the surface, yet there's real tenderness underneath it, and let me tell you I really identified with that group of addicts living underground to stay clean."

"Oh, I guess it kind of takes you back, huh?"

Bootsy makes a face that says, "You don't know the half of it."

"So, what's going on?" she asks. "Gil developed this?"

"Well, he was interested in it for a while, but we never made a deal."

"Oh, did he throw something at you?"

"No, no. But we had some . . . creative differences and I've heard that he's in trouble, so I kind of . . . backed out."

"Yeah," sighs Bootsy, taking a moment to mourn for Gil. "Well, you did the right thing, Nick. I think I might be able to do something with this, if you'll give me the chance. Has anyone else seen it?"

"Well, not that I know of, except for Don Flynn's company. He has the outline now."

"Don Flynn," Bootsy muses. "Y'know what he's got that I like?"

"No, what?"

"Real honest-to-God hackmanship. He really understands the lowest common denominator."

"Well, I don't want my script being produced by someone like that."

"Of course you do. You want to get it made, don't you?"

"Well, yes . . ."

"Then you want to go with Don Flynn."

"Oh, and Killian Louth said he was interested," says Nick.

"Really? When?"

"Gil pitched it to him a few weeks ago in L.A."

"Kyle!" erupts Bootsy.

"Yello!" says Kyle, magically there again.

"Hey, baby, get me Don Flynn on the phone, will you?" she says sweetly. "And then call Sam Waterman's office and tell him I want to talk him as soon as he gets in. It's urgent."

"Sure thing," says Kyle.

"I actually sent it to Jenna Wahl," says Nick, trying to be helpful.

With the phone already to her ear, Bootsy pulls a sour face. "I only deal with Don himself," she says.

Still another upshot of unemployment in New York is that the liberated worker need not fight as fiercely for a seat at the movies during a weekday afternoon matinee, as she must during the more competitive evening and weekend showtimes.

Lizzie is appreciating this thoroughly as she sits down to a critically touted independent feature starring a box-office goddess who, in a pitch for "seriousness," engages in an extended, raunchy sex scene shot in a single take. The critics have called it "daring" and "provocative" and Lizzie has been eager to see it for herself. She hopes that it helps inspire some passion and drive, but sadly, Lizzie can't see the picture for the deal.

To Lizzie, the movie is nothing more than a clunky, unfinished script that got hurried into production prematurely and then rushed into the theaters to accommodate the narrow opening in a movie star's busy schedule. Lizzie fidgets in her seat throughout the movie and checks her watch every ten minutes, and even more frequently during the vaunted, strenuous, tedious sex scene. Lizzie swears that she can actually see, between the frames, the producers' desperation to get the thing in the can before the star has a chance to listen to her agent, or her mother, or her Pilates instructor, and back out of the project altogether.

"This is what working in the movie business does to you," Lizzie says to herself later, as she flicks her ticket stub into the garbage can and exits the theater. She could take the subway home, but there's really no rush and Lizzie can't justify wasting two more precious dollars. Instead, she steps straight into a melancholy, rain-soaked montage underscored by the low, lonesome moaning of a bluesy saxophone.

Here is Lizzie on the slick wet streets of the Lower East Side, and there she is standing at a shop window in Nolita, with that mysterious New York sidewalk steam billowing behind her for atmosphere. Lizzie stands there eyeing all the cute, exorbitantly expensive little purses that are now even further beyond her reach than they were a week ago. Here is Lizzie now, ducking a sudden downpour in a doorway with a homeless man. He offers her a drink from his bottle concealed inside a soggy paper bag. She actually considers it for a moment, then declines, graciously. And there she is again, back on the Brooklyn Bridge, looking tiny in the frame of one of its soaring gothic arches.

The rain has petered to a moody drizzle and Lizzie pauses to look back at the Manhattan skyline, now smothered beneath a wayward cloud that has collapsed to the ground like an exhausted Thanksgiving Day Parade balloon. The saxophone builds to a caterwauling wail, while a tide of strings swells up around it. The music grows ever more insistent, prescriptive even, telling all the world to feel bad for this poor New Yorker on this damp, colorless spring day, and to weep for all of her lost opportunities and her misspent youth.

"Oh, forgodsake!" says Lizzie, breaking the schmaltzy spell.

Lizzie has never been one to endure pity comfortably, not even self-pity. "The only thing worse is one of those damn movie scores that tells you how to feel from scene to scene," she grumbles, as she digs her flip phone out of her purse.

She sends Iago a text message that reads *"i need u,"* and then, with the closest thing to a genuine sense of purpose Lizzie has felt all week, she crosses the bridge into Brooklyn.

After an antsy, interminable hour of tapping her nails, checking her messages and even testing her phone connection, Lizzie finally gives up on Iago. She imagines that he is flirting right now with some other poor office drudge, a young woman overdosing on the same stress and professional frustration that plagued Lizzie for years. Lizzie imagines that there's a whole network of these women trapped in flimsy cubicles and windowless offices throughout the city who rely on Iago to dull the pain of their menial existences and ward off their own Sandy Dennis issues. And how can she blame them?

There is another alternative, and for the last fifteen minutes, Lizzie has been staring at Mike's card, the one with his cell number written on the back. Although she has been resisting it mightily for days, she can hold off no longer.

Mike is all understanding and concern when he hears that Lizzie has been fired, but he is sure that it will ultimately prove healthy for her. Lizzie isn't convinced, and when she tells him that she will no longer be able to afford his services, Mike reminds Lizzie that he would very much prefer to see her outside the spa, without payment.

"Believe it or not, some of us love what we do," he swears.

"Then maybe you would love to do what you love to do at my place," she says.

"Maybe I would," he teases. "But you'll have to give me your address."

While waiting for Mike to finish his shift at the spa, Lizzie takes a long bath that relaxes her for the first time all day. She slips into a satiny kimono, then goes about lighting every candle in her apartment. It looks more spooky than sexy, however, so she immediately starts extinguishing them. When she is about halfway through, her doorbell finally rings.

"Fifth floor! Sorry, no elevator!" she yells into the intercom and hits the door release.

She snuffs out a few more candles, uncorks a bottle of wine and rinses two glasses. She wonders what could be taking Mike so long, when she finally hears his knock. Her kimono fluttering behind her, she runs to greet him.

"Mike," she says breathlessly, swinging the door open. "*And* Iago!" she adds, stunned. "Wow! It's so good to see you! Both!"

"He let me in," says the glum duet, looking extremely uncomfortable.

"Did he?" says Lizzie. "So, you've already met then."

Across the hall, the Sandy-Dennis-in-residence is peeking out through her door, telegraphing her disapproval of extended hallway greetings.

"Well, I don't live in the hall," says Lizzie, pulling them inside. "Come on in."

Mike and Iago step into the dim, candlelit living room, with Lizzie cringing behind them.

"Oh. The power went off earlier," she says, lying badly and switching on the lights. "Damned old wiring."

Iago and Mike just stand there stiffly, awkwardly.

"So . . . Iago . . ." says Lizzie. "How did you know . . ."

"Gil told me you were fired and your paycheck has your address."

"Oh! Right! My paycheck!" she says, smacking her head to show what a dunce she can be. "Good thinking!"

The men look at her with all the good humor of customs agents.

"So . . . uh . . . have a seat while I go throw something on," she says, her mind flashing on the bedroom fire escape and wondering if she could get away with it. "I'm sorry I don't have much to offer."

"Wine is good," says Iago, indicating the bottle of wine chilling in an ice bucket beside two long-stemmed glasses.

"Hah! Look at that! Let me get another glass," Lizzie says, heading for the kitchen. "Sorry that I don't have anything to go with it. Unemployment, you know."

"So let's order out," says Mike, flashing his cell phone. "Does everyone like pizza?"

"I do," says Iago.

"Oh! Yay!" shouts Lizzie with badly forced cheer. "Pizza-a-a!"

Cut to Lizzie enduring one of the most uncomfortable meals of her life. Iago knows why Mike is here, and Mike knows why Iago is here, and Lizzie knows they both know, and they both know that Lizzie knows they know, but no one dares to bring it up. The truth just sits there, in the middle of the floor, like a large pizza, half sausage-and-mushroom and half tomato-and-basil for Mike, the vegetarian.

The dinner conversation starts out haltingly, clumsily, like a group therapy session for stroke victims. It seems to Lizzie that both men are digging in their heels, each one refusing to cede territory to the other. The evening takes an unexpected turn, however, when Mike reveals that he is that rarest of breeds—an American soccer fan. He grew fond of the sport, he explains, during a youthful, soul-searching year working on his uncle's vineyard in Sicily. Lizzie is much more interested in the vineyard, but like so many Brazilian men, Iago is fanatical about soccer, or, as he calls it, "foochieball." All the chatter of teams and games and players adds a level of overwhelming boredom to Lizzie's discomfort, as she wonders how she's going to handle this delicate diplomatic situation once the pizza is gone and the dishes washed, dried and stored.

"Lizzie, you're not saying much," says Mike, reaching for his third slice of pizza. "Not a soccer fan?"

"Oh, well, not yet," she says. "But keep talking. I'm learning so much."

"Yes, Lizzie, you seem so far away tonight, unreachable, like the stars," says Iago.

"That far away, huh?" she says, as the two men stare her down, like cops waiting for a suspect to crack.

"Okay, look," she says, when she can finally take no more. "I'm really grateful that you guys rushed over here. I really needed a . . . friend . . . tonight, but I didn't mean for both of you to come. It was a terrible mix-up and it's awkward for all of us. I feel totally stupid and I'm very, very sorry."

"We understand," says Iago.

"We figured it out downstairs," adds Mike.

"You did?" she asks.

They look at her with challenging, stony expressions.

"Oh, now don't tell me you came up here expecting me to make a choice."

"No, not at all. This is an intervention," Mike announces.

"Well, that's funny," says Lizzie. "I thought it was a pizza party."

"We think that you are out of control, Lizzie," says Iago.

"Okay, I admit it," she says, rolling her eyes. "I was feeling sad and a little frustrated and I wanted some . . . companionship."

"Companionship?" presses Mike.

"Okay, sex. I wanted sex. Long, hot, wet, noisy, cathartic sex. Okay? Because it makes me feel good. Is that so wrong?"

181

"It's not wrong at all," says Mike. "We've all abused sex at different points in our lives."

"I'm not abusing sex."

"Only because we won't let you," says Iago.

"That's right," adds Mike. "We can't enable your addiction any longer."

"My what?"

Iago takes over for Mike. "We think that you need to get in touch with your unhappiness and find some release, Lizzie. But *creative* release. It has been so long since you have written, that you have dried up inside."

"Oh, now that's vivid," she says.

"So we're shutting you off," says Mike.

"Shutting me off? How arrogant is that?"

"You need to get a grip," lectures Mike, sounding much too parental and patriarchal for Lizzie. "Your friend and I both think that you're searching for false fulfillment. It's time for you to ask yourself what's at the root of your craving."

"Hmm, maybe I can draw you some dirty pictures."

"Maybe you have some self-esteem issues," he proceeds self-helpfully.

"Oh, thank you Dr. Phil, and thank you both for your concern. I'm sorry for the confusion. I really didn't intend to put anyone in an uncomfortable situation or hurt anyone's feelings and I agree that we should call the whole thing off," says Lizzie, closing the pizza box. "Unless . . ."

Lizzie looks at Iago, then at Mike, who looks at Iago, who looks at Lizzie then back at Mike, who looks at Lizzie, then finally gets the idea.

"Oh, fuhgeddaboudit!" Mike says, suddenly more than a little bit Brooklyn. "This is exactly what we're talking about! This is a classic symptom of your problem."

"Oh come on," says Lizzie. "As if you've never considered doing it with two women. Why is your urge healthy and mine pathological? How come you're a red-blooded male and I'm a rabid nymphomaniac? Hm? I bet you've been with two women before, Iago."

Iago gives a shrug of no contest.

"You see!" she says to Mike. "Are you going to let him get away with that, and the World Cup, too?"

Mike throws up his hands in exasperation, and Iago, the good cop, tries again.

"Lizzie, I would love to share your beautiful body with this man," he begins.

"You would?" says Mike, suddenly worried.

"But I cannot do it, Lizzie, because I agree with him. I think you want it for black reasons. Not to celebrate your freedom and the innocent joy your body holds inside, but because you are very unhappy. You want it for narcotic purposes, to numb you, like a dying man wants for morphine. And I think this would be bad for your spirit. I am your friend, Lizzie. I want you to be happy. Not just for a few moments, not just for tonight, but forever."

"Oh-h-h-h. That's so sweet," says Lizzie, genuinely moved. "You really are such a good friend, Iago. Now why don't you both get out of those clothes and let's get this party started."

"I am sorry, Lizzie," says Iago, kissing her on the head and picking up his messenger bag. "I have said all I can say. Now it's time for you to think about this."

"Huh," she says, realizing that Iago is serious.

"Then how about a big, healing hug," she says, turning to Mike.

"No can do, pal," he says, giving her a chummy little punch on the shoulder instead and following Iago to the door.

"We look forward to seeing whatever you create," says Iago.

"Yeah," says Mike. "Be strong and do good work."

Conceding defeat, Lizzie follows them to the door. "Thank you. Thank you, both," she says waving to their backs. She lingers at the door, leaning on the frame and listening as they rumble down all four flights. She waits until she hears the familiar click of the lobby door shutting behind them, then she closes her door and turns to face her empty apartment.

"Bastards," she spits, kicking the pizza box clear across the living room, which isn't all that far in a 500-square-foot apartment, but for Lizzie, it will have to do.

Lizzie knows that Iago and Mike are right, that she *is* lost and lacking something vital at the center of her life. Ever since she filled out her W-4 for Gil Gorman Productions, Lizzie has been a woman without a premise, and just like a movie without a premise, she has been totally rudderless. Now that she has finally found what she has been missing for the past six years, the time to write, she doesn't know what to do with it or exactly how to reclaim that part of herself she betrayed on that dark, regrettable day.

Determined not to let her experience as Gil's D-Girl ruin her chances at happiness forever, Lizzie goes in search of a premise straightaway. She spends the rest of the night poring through old notebooks and manila folders filled with dingy, dusty articles she clipped long ago.

There's the story about the stigmatic girl who predicts the end of the world, and the local media circus that invades her small Arkansas town. There's the story about a woman who embarks on a grueling immigrant's journey from the Middle East, to Europe, to America, on the run from her abusive husband *and* sons. There are the character sketches for a multiethnic teen romance about kids in Queens trying to go to the senior prom, against the orders of their strict, traditionalist immigrant parents. There's the story about the hundred-pound girl who aspires to be the international hot dog–eating champion in a famous Coney Island competition. There are articles about professional autograph hounds, tornado chasers, a support group for nannies, and a Russian spy dispatched to assassinate John Wayne in the 1940s. "*Brigadoon* in Golden Age Hollywood?" Lizzie has written in the margin.

There are notes for an intergenerational comedy about an unreconstructed, free-loving, rock-and-roll legend who must suddenly learn to be a mother and a grandmother when the daughter she gave up for adoption shows up at her Laurel Canyon gate.

There are extensive notes, a bibliography, and even a rough outline for a story about a pre-revolutionary colonist who is captured by Indians, who treat her far better than her

Puritan minister husband. "*Dances with Wolves* from a female perspective—Nicole Kidman?" reads an overly opti-
mistic note that Lizzie has scribbled at the top of the page.

They are all decent, viable premises, Lizzie thinks, but she
can't reconnect with the long gone impulse that piqued her
interest and inspired her to clip these articles and make these
notes in the first place. Lizzie reads them over and over
again, until she feels drugged and drowsy with quandary.

When Lizzie wakes up the next morning, she finds the articles and notes gathered all around her. "*Dances with Wolves*
from a female perspective?" she says. "What the hell was I
thinking?" She gets out of bed, crumples the outline into a
ball and tosses it into her fireplace, which has not worked
since 1934.

Before Lizzie has finished her morning coffee, she has
convinced herself that the chances that anyone would buy,
let alone actually produce, any of her stories in a marketplace
driven by hype, prurience, violence and infantilism are simply too slim to waste her energy further. She scans the want
ads and zips through several job search sites just to make
sure that there are indeed no jobs she is qualified for, then
she goes on another long premiseless peregrination, this time
in Brooklyn.

Lizzie wanders along Smith Street, drifting in and out of
the tiny boutiques that seem to crop up overnight and subsist
without actual paying clientele. She makes superficial chit-
chat with shopowners, complimenting them on their taste,
wishing them luck, but buying nothing. She wends her way
over to Park Slope, past the pretty brownstones with their

gaslights flickering redundantly in the middle of the day, until she finds herself at the Brooklyn Botanical Garden. Wandering the nearly deserted midweek paths gives her the delicious feeling of playing hooky and getting away with it.

Her spirits buoyed now, if only a bit, Lizzie grabs a bus home. After a late lunch, she stares face-to-face with a still empty day, so she decides to do that other thing that premise-poor New Yorkers do: She cleans her apartment.

Lizzie moves bookcases that haven't been upset since she settled into the place four years ago. She vacuums ledges and moldings and long-neglected corners. She even fashions a makeshift tool from a broomstick and an old sock and flosses in between the chambers of her radiator. She scrubs her tub and her sink and her tiles and her grout. She washes her windows, not that there are so many, but it's the most gratifying task of all, bringing a honey-colored sunset into crystal sharp focus.

When the apartment is vibrantly clean, Lizzie sits there enjoying the smell of scented solvents mixed with the fresh spring air, until she notices a stack of newspapers, magazines and old scripts lurking in the corner, slovenly, unbundled, and mocking her sense of accomplishment. So Lizzie sets to that most Sisyphean of modern domestic chores—the recycling.

As she wrangles the papers into a tidy bundle and prepares to subdue them with ropy twine, she notices Nick's script, the first draft that Lizzie thought for sure would kill her. For days, she has surpressed all the details of the job from her mind, the way so many trauma survivors do. But now, Lizzie finds herself thinking back about Nick, and his script, and the absurd set of circumstances that delivered her into her impoverished, angst-filled freedom.

Suddenly, Lizzie feels something she has not felt in years—a jolt of genuine inspiration. With great urgency, she kicks the recycling bundle aside and boots up her computer. It is as if Lizzie can actually feel her atrophied imagination tingling, awakening, limbering up, and sprinting off at breakneck speed. Wild-eyed and nearly euphoric, like Rosalind Russell in *His Girl Friday*, Lizzie tippity-tippity-taps away, matching it stride for stride.

9

SUMMER IS NEW YORK'S CRUELEST SEASON, WITH ITS
rank air, its pressure-cooker subway platforms, its
fetid sidewalks and its gutter-flooding thunderstorms. Every
June the city erupts in an avante-garde symphony of sirens,
jackhammers, sandblasters, power chisels, death-rattling air
conditioners, demented soft-serve jingles and the hostile
beats and tortured melismata that emanate from the open
windows of passing vehicles, which never pass quickly
enough. The residents become surlier, the tourists crankier,
the rodents more frantic and outgoing. Only the waterbugs—
each one the size of a baby's shoe—seem to thrive in this
nightmarish milieu.

Normally, Lizzie would be suffering from all of this,
counting the days until autumn. But on this long hot day in
June, she has been so infatuated with her new screenplay
that she has barely noticed the city's seasonal incivilities at
all. It is the story of a writer very much like Lizzie, one who

sells her soul to a producer, very much like Gil, who orders her to turn a hopeless amateur, very much like Nick, into a Hollywood player. It feels like revenge to Lizzie, only sweeter, as she finds it deeply satisfying to spin the tale of her discontent into a work of fiction.

On the subway into Brooklyn, Lizzie is mulling over titles for her new script, and by the time she finally settles on *My Fair Loser,* she realizes that she has missed her subway station by two stops. Rather than feeling put out by this gaffe, she just laughs it off and takes it as a sign that her work is going well. She even feels a little rush of pride for her own dedication and can't wait to report it to Daniel later.

Lizzie backtracks home, eager to get to her script, but she feels instantly deflated when she receives her first insurance statement in the mail. Thinking that there must be an error in the math, she calls her provider immediately, but the premiums are correct.

Already, Lizzie has taken Judy up on her offer for freelance reading work, but there isn't much of it, and story analysts are paid paltry wages for their troubles. Lizzie could read scripts day and night, all week long, just to live hand-to-mouth. She has already cut her budget as drastically as she can, too. Lizzie has given up taxis, pedicures, and cable TV, and she has started buying embarrassingly large blocks of toilet paper and family-sized everything. She has even been learning to cook, which isn't easy in a kitchen not much larger than a tanning booth.

Now Lizzie finds herself facing the grave, hard choice that so many struggling writers and artists have to face eventually: keep working and hope she doesn't get hit by a crosstown bus, or find some way to afford life's unforeseen catastrophes.

"This great nation of ours," says Stephanie out of the side of her mouth when Lizzie commiserates with her later.

They are sitting on Lizzie's roof, sharing a bottle of wine, courtesy of Stephanie, as the hazy molten sun takes its merciful leave over New Jersey.

Since her own dismissal, Stephanie has reverted to smoking and catering work, not that she needs the money just yet. Stephanie is enjoying all the severance benefits that Lizzie was denied, but she is one of those people who can't bear to be idle.

"I'm a social animal," she says, lighting up a cigarette and savoring her first drag.

"I wish you wouldn't do that," Lizzie says.

"Ah, catering's not so bad. It's flexible, the pay is decent, and you get to meet a lot of cute, interesting people on their way up."

"No, I mean the smoking."

"Oh, I know. It's a nasty habit. No one should smoke, unless they're in jail, or a Communist country, or the food-and-beverage industry. Then you get special dispensation," she declares, sending a thin stream of smoke Lizzie's way.

Lizzie recoils. "Please," she says, waving the smoke away. "I'm about to join the ranks of the uninsured. I can't afford cancer. Not even secondhand."

"Listen," says Stephanie. "You're not going to make any kind of money reading scripts. You know just as well as I do that story analysts read for the 'privilege' of it these days. Unless you need a foot in, there's no future in it. And you need a foot out, Lizzie. So, why don't you pick up some catering shifts."

"Oh, thanks, Steph, but I haven't done that since college. I just don't think I can. I don't have any recent experience."

"Experience? You can walk and carry things at the same time. I've seen you do it. All you need now is a pair of black pants, a white shirt and some comfortable shoes."

Although reclaiming her voice has been a sure step forward for Lizzie, reading scripts for Judy has felt like one step back, and Lizzie doesn't want to make it two. Just a month ago Lizzie had her own office, business cards and stationery with her name and title under the company logo. She simply isn't ready to wait on people who still have their own offices, business cards and personalized stationery just yet. Nor is she ready to suffer any of the other indignities of professional servitude—nonspecific skin rashes, seasonal allergies, occasional infections and inoperable brain tumors be damned.

Lizzie spends the rest of the night trying to concentrate on her script and obsessing over her finances. When the phone rings early the next morning, she answers, "Gil Gorman Productions," a habit she still hasn't broken.

"Oh, honey, you've got to stop that," says Janie, who has grown more fretful than ever since Lizzie's unemployment.

"Oh, sorry. Hi, Mom."

"How's the job search going?"

"The job search?" says Lizzie, staring at the beginnings of

an outline on her computer screen. "I'm experiencing a one-woman jobless recovery."

"Well, it's good to know that you have a sense of humor about it," says Janie, with no sense of humor of her own.

"I'm very happy to be writing, Mom. Thanks for asking."

"Well that's nice. I'm very happy to hear it, but you know that your father and I are worried about you. We don't think you should stay in that expensive apartment."

Lizzie looks around her humble, beloved little apartment with its wall of mullion windows and its chimney-and-rooftop view. Just the thought of leaving it pains her.

That's when Janie utters the words that strike fear in any young, fiercely independent city-dweller's heart, and they echo chillingly through Lizzie's head: "HONEY, honey, honey, honey. You know that you could always move HOME, home, home, home home, home . . ."

Shock cut to suburban Lizzie, a hundred pounds heavier and wearing unflattering eyeglasses from twenty years ago. She is crouched on the egregiously carpeted floor of her parents' living room and mouth-breathing over a large jigsaw puzzle of an adorable litter of cocker spaniel puppies romping in a wicker basket.

"Liz-zie," Janie yoo-hoos from the kitchen. "It's six o'clock, honey. Time for dinner."

The citified Lizzie wouldn't dream of eating dinner before eight o'clock, but Lizzie of the Hinterlands is already salivating. She clutches onto the arm of her father's La-Z-Boy recliner and begins to rise in an elaborate four-stage operation.

Propping herself up on one knee, she grabs onto the chair with her other hand, then she cranes herself up slowly, laboriously, until she has achieved the full upright position. Finally, she holds onto the back of the chair to steady herself and catch her breath, allowing the hard won oxygen to make its way to all of her body's distant places. Once stabilized, she earth-moves toward the kitchen, her back-fat testing the seams of her pink and orange Dunkin' Donuts uniform, the only clothes she ever wears now.

Smash cut back to the svelte, big city Lizzie pacing anxiously in her cute, vintage Lilly Pulitzer sundress and chewing on the arm of her very stylish eyeglasses. An hour has passed and she is still reeling from her mother's phone call. She grabs the phone and punches in a number.

"Stephanie?" she says, her voice wobbly with panic. "How much does that catering job pay again?"

Loaded down with his duffel bag, his laptop and two sacks of groceries, Nick is fumbling at a locked door, which finally gives, and he stumbles into a small, furnished room. Beige is not just the dominant color here, it is the only color in this impersonally designed kitchenette, which normally rents to travel-weary corporate drones.

Just this morning, Bootsy Barron closed Nick's deal with Don Flynn, who has taken a fairly generous one-year option on Nick's pitch. But to spur Killian's "interest" and accommodate his availability, Don Flynn has given Nick a ridiculously short deadline to produce a first draft, which Jenna Wahl is overseeing.

Bootsy has also given Nick a loan against his first payment, enabling him to rent his own apartment, at last. Small and bland though it may be, to Nick it is the Sherry-Netherland, the San Remo and the Dakota rolled into one. He goes around opening the refrigerator, the closet, the bathroom door, the medicine chest, saying "my refrigerator, my closet, my bathroom, my medicine chest."

"My window," Nick says proudly, as he draws the curtains and comes face-to-face with his neighbor, ten feet across a lightless airshaft, performing a t'ai chi routine in his underwear. "My neighbor."

Nick throws himself onto the bed, which is all the furniture there is besides a small table, two side chairs, a combination bureau/desk and a nightstand.

"My God," says Nick, staring up at the ugly overhead light. "What have I done?"

Anyone who believes that America is a classless society has probably never catered the ninetieth birthday party for a Park Avenue dowager. Lizzie knows better.

At the moment, she is relearning this hard lesson in social stratification in a professionally appointed, industrial-sized kitchen in the dowager's sprawling East Side triplex. Lizzie is serving a posh luncheon to the elderly woman and seventy-eight of her closest friends and family members. All of the guests could, and should, be at their summer houses, and they all seem to be silently resenting the inconvenience of the woman's peak-summer birth and long life.

Scooping out little balls of melon and arranging them

around dollops of sorbet, which Stephanie is plopping into crystal champagne coupes, Lizzie is trying to shut out her own class resentment and ignore the cruel fact that this kitchen is more than twice the size of her apartment. She is also trying to block out the very absurdity of having anything at all to do with a melon baller, the most frivolous of all kitchen gadgets. She is trying even harder to resist the idea that this is exactly where she was six years ago when she went to work for Gil. With each little juicy little blob of melon she drops into the glass, she reminds herself that this work is keeping her housed, fed and insured, even if it is draining her energy and writing time.

Later, when the pots and pans have all been scoured and the caterers have removed all signs that they were ever here at all, Lizzie rides the service elevator with Marty, the catering captain. A former chorus boy who is too old to hoof and too young to die, Marty has grown bitter catering functions for the last twenty years.

"I hope you can come to this," he says conspiratorially, handing her a flyer.

Lizzie fears an invite to a maudlin fortieth birthday Sondheim sing-along, but she is relieved to find that it's only a notice for a meeting to explore unionizing cater waiters.

"I'll do my best," she tells him, as she steps from the cool, marble lobby into a wall of hot, halitosic air.

Lizzie heads straight to Judy's office to pick up a reading assignment. As is typical of their recent unfair trade practices, Lizzie gives Judy a container of leftover melon balls and profiteroles, and in exchange, gets a script to read and report on overnight.

"Look whose name showed up on our screening list for Thursday night," Judy says, biting into a little ball of honeydew and passing the invite list over to Lizzie.

"Sylvia Miles? So? She'd attend the screening of a back porch."

"No, farther down."

Lizzie scans the list and stops when she sees Nick's name. "Huh. So, he's still around," she says. "How did he get on the list?"

"Bootsy Barron's office. She's representing him now."

"Wow," says Lizzie, genuinely impressed and more than a bit envious. "So my tip must have paid off."

"What tip?"

"Oh, nothing."

"Do you want me to put your name on the list, too?"

"Oh, I can't make it Thursday. I have a function during the day, and a union meeting afterward."

"Well, pardon me, Norma Rae."

"It's important. A girl's got to stick to her priorities."

"I understand," says Judy, who catches Lizzie looking more sad than summer bedraggled. "Do you ever miss it, Lizzie?"

"Working for Gil? Do you?"

"No, I mean working with Nick Inkersham. You seemed so happy when you were working with him."

"I did? Hm. I haven't really thought about him all that much," Lizzie lies.

In fact, Lizzie has been thinking about Nick more and more every day. After all, he's the model for the love interest in the new romantic comedy she would rather be working on. With her work now stalled for an entire week, Lizzie has also been wondering how Nick ever got himself past his own fatigue and all the negative, self-defeating voices in his head to be so productive. Now that the sting of his betrayal has subsided, Lizzie has to admit that she can't really blame Nick for walking out on Gil's deal, either. Forced to make an honest struggle of it herself, she appreciates just how much he must have sacrificed and how hard he must have been working. Every day she admires him a bit more for being so devoted to his script, and his pride, that he wouldn't see either compromised.

That night, Lizzie reads the assigned script and the next morning, she files her report with Judy. In the afternoon she sits down at her desk, determined to make an honest writer of herself, but nothing comes. Lizzie is at that part in the plot where her fictional screenwriter walks out on her fictional D-Girl, but she doesn't know where to take her heroine from there. Her mind is weary and distracted, and after two hours of getting nowhere Lizzie admits that she needs the sympathetic ear and shoulder of another writer.

She picks up the phone and considers calling Daniel, but she knows how he does it—with the loving support of an apple-cheeked veterinarian wife. Taking a deep breath, she dials Judy instead and is greatly relieved when she gets Judy's voicemail.

"Hi, Judy. Yeah, um . . . just making sure that you got that coverage I e-mailed you earlier," she dithers, like Diane Keaton in *Annie Hall*. "And you know . . . wow . . . yeah . . . that union meeting has been postponed. So if there's still room on the list for the six-thirty screening, why not? Right?"

Establish an unassuming midtown highrise with one brightly lit window blazing in the lonely night. Lap dissolve in, artily, expensively, gratuitously, to find Nick, now very well settled into his fortress of beigeness.

He sits at the table with his laptop, a mess of papers, and an assortment of half-eaten junk foods in front of him. He has not slept in days it would seem, and he is focusing on something with deep, devoted concentration. Across the air-shaft, Nick's neighbor is going through his t'ai chi ritual once again, and Nick is mesmerized.

He is halfway into his script for Don Flynn, but he has no idea what to do with Jenna's notes. Every day she calls with some strange new directive, and this week, she has ordered him to add a role for a humorless white rapper, "a friend of Don's," who will only provide the soundtrack if he can co-star in the movie. Nick has also been struggling to add explosions and battle scenes to his plot, which now features a war between a gang of drug dealers and a tribe of bloodthirsty mole people. He barely recognizes his own characters, or his story, and he has lost all interest in the one he is being forced to write.

Bootsy has provided plenty of sympathy, but Nick can't

tell if it's sincere or not, and he is learning the hard way that her allegiance is to her agency first, and her clients second.

The closer Nick gets to his inhumane deadline, the more paralyzed he becomes. He feels terribly alone and vulnerable as he watches the man across the airshaft fighting off invisible, slow moving demons.

"So this is Development Hell," Nick says to himself.

Several hours later, Nick starts awake in his chair to find that his neighbor has either vanquished his foes, or simply gone off to work. Nick is even further behind in his own work and he realizes that Lizzie tried to warn him about the mess that he's in. With nothing left to distract him, Nick finally decides to seek help and he dials up a number on his phone.

"Gil Gorman Productions," says an unfamiliar voice.

"Lizzie?"

"I'm sorry, sir," says a young woman who seems to be speaking through ill-fitting braces. "You must have the wrong number."

"No, Lizzie, it's me. Nick Inkersham."

"Sir, there's no one here by that name."

"Oh," says Nick, realizing that this isn't Lizzie putting on a new voice. "Well, I'm looking for Lizzie Hubbard. She was the director of development there just a month ago."

"Oh," says the terrified young intern in charge of answering Gil's telephone this week. She is painfully aware that three of her classmates have already been relieved of their internships here in the past month, and she is fearful of making a misstep and losing some desperately needed credits.

"I don't think she works here anymore," she whispers bravely.

"Well, yeah, but do you have any idea where I might find her?"

"No, sorry."

Nick hears Gil in the background. "Hey! Hey!" Gil screams. "What the *hell* is this?"

"Oh, I gotta go," says the intern, on the verge of tears.

And Nick sits there, with the dial tone droning in his ear.

After another afternoon function in a Wall St. law firm, Lizzie, still dressed in her black and white uniform, races uptown to make the screening. She has been so excited about "bumping" into Nick that she has almost forgotten about actually bumping into the people who just a month ago were her peers, a status-conscious group if ever there was one. Lizzie knows that some choose to avoid her altogether, or worse, offer their belated condolences for her downfall with too much pity and condescension. Lizzie can't bear the thought of either treatment, so she takes a seat in the back of the theater, scrunches down low and pretends to read a list of the movie's credits.

No movie screening ever starts on time, something Lizzie learned years ago, and she curses herself for being so punctual. The wait seems endless, but when Nick arrives her heart actually flutters a bit. His hair has not been cut since she saw him last, and over his baggy pants he is wearing the jacket that she bought for him in L.A., but it now looks slept-in and beat up in a way the designer never intended. Only Nick could manage to look rumpled in Jil Sander, and Lizzie finds this quality remarkably endearing and reassuring. He isn't at all the slick monster that she feared he was becoming.

Lizzie doesn't know how she's going to be received, and she has accepted the possibility that Nick may not be welcoming at all. Steeling herself for the worst, she gets up to greet him, but Bootsy Barron beats her to it.

Lizzie watches as Bootsy bounds over and whispers something in Nick's ear as if she were imparting state security secrets. Then she squeezes his arm and shoulder reassuringly, several times, like a trainer soothing a fidgety fighter between rounds. Bootsy goes back to her seat and her bored corporate husband, who is already settling in for a nap.

Lizzie takes this as her cue and rises once more, just as Jenna Wahl breezes in, following her own pointy chin straight to Nick. Lizzie scrunches down again and watches as Nick stands up to meet her. Jenna offers her cheek, demanding a kiss that won't smudge her makeup. Nick obliges, and Lizzie watches as they settle in together, much too cozily for her comfort.

Suddenly, Lizzie has lost all interest in seeing Nick, *and* the movie. She waits until the lights finally go down, then quietly slips out the side door, while the opening theme blares behind her. Lizzie walks straight into Leroy Gillis, the classically trained, hard-working stage actor who plays the villain in the run-of-the-mill thriller unspooling on the other side of the door. With the scarcity of strong roles for black actors in movies, Gillis has to rely on vehicles like this to support his family and his theater habit.

"Couldn't even make it past the credits, huh?" he asks blamelessly.

"Oh, no . . . it's not that . . . it's just . . . I'm so sorry," says Lizzie.

"Believe me, no one is sorrier than I am."

10

B Y August, Lizzie has written off Nick entirely. Judy has confirmed her suspicions that Nick did indeed take the script that Lizzie developed to Jenna-5, and it sickens Lizzie even more than the brutal heat.

At this point in this relentless summer, Lizzie has all she can do to keep herself hydrated, housed, fed and insured. In a matter of days there will be only two kinds of people left in the city: those who can't afford to escape, and those who pretend that they'd rather not. Lizzie knows that the freelance reading assignments and the catering work will dry up completely as those who tend to write the checks for freelance readers and catered affairs flock to the beaches, the country, and the better plastic surgery clinics. In anticipation of this annual mid-August exodus, Lizzie has been taking every freelance assignment that comes her way, making hay while the sun blazes, much to the further neglect of her writing.

Feeling terribly disloyal to herself, Lizzie is relieved when she finally finds a night off to work on her script, until Marty calls asking her to fill in for another waiter who has fallen ill from heat stroke.

"I'm sorry, Marty, but it's not a good time for me. I'm trying to write and it's such short notice and I don't have any clean black-and-whites. . . ."

"Oh, that's okay. You can just wear your street clothes for this one."

"But I have other work to do, Marty. What about Stephanie? Have you tried her?"

"She's already booked for a party at Wave Hill. There's really no one else. You're my last hope."

Ever since Lizzie skipped Marty's union meeting, he has done everything he can to make her feel guilty, and it has worked.

"Okay," Lizzie sighs. "I'll be there."

"Please don't humor me if you don't plan on showing up, because I've been lied to enough in my life."

"I will *be* there, Marty," she promises through her teeth.

Lizzie reports to The Roseland Ballroom per Marty's instructions and finds the catering crew already frantically engaged in an elaborate setup. Marty is wearing a headset and a pager and self-importantly flipping through pages on his clipboard.

"This one is going to be a pain in the hooey," he says. "C'mon, let's get you dressed."

"What's going on?" Lizzie asks.

"It's the after-party for *Manifest Destiny*."

"The Killian Louth movie?"

"The same," he says, then he barks out militaristic orders to the florists who have just arrived.

"Oh, I'm sorry, Marty. You should have told me it was a function for that premiere. I can't do it. I know too many people in the business and I know Killlian Louth."

"Oh, you big namedropper. I know Miss Angela Lansbury, Miss Patti LuPone, Miss Elaine Stritch *and* Miss Nathan Lane, and I'm still here! Dammit!"

With that, Marty hands her a shrink-wrapped package and breaks into "I'm Here" from *Follies*. Lizzie opens it to find a silvery spandex jumpsuit just as three waiters walk by dressed as the cannibalistic aliens from the movie.

"You've got to be kidding me," says Lizzie. "I can't wear this."

"Don't worry," says Marty mid-song. "Spandex stretches."

Lizzie ignores the dig. "Can't I switch positions with someone in the kitchen? I can't work the floor in something like this. You have to understand, Marty. I have suffered a long fall from grace. I used to work with these people. Think about it. Have you ever had to serve finger foods to Angela Lansbury?"

"Worse than that, I had to serve cocktails to Elaine Stritch, *on a bender*. Both of us. But don't worry, no one will know, and I won't give you away," he says, handing Lizzie another plastic package.

Inside, she finds her uniform's accessories, a pair of webbed latex gloves that glow fiber-optically at their knobby fingertips and a stretchy pullover mask with two breathing holes and reflective ovoid eyes.

"This is supposed to make me feel better?"

"Well, maybe if you'd put some support behind the union, sisterwoman, we wouldn't have to deal with these indignities," Marty says, then he exits, stage left.

In the kitchen, Lizzie tugs at the seat of her tight, crotch-riding onesie as she lines up with the other servers waiting for the hors d'oeuvres that will be passed to the guests. They all agree that Lizzie wears the costume best, as her curls really "fill out" the mask and replicate the movie aliens' bulging skulls with uncanny verisimilitude. In this endless, airless, thankless summer, Lizzie is happy to take good fortune and compliments wherever she can find them.

Once her tray is loaded up, Lizzie charges through the kitchen doors and into the ballroom, where she finds herself struggling against a frontline of hungry troops storming in for the free food, the open bar and the final schmoozing opportunities of the summer.

Despite its delayed release, the expectations have been high for *Manifest Destiny,* which is the last big-budget movie of the season. Lizzie, however, can read the disappointment in the faces of the guests as they mob her and grab at the shrimp scattered on her tray, their due reward for having suffered through such a preposterous, over-hyped, shameless piece of junk.

As itchy and uncomfortable as it may be, Lizzie is grateful for the mask, as she spots people she once counted as her peers among the smattering of celebrities like Regis Philbin, Salma Hayek, Ethan Hawke, Mary Tyler Moore, Adrien

Brody, and of course, Sylvia Miles, the great character actress who never misses a New York screening. These gods and demigods of the entertainment industry find themselves on a shockingly even playing field with the hopelessly mortal salaried employees beneath them and the friends they have dragged along, as they all fight for stingy tidbits of food and merely drinkable wine while it lasts.

Through the din of the crowd, Lizzie suddenly hears a familiar braying sound: "Excuse me . . . excuse me! Is that the shrimp? Some of us haven't gotten any of the shrimp!"

She moves away from it as quickly as she can, but it is nearly impossible in the thickening mob and even Gil Gorman at his most winded can catch her easily. Clenching her jaw inside her mask, Lizzie holds the tray out for him. After Gil snatches two shrimp and places them on his little cocktail napkin, she turns on her heel, but he says, "Don't go anywhere!" and Lizzie freezes, from force of habit.

"Just stand right here for a while," he says, trembling from low blood sugar and making fast work of the shrimp.

"That damned movie was almost three hours long," he explains, as he plucks another shrimp off the tray and sucks it whole, tail and all, off its little toothpick spear. "Y'know, I don't think I've ever seen a movie longer than two hours that needed to be longer than two hours. Okay, the *Godfather* pictures and *Nashville*. Maybe those noisy Hobbit things," he reasons aloud. "But *Manifest Destiny*? Gimme a break!"

Suddenly someone calls out Gil's name, and he and Lizzie turn to see Nick, waving over the head of Wallace Shawn, who is chatting with Gwyneth Paltrow and Chris Martin.

Lizzie tries to get away again, but Gil grabs her shoulder and hollers, "Nick! Good to see you! Have some of these shrimp before this alien takes them back to his planet!"

"I thought these aliens only ate people," says Nick, as he squeezes up to them and grabs a shrimp from the tray. "So what did you think of the movie?"

"It's not my genre," Gil says, which in the movie business is a diplomatic way of saying that he hated every frame of it and wishes that everyone involved had never been born. "What did you think?"

"It is what it is," says Nick, using another way to say the same thing.

Nick has obviously assimilated and Lizzie has heard enough. She turns to go, but Gil stays her again and grabs another shrimp.

"Look, Gil, I want to tell you how sorry I am for the way things went," says Nick.

"Bygones, Nick. Bygones. I don't hold grudges."

Behind her plastic eyes, Lizzie rolls her very real ones.

"Besides, it all worked out. Haven't you been reading the trades this week?" says Gil, nearly glowing. "Killian is finally signing on to *Split Second*."

"Congratulations!" says Nick, patting Gil on the shoulder. "That's great!"

"And the best part of it is that Don Flynn had to shelve *Contents Under Pressure*," Gil cackles over Lizzie's tray.

Lizzie now understands what's behind Gil's expansiveness and his forgiving attitude. It is obvious that he came to this party to gloat, the winner's prerogative, and Lizzie feels a renewed sense of relief at being out of the movie business, with all of its high school nastiness and pettiness.

"So you see, Nickyboy, everything has a way of working out. My movie is moving forward and your movie is moving forward. Everyone's a winner."

Lizzie is finally able to extricate herself from this unappetizing sandwich and turns to go.

"Well, my movie is moving forward, but not with me," says Nick. "Don Flynn is replacing me on *The Way*."

Lizzie turns back and shoves her tray in between them again, eager to hear more about Nick's misfortune.

"No, thanks," Nick says to the last, lonely little shrimp, which Gil can't resist.

A rattled, sweating Marty suddenly squeezes by and notices the empty tray. "What are you doing? We needs more runners," he says into Lizzie's pointed rubber ear, turning her toward the kitchen. "Now!"

As Lizzie extends the empty tray high above her head and inches her way through the crush of bodies, Gil moves in closer to Nick.

"I just found out yesterday," Nick explains. "I guess I deserve it, though, for walking out on you after you showed such faith in me. I'm really sorry, Gil."

"Well you do deserve it, and you're very gracious for admitting it. Most people wouldn't. I'm sure it's a hard lesson for a writer, but it's not the end of the world. Losing your own script is a painful thing, but you can't let it defeat you. You have to be resilient in this business and you have to keep all your victories fresh in your memory and all your opportunities trained in your sights. Remember, you sold a story. You have a credit. That's more than most and a lot further along than you were a few months ago. You've got something to build on. You'll do well, and I'm still interested in anything you write, Nick. The door is always open."

"Thanks, Gil. I really appreciate everything. Y'know, I'd like to apologize to Lizzie, too. She put in so much time on the script and I learned so much from her. I feel like such an ass. Any idea how I can get in touch with her?"

"Lizzie who?" says Gil, scanning the crowd, seeking out more important, more powerful people to talk to, or perhaps another alien bearing gifts.

Follow Lizzie as she fights her way through the underfed crowd, which is growing more restive than festive as the evening wears on. She barges into the ladies' room, slams her empty tray down on the marble counter and strains to reach the zipper on the back of her costume, but it gets snagged on her mask.

"Here, let me help," says the woman in line behind her, and Lizzie feels the zipper release.

"Oh, thank you so much," Lizzie says, as she tears the mask off and stands face-to-face with Jenna-5.

"Lizzie," says Jenna, barely able to conceal her delight. "What a surprise."

"Oh. Hello. The surprise is all mine."

"I heard that Gil let you go. It must be awfully hard on you," Jenna says, taking in Lizzie's costume.

"Not as hard as it looks."

"Well, I'm sure you must have seen it coming. Let's face it. Gil's day passed a long time ago. I'm surprised he's held out this long."

"So am I," says Lizzie. "Considering the way people have been stealing his ideas and his writers."

"Oh, please. I won't be blamed for his sloppiness. That's just show biz, and you know it. Or maybe you don't. Maybe you've finally found a line of work that suits you."

"Yes, well maybe I have. I'm writing now, thanks for asking."

"Oh, is this part of your research?" says Jenna.

"No, this is part of my dues, and I'm happy to be paying them. Because even though I am dressed like an alien and slinging finger food, I know that I am doing it in the service of some higher goal. I know that at the end of *my* day I have made something other than a screaming phone call or a cut-throat deal, and I have done something other than make an intern cry, or a screenwriter consider suicide. I'm not whoring myself to some pseudo-creative job that sucks the soul out of you. But you would have to have a soul to understand that in the first place, now wouldn't you?"

"Next," says Sylvia Miles, holding the stall door open for Lizzie.

She thanks the two-time Oscar nominee politely, then bangs the door shut. Inside the stall, Lizzie heaves a deep sigh and peels herself out of her ridiculous costume, but she finds that it is hard to cry and pee at the same time.

* * *

Cut to Gil, later, nudging his way through the line at the bar and nearly knocking Jenna off her high heels.

"Gil, you're a menace," she says.

"Only when it comes to closing deals, Jenna."

She imitates a laugh.

"So, no hard feelings about *Contents Under Pressure* over at Don Flynn's house, are there?" he asks.

"Why would there be?"

"Exactly. The trades make such a big deal over these things, but it's just business. You and I understand this."

"I suppose," says Jenna, fanning herself with a movie program. "But we really just don't have enough faith left in the premise to risk such high above-the-line costs."

"Hmpf! Well, I still think it'll make a great summer tentpole for the studio. Especially with Killian attached."

"Mmm, I wouldn't get too attached to my attachment, if I were you," she says, and she leans in close to his right ear. "Because I think that Killian might be yanking his pole out of your tent any day now."

"What is that supposed to mean?"

Jenna answers with a mean little smile. Taking a glass of Chardonnay from the bartender, she makes a little "cheers" gesture to Gil, and sashays away. Gil stands at the bar watching as she insinuates herself back into the crowd.

"Red or white, sir?" asks the bartender, but Gil ignores him and charges off.

Gil shoves his way through the throng, saying "Excuse me," and "Pardon me," to anyone who is a celebrity or an executive, and "Blocking!" to anyone who is not. He scans the room, searching for any sign of Killian Louth, when he walks straight into the next best thing, Sam Waterman, the éminence grise of superagents and the man in charge of Killian's career. He is chatting in a corner with his elegant, deeply tanned helpmeet, Dolores, a central casting version of the classic Hollywood wife.

"Gil, so good to see you. But tell me, how the heck do you people tolerate this weather? It's like Bangkok!"

The only time Gil ever talks about the weather is when it threatens to hold up production or cross-continental flights, so he ignores the chit-chat. "Sam, I've just heard a rumor."

"In this room? Don't believe it."

"I don't want to believe it, because I've heard that Killian Louth isn't going to sign on to *Split Second* after all."

Sam becomes stiff and self-conscious, a corrupt politician caught by a secret camera. "Now Gil this is hardly the place to talk business. My wife is easily bored."

"Sam, don't bullshit me. Everyone in this room is talking business. You know it, I know it, and I'm sure your wife knows it. Hi, Dolores."

She wiggles her fingers at Gil politely, uncomfortably.

"Gil, why don't you call me in the office tomorrow," Sam suggests.

"Because you're here right now. You know what people are saying about me, Sam. I'm a dying man. I can't wait for a better time or place. Are you going to lie to a dying man?"

"Listen Gil, you know I'm not at liberty to discuss this. I like you. I always have. You're one of the good ones, Gil, but I'm obligated to my client."

"So when were you planning to tell me?"

"I'm not telling you anything."

"Yes, you are. You're telling me right now."

Sam's pained look gives him away, while Dolores inspects her fingernails, the clasp of her tennis bracelet, the veins on the back of her hand.

"You see, Dolores even knows," says Gil. "Who else knows? Does everyone in the room know? Is that why they all came here? To have a good laugh at me?"

"Now, stop being dramatic, Gil. Get a grip. Be a pro."

"Why, Sam? Why is he backing out on me?"

Sam heaves a sigh of defeat and finally lets go of his professional front. "You know how it is, Gil, we're all at the mercy of these damned people and their damned whims. Killian could change his mind tomorrow; that's why I didn't tell you. But frankly, he's getting a better deal from Don Flynn. He made Killian an offer on some script that he just bought and Killian liked the story. They agreed to beef up his role, let him pick the writer, the co-star, the music, even direct it if he wants."

"Hmpf! What's the project?"

"Some cockamamie thing about a drug addict named Hercules who's the mayor of some secret world underneath the city and some kid falls down a hole or something. Bootsy brought it in. I haven't read it myself yet—"

"*The Way*? He's signing onto *The Way*?"

"Well that's the working title, but they'll change it. Look, I'm sorry, Gil. It's nothing personal, it's just business."

"Of course," Gil mutters to himself. "Of course, it's just business."

"Killian really admires your output," Sam says, sliding back into slick mode. "He would love to work with you in the future. . . ."

Gil has heard this line a thousand times before and he can't bear to hear it again. Dazed and devastated, he just turns his back on Sam and Dolores and sleepwalks back into the crowd.

Cut away to Lizzie as she bounds into the kitchen. Panting with exhaustion, she yanks the mask off of her head and staggers to the dishwasher's station. She turns on the faucet and splashes her face with cold water.

"Hey! You! Ayn Rand!" yells Marty. Lizzie turns to see him loading up a rolling food cart. "They need more food in the VIP room. Put your face back on and follow me with those hors d'oeuvres."

Lizzie groans and pulls the mask over her face. She grabs the tray, hoists it high above her head, and follows Marty out. When she steps through the doors into the VIP room, the K-Lads set upon her like a pack of feral dogs. Lizzie barely manages to steady the tipsy tray.

"It's about time," says Finbar. "It's like another potato famine around here."

The others chortle, and they all begin scarfing down the hors d'oeuvres and licking their fingers. Lizzie notices Special K himself in a roped-off section of the room flirting his way through an exclusive interview with an *E!* reporter. Finbar tries to grab the tray away from Lizzie, but she resists.

"Hey," she says, getting tough, like Gena Rowlands in *Gloria*.

"C'mon E.T, give it up!" he says, just as Gil charges through the double doors, his head hung low like a bull.

"Killian!" Gil roars. "Killian Louth!"

Confused, Killian turns to him with a phony, just-bleached smile. Gil stops, reaches down, and yanks the carpet out from underneath Killian, sending him toppling into the sound man. The interviewer scrambles away screaming as Gil dives on top of Killian, pummeling the star with his fat little fists. The steadicam man seizes the opportunity, circling them to get the kind of shockingly graphic close-ups that would make any pornographer proud.

Lizzie staggers backward when Finbar quits their tug-of-war for a better fight, as all of the K-Lads rush to Killian's aid. They try to pull Gil off Killian, but Gil sinks his teeth deep into a freckled forearm and keeps pounding away at the actor's chiseled head.

"He's trying to eat me," Patrick squeals. "The fat bastard!"

With Dwayne's help, the K-Lads finally manage to winch Gil off their friend, then hold him still so that Killian can even the score.

Perhaps it's a vestige of her loyalty to Gil, or perhaps it's just a summer full of slow percolating rage finally reaching its boiling point, but Lizzie looks at her tray, then at Killian's head, and decides they were meant to be together. She winds up and whacks him with everything she's got, and today,

Lizzie has got a lot. At the sound of the gong, Killian teeters, then totters, then keels to the floor.

Finbar grabs Lizzie by the stretchy scruff of her costume and they go whirling, dervishly, about the room.

"Hey, you! Unhand that worker!" screams Marty, who has been watching it all. "I said desist! Desist!"

But Finbar will not desist, so Marty yells *"Stri-i-i-i-ke!"* as he wheels the food cart straight into Finbar, driving him into the wall.

The K-Lads set upon Marty now, but from within Dwayne's expert headlock, Marty chants "Strike! Strike! Strike!" pumping his fist in the air.

In an instant, an alien invasion of underpaid, uninsured, unsteadily employed and unfairly costumed cater waiters heed his call and come crashing into the room for a full-scale donnybrook. The building's security people follow and try to restore order, but they're badly outnumbered and they learn quickly and painfully about the military disadvantages of fighting two enemies at once.

By now, the ruckus has also caught the attention of the not-so-very-important people in the main ballroom who have come to rubberneck, and some of them also get caught in the fray.

Concerned for her newly acquired star, Jenna comes to in-spect the situation with all the officiousness of a senator at a disaster site. She dodges a volley of mashed potatoes and watches in horror as cheap, functional function furniture goes flying through the air, shattering like breakapart movie props. Convinced that Killian is trapped somewhere inside the thick monkey pile of bodies, Jenna scurries about on her matchstick legs pleading for someone to do something. She notices an alien figure with a distinctly bulging skull hanging from an oversized gold chain on the back of a K-Lad, who is grappling with a now bloodied, but ever bellicose Gil.

"Leave him alone, you bully bastard!" yells Lizzie, as the K-Lad tosses her off his back.

While Lizzie gets her bearings, Jenna feels a surge of viciousness she just can't resist. She scootches over and yanks the mask off Lizzie's head. Her eyes even wilder than her curls, Lizzie rises up and moves toward her, threateningly.

"Oops," says Jenna, giggling as she steps backward.

From the vise of a crushing wrestling hold, Gil notices Lizzie for the first time. *"Hubbarrrrd!"*

Switch to a dreamy slow-motion as Lizzie turns to see Finbar at her back, his face a grotesque mask of savagery as he lets loose with an Irish roundhouse. His meaty fist cuts through the air, ever so slowly, and even rather gracefully, heading straight for Lizzie's nose. She ducks, and instead, the blow connects with Jenna's sharp little chin. Suddenly airborne, her mouth shocked into a perfect O, Jenna rockets, ass-backward, onto the rolling waiter's cart and goes sailing, sailing, sailing, out through the ballroom doors.

Back in real time, Finbar tries for another swing at Lizzie, just as Marty traps him inside an expandable tray stand. His arms stuck at his side and desperately trying to free himself, Finbar goes into a frenzied riverdance. Lizzie grabs a handy bottle of champagne and casually cracks it over Finbar's head with slapstick timing and grace. Finbar collapses, and Marty shakes her hand, Oliver Hardy to Lizzie's Stan Laurel.

Two more K-Lads charge them from behind and shove them onto the pile of bodies, with Killian and Gil now somewhere deep at its core. Together, this violent, writhing, flailing ball of humanity rolls as one, like a giant, many-limbed microbe, out toward the ballroom and straight into a wall of NYPD riot cops, who charge at it from all sides like an army of antibodies. The police work with madcap Keystone energy to disentangle the angry cater waiters from the bogus gangstas from the deposed and obsolete development executives from the assorted party guests who simply couldn't pass up a good brawl.

In the meantime, Nick and the more peaceable guests have been herded outside, where they are corralled behind police barricades. He strains to see over the heads of the other gawkers and the press photographers who have already elbowed their way to the front. Nick is surprised to see Gil, in handcuffs, being ushered out by two New York City cops.

Flashes strobe like heat lightning, as the photographers desperately try to keep track of something so unplanned.

Nick is even more surprised when he sees Lizzie emerge with a police escort of her own. Feeling notorious, Lizzie gives her curls a defiant shake. She is enjoying her perp walk and the red carpet moment she has always dreamed of, even if she is heading the wrong way.

Nick calls her name, but he is drowned out, and Lizzie is upstaged, when the EMT workers come out bearing Killian on a stretcher. The teenaged girls who have been waiting outside all night for a mere glimpse of him sob and wail at the injustice of having crossed bridges, tunnels and ten o'clock curfews only to see him swathed in bandages.

Nick jostles his way through the teeming, squealing crowd, who have finally gotten what they didn't pay for—a night of fresh, well-played entertainment. He breaks free from them just as Lizzie is being shoved into a paddy wagon along with Marty and the other caterers.

"Hey! Wait!" he yells to a pair of stern cops who slam the doors shut, then give a signal to the driver. "Hey!"

Blue lights sweep across Nick's face and the siren overpowers his voice as he sprints after the truck, calling Lizzie's name.

Lizzie has never been inside a police station before and what surprises her most about this one is the twenty-inch television mounted high on the wall, as if it were a hospital room, or a cheap European hotel. It is playing a somber urban cop show in which a team of brooding, seen-it-all homicide detectives wrestle with the blindness of justice, the moral grayness of the universe, and their own tortured psyches from one moodily lit scene to the next. It couldn't be more different from the fluorescently lit scene being played out by the very real cops in front of Lizzie. The drama that is unfolding in miniature is above their heads in every sense, as they shamble and shuffle about their duties as dispassionately as any civil servants anywhere in the world. It's a lot like the post office, Lizzie decides, but with shorter lines, better hours *and* TV.

All of the women cops on the show look hopelessly like actresses, preternaturally glamorous Zone dieters forced into dark pantsuits and sharp-collared blouses. They are not at all like the kindly Sgt. Scarlett, who speaks with a warm Jamaican accent and wears her standard issue NYPD uniform with pride. As Lizzie follows Sgt. Scarlett down a long hallway, she is trying to decide whether to use her one call for Judy, or Stephanie. Lizzie can't wait to give them her first-hand account of the disastrous premiere, but she finally decides that Judy might be better able to make bail. She just hopes that Stephanie won't be offended.

Sgt. Scarlett shows Lizzie to a glass booth, where another cop instructs her to sign some papers.

"Oh, but I didn't get my call," says Lizzie. "I'd like to talk to my attorney before I sign anything."

"No charges are being filed, and there's a pay phone outside if you want to call somebody," says Sgt. Scarlett, helpfully.

"Oh," says Lizzie, a little disappointed by this anticlimactic turn of events. "But don't I have to post some bail, or something?"

"No, I already told your friend out there that it's not necessary."

"Really? Which friend?"

"That guy over there, the skinny one."

Lizzie turns to see Nick in the waiting area. He waves to her.

"Forget it," says Lizzie, offering her wrists for cuffing. "I'd rather stay here."

"It's not a hotel, honey. You want to stay here, you gotta go outside and break some laws. Then we'll see what we can do. Okay?"

Lizzie gives in and signs all the release forms, bearing down hard. The other cop hands over a Ziploc bag containing Lizzie's sole belongings, the gloves that complement her alien costume. Lizzie thanks him, then bounds out to freedom as fast as her cloven extraterrestrial booties will carry her. Nick springs up from his chair, but she brushes straight past him.

"Lizzie! Lizzie!" he calls, following her into the murky night air. "Oh, c'mon. Give me a break."

"Oh, pardon me, is that your knife in my back?" she sneers, and keeps on walking.

"Okay, okay, I deserve that. You have every right to be mad at me."

"Well, thank you so much for your kind permission."

"But maybe if you'd let me explain and apologize, you wouldn't feel so angry and hostile."

"It would let you off the hook, wouldn't it?"

"It would let us both off the hook."

"Okay, thanks for coming to bail me out," she says flatly. "Luckily, it wasn't necessary, but you can now consider your account settled. And closed."

"No, I can't. Look, I am sorry for walking out on you and I am sorry for not listening to you and I am just sorry for everything. It was the stupidest thing I've ever done in my life and I hate the way things have turned out. You were right about Don Flynn and Jenna and everything."

"Oh, did she do you wrong?"

"Yes, as a matter of fact, she did."

"Hurts, doesn't it?"

"As a matter of fact, it does, and there's nothing I can do about it, but there is something I can do about this. I lost my script forever, and I don't want to lose my friend too, if I can call you my friend."

"Ugh," says Lizzie, bustling ahead. "If you think I can still move your career forward, you're wasting your time, because I don't work for Gil, or anyone, anymore. I'm in no position to move anyone's career forward, not even my own."

"I don't want you to move my career forward."

"Then what do you want from me?"

"I'm asking you to forgive me."

"Oh fine, you're forgiven," she says insincerely.

"Not like that. I'd really like to be forgiven, eventually, over time if you need it, but really, truly forgiven, the way that friends forgive each other."

"Why should I?"

"Because I made a huge mistake, and I'm admitting it. Sometimes people screw up. Haven't you ever screwed up?"

"Okay," Lizzie says, rolling her eyes heavenward. "I'll try to forgive you."

"Yeah, but you rolled your eyes, which doesn't suggest that you really will try."

"Okay," Lizzie says, fighting the temptation to roll her eyes again, "I will really, really try to forgive the very shitty thing you did."

"Okay, thanks. And maybe try to come to some appreciation of why I might have done it in the first place? Like my inexperience? My years of hard work? My desperate need for food, shelter, clothing? Your bad attitude?"

"Don't push it," she says, marching on, but Nick keeps following her.

"Okay," Lizzie says impatiently. "So, I'm working on the forgiveness thing, but it's going to take a little while. Maybe even a lifetime."

"Okay. Thanks. I'll try to to be patient," says Nick, keeping up. "So, maybe sometime this week, I could check on your progress? See how the forgiveness is coming along? Maybe over dinner or a movie, or something? My treat."

Lizzie stops and looks at him incredulously. "Are you asking me out on a date?"

"If . . . that's what you want to call it, I'd be honored."

"Is that how you got Jenna-Five interested in your script? What kind of an operator are you?"

"Jenna? I never went on a date with her."

"I saw you together at a screening."

"What?" says Nick, thinking back. "That wasn't a date! She invited herself because she had a meeting with the writer's agent the next day and she couldn't get on the list."

Lizzie makes a mental note to check this out with Judy later, but she has to admit, it sounds good. It would be very much like Judy to keep Jenna off her invite list.

"You thought we were on a date?" Nick laughs.

"It looked like a date," says Lizzie, who starts walking again.

"It wasn't a date! Look, Lizzie, I had a great time working with you and I learned so much from you, and all summer long I've just been thinking about L.A. and how exciting it all was, and it was really because of you. You were so funny and I have to say . . . well . . . it felt great being next to you that night, so I thought now that we're not working together maybe—"

"Wait a second. I thought you were asleep that night."

"I was. Well, half asleep, like in that kind of waiting room for sleep, when you're not quite dreaming, and you're still sort of aware of what's going on around you and—"

"You copped a feel?"

"I didn't cop a feel, Lizzie. I wouldn't do that."

Lizzie smirks at him.

"Okay, I copped, like, half a feel. No, the half of me that was asleep might have copped a feel, but the half of me that was awake did not cop a feel. That guy is totally innocent. He had no fun whatsoever. So I guess that makes me sort of like a sleepwalker, or a sleepfeeler, but—"

"Look," says Lizzie, stopping again. "I've had a really rough night. I had to dress like an alien and wait on people who I used to work with, then I got beat up by a bunch of thugs, and then I got hauled off to jail in a paddy wagon. Now someone who has backstabbed me and nearly date-raped me is insisting that I go on a date with him! I'm sorry, but my threshold for absurdity was reached hours ago."

"I think 'date rape' is a little strong," Nick says. "I take issue with that. It was more like date-spooning, with maybe some date-nuzzling thrown in. Is that really so wicked?"

Lizzie can't say that it is.

"Look, Lizzie, I thought we really had some kind of connection developing. We worked so well together and we were having fun. I can't say I've ever experienced that before with anyone, and I've missed it. I really have. It's . . . it's like you made me a better person, or something."

"Oh forgodsake, that's from *As Good as It Gets*," says

Lizzie, who has heard enough and starts heading for the subway.

"No, no, no, I mean, it's like . . . you complete me, or something," says Nick, running after her.

"Okay, do you think I haven't seen *Jerry Maguire*? You've already cost me my job, please don't insult me on top of it," she says, crossing Eighth Avenue against the light.

"Lizzie! Will you stop for a second?" he pleads. "Damn you!"

Nick sprints into the crosswalk as a yellow wave of taxis bears down on him, honking contemptuously. He leaps to the curb and catches up with her.

"Jesus! You know, I thought that walking out on Gil's crummy deal was the stupidest thing I ever did, until I tried this," Nick says. "You're so damned stubborn! What a fool I was for thinking that I could ever get through to you. No one will. Ever. Let's face it. You're just too sarcastic and too smart and too arrogant and too . . . hard for your own damn good."

Lizzie rolls her eyes.

"And that way that you roll your eyes to show how superior you are to everyone; how you can't even be bothered with us lesser beings because we aren't even worth your energy . . . or your breath."

Lizzie stops and looks at him, stone-faced.

"I really don't know what the hell I was thinking," Nick continues. "I don't care if you forgive me, or not. It's not worth it. In fact, I should thank you for making me see that the mistake I made wasn't cutting out on you; it was trying to make up with you. 'Cause frankly, you're scary. That's right, you scare me. The whole time I was working with you it was like . . . I was being chased by a herd of hungry mastodons or something . . ."

"Mastodons?" says Lizzie, still the D-Girl.

"That's right, mastodons! And it was like . . . I was either going to be crushed to death, or get devoured alive, or, or, or overdose on my own freakin' adrenaline. And you know what's really pathetic? I liked it! Isn't that disgusting? It gave me a charge. Pitiful, right?

"It was like there was an electrical current running through my spinal cord and all this energy pouring into me from all over the place and I couldn't think straight and I couldn't speak right. Everything always came out so . . . so clumsy and, and, and I couldn't formulate even the most simple thoughts because all I could focus on was you.

"You! Being with you . . . and watching you . . . and listening to you . . . and pleasing you . . . and wondering what you were thinking, and waiting for you just to look at me, just to look into my goddamned eyes, just to spare me a glance! And it was the most exciting thing I have ever felt in my whole life! And I wish that every minute of the rest of my life could feel that way . . ."

Now it's Nick who can't look at Lizzie. He tightens his jaw and gazes off toward the lights pulsing and flashing in Times Square while Lizzie stands there, staring at him, unblinking, and just as stunned as he is by his naked outburst.

There is nothing she can say to Nick right now. There is nothing she even feels like saying to him, but suddenly the dark breach of space between them feels terribly wrong. Lizzie reaches out her webbed green hand, ever so tentatively, its bulbous fingertips glowing fiber-optically in the night.

"C'mere," she says, smokily like Lauren Bacall, huskily like Kathleen Turner, seductively like Veronica Lake; and grabbing Nick's shirt, she pulls him to her for a kiss.

The gesture shocks Lizzie almost as much as it shocks Nick, but breaking the kiss would be too embarrassing now, harder than the kiss itself. So Lizzie and Nick settle into the refuge of their kiss deeper, and deeper, and deeper still.

A small team of carb-raised Midwestern tourists trudge by, fanning themselves with crumpled *Playbills*. Groaning and swearing that they will never come to the city in August again, they cut a wide detour around Lizzie and Nick, who are off together somewhere far away. They don't even notice when they're besieged by a crinkly plastic sack that has caught the tail of a sudden northwest breeze. Lizzie and Nick just keep following one kiss with another, even as the little sack swoops and swirls all around them like a puckish little sprite.

Leave Lizzie and Nick now and follow this giddy little cupid of the gutter. Crane up and travel with it as it drifts higher and higher into the Broadway canyon. It flits and it floats and it flutters about, performing a weightless ballet. It flattens itself against a window, stealing a peek of the dreamers inside, then it reels back into the void. It twists and it twirls and it spins and whirls, Ginger Rogers to a Fred Astaire wind. It dips for a bow, and then rockets straight up, on its way to a date with the moon.

11

CAN YOU FEEL THAT?" SAYS NICK, IN ECSTASY.

"Oh, yes," says Lizzie. "It feels *so* good!"

"I've been waiting so long for this."

"So have I," she says. "I hope it never stops."

"Don't worry, baby. This is going to last for days," he says. "Oh. Wait. Is this another one?"

"Oh, yesssss," says Lizzie. "Get ready."

"Oh, I'm ready. C'mon now. Come to Papa," Nick urges. "You can do it."

"Oh, here it is!" shouts Lizzie. "Now! Oh! Oh!"

"Oh! Oh! Oh! *Yeah!*" Nick rejoices.

"Oh! Oh! Oh! OOOOOOOOOOOOOOhhhhhhhhhhhhhh!" They sing out loud in rapturous harmony.

They are, of course, talking about the Canadian cold front that made a heroic rescue of the entire northeast two nights ago. They are lying across Lizzie's bed in front of the window, where a deliciously refreshing breeze is tickling the sheets and their cool, bare flesh.

231

Almost every August, usually late in the month, the warm weather breaks for at least a few days with a brisk, clean blast of air from the north, yet the weather forecasters seem to have no term for this event. There is nothing like Indian Summer or the January Thaw or the Pineapple Express to mark this blessed out-of-season phenomenon. And so, for the past hour, Lizzie and Nick have been lying in this position trying to rectify this meteorological oversight.

"How about The Big Chill," he suggests.

"Too on-the-nose," says Lizzie. "What about The Canadian Invasion?"

"That seems unfair to Canada. After all, this is a gift they're sending us," reasons Nick.

They finally settle on The Autumn Overture, which they both like for its overwrought elegance and because it sounds like the title of a movie Douglas Sirk never made, but should have.

"Oh, look," says Lizzie. "I think I actually have a goosebump!"

"Will you look at that," says Nick in mock amazement, squeezing her tighter.

Lizzie rests her head on his chest, self-soothing to the deep glug-glug of his heartbeat. She can hardly believe the comfort derived from this sound of life, which she surely would have cursed just a few days ago, and she is in awe at the wondrous turn her life seems to have taken.

Since the night of her arrest, Lizzie and Nick have barely left her apartment, or her bed. They have spent most of it just like this: naked, marveling at the cool air, and absent-mindedly caressing each other, with occasional breaks for napping, eating or swapping their back stories; and even more frequent breaks for acting out their own torrid love scenes. It has all left Lizzie with an indescribable, otherworldly sense of peace.

Lizzie felt something similar with Daniel, but she chalked it up long ago to the romantic illusions of youth and inexperience. Just as she had come to believe that she would never enjoy another goosebump again, Lizzie had come to believe that she would never feel this kind of passion again.

Lizzie certainly never expected that Nick would be the man to awaken her long-dormant heart. He isn't attracted to Lizzie's discontent, like Mike, or to some idealized vision of her as a misunderstood artist, like Iago. Nick sees Lizzie for the pain in the neck that even she knows she can be, and yet he seems to love her because of this, not despite it, and it is the most powerful aphrodisiac Lizzie has ever experienced.

As Nick sings an off-key rendition of "The Impossible Dream," Lizzie begins planting a row of kisses along the middle of his chest, up to his neck, and past his knobby Adam's apple, stopping at the tip of his chin. She climbs on top of him and looks into his eyes, devilishly.

"Why, Madam, what kind of man do you think I am?" he asks, distracted from his quest to follow that star for the moment.

"Mine," says Lizzie, now more B-Girl than D-Girl. "And I intend to do whatever I please with you."

"Vixen!" he hisses, and Lizzie finally delivers her kiss.

The phone rings, but Lizzie and Nick are having too much fun to stop now.

"Hubbarrrrd!" shouts her answering machine, a potent interruptus if ever there was one. "Hmpf!"

Lizzie and Nick stop and press their foreheads together, waiting, longing, praying for the hang-up.

"Hubbard," Gil croaks, sounding uncharacteristically weak. "Would you please pick up the phone?"

"Did he say 'please'?" says Lizzie, seriously confused.

"Hub . . . " Gil tries to raise his voice but it breaks into a series of coughs and hacks. "Arghh! Hrumpf! H-rrrumm! Ha-a-a! Hmpf! Well, yes. I just wanted to let you know that I'm in the hospital and this may be your last chance to talk to me, but if you've got more important things you'd rather be doing, I understand."

Lizzie gives Nick an apologetic look and picks up the phone. "Gil, what's going on? Why are you in the hospital?"

"Haven't you heard, Hubbard? It's where they send sick people. And some of them don't ever go home."

"Yes, Gil. I know how it works, but what's wrong? Specifically."

"I don't want to tell you over the phone," he rasps.

"Well, is it serious?" she asks, rolling off Nick.

"It's very serious, Hubbard. It's major, and I need to see you."

Lizzie shoves the receiver into the pillow, where Gil babbles on in a muffled tone.

"I think I have to go see him," she says, crinkling her nose.

"I can come with you," says Nick, strumming a soundless tune on her belly. "We haven't done it on the subway yet."

"Let's save that for another time," says Lizzie, kissing him again.

"Anytime you want," he says, returning her kiss. "Or until my Metrocard expires."

"Hubbard!" yells a tiny voice buried inside her pillow.

"Oh, sorry, Gil," says Lizzie, picking up the phone with one hand and holding a finger to Nick's lips with the other. "Which hospital are you in again?"

While Gil gives her the information, Nick cups her hand in his and kisses it over and over and over again, as if it were the dearest, most precious thing he has ever held in his life.

When Lizzie opens the door to Gil's private hospital room, the first thing that strikes her is the thick, funereal scent of too many flowers crammed into one small space. It actually takes her a moment to pick him out in this insanely fecund jungle of oversized floral arrangements, potted exotica and baskets of shiny, hand-polished fruit. But there Gil lies, still bandaged, bruised and butterfly-stitched from the brawl and blowing his nose madly.

"Hubbard!" he honks from underneath his hankie.

"Gil," says Lizzie, still trying to take it all in. "They put you in *The Little Shop of Horrors*."

"Isn't it something? Those are from Geffen," he brags, pointing to an elaborate arrangement of orchids. "Aren't they pretty? And those are from the Weinsteins. Let's see, that's Joe Roth, Katzenberg, Amy Pascal, Lynda Obst, Bruckheimer, Art Linson, Merchant and Ivory, but you could have guessed that one," he says, pointing out a beribboned fruit basket that is perfectly Victorian in its overabundance.

"Oh, that's Sherry Lansing, Bob Shaye, Danny DeVito, Ron Howard." He goes on naming the fruits and flowers, like a starstruck Adam in the Garden of Eden. "Scorsese, Demme, Minghella, Warren and Annette, Demi and Ashton—*and* Bruce, Robert Downey, Jr."

"And they're all going!" announces a monochromatic arrangement with a profusion of Casablanca lilies.

For a moment, Lizzie thinks that she really has stumbled into *The Little Shop of Horrors,* but through the plants peeks an actual mammal, who also happens to be Gil's nurse.

"Hi, I'm Chip Farrabee," he says.

"Um . . . hi. I'm Lizzie."

Nurse Chip is balancing the flowers in one hand as he hacks his way through the dense understory of the indoor forest with his other. He emerges wearing a smock covered with gay pride rainbows and triangles, and upstaging his name tag is a large button that says AMEND THIS!

"Put those back!" commands Gil. "Do you know who sent those to me?"

"Someone named Francis Ford Coppola," says Chip, reading from the card.

"Coppola!" Gil corrects him. "Francis Ford Coppola! Don't you know who that is?"

Chip apparently does not.

"The Godfather? The Conversation? Apocalypse Now?"

"Those are movies, right?" guesses Chip. "I don't go to the movies. They're either too violent or too silly, and Francis

Flipping Cupola should have known that one, you're allergic to lilies; and two, having this many plants in any room isn't healthy, even for a healthy person."

Chip bustles out with the flowers.

"Do you believe him, Hubbard?"

Lizzie does not believe Nurse Chip, but she learned long ago not to get involved in the public mini-dramas that Gil can't seem to avoid, or resist.

"Gil, what is going on?" she demands.

"Oh, Hubbard, the phone's been ringing off the hook and I'm getting all these gifts. It's so exciting! And did you see the reviews for *Manifest Destiny*?"

"No-o-o," she says, not interested in them either.

"What have you been doing? Haven't you been reading the trades?" he nags.

"No, Gil, I don't read the trades anymore because I'm no longer *in* the trade."

"Hmpf!"

Gil reaches for a stack of newspapers and magazines with a groan, then hands them over to her.

"It's bombing everywhere," he says gleefully. "*Variety* even called it a 'low Plains drifter.' Isn't that good?"

Chip power-walks in and grabs another arrangement, this one full of stargazer lilies.

"Hey, that's Robert Redford!" Gil protests.

"No lilies!" snaps Chip, power-walking right back out.

"You did a great job at that premiere the other night, Hubbard, and I want to thank you for coming to my aid. You really proved your loyalty."

"Loyalty?" says Lizzie. "I just can't stand to watch an unfair fight. But I wish you'd tell me what you're doing here? You sound terrible and you look worse."

"Well, you know I'm allergic to lilies, Hubbard."

"They don't hospitalize people for that, Gil, and if they did, they wouldn't put them in rooms full of them."

Gil heaves a sigh, then signals her to close the door. "There's nothing wrong with me, Hubbard," he admits in an impatient whisper. "I'm here because Laszlo recommended it."

"Laszlo Baranszky? Okay, Gil, you know that he's a lawyer, not a doctor."

"No kidding, Hubbard. And he's a damn good one, too. He thought it would be a good idea for me to have a little 'breakdown' for my defense, because that damned Louth is suing me. That Irish ham is out to ruin me, and Garth Van Allen already cancelled my deal because of it."

Lizzie wants desperately to roll her eyes, but she promised Nick that she would try to break her unbecoming habit. For want of a glass of whiskey, she reaches for one of Merchant and Ivory's apples, which looks much better than it tastes.

"So," she says, eating the apple anyway. "You've finally found your way into the cuckoo's nest."

"And I'll tell you it was harder to get into than Proust. Laszlo pulled some strings. According to this shrink he works with I have a temporary psychosis caused from physical and mental exhaustion made worse by a bipolar something-or-other. Y'know, like an Anne Heche kind of thing. That's going to be Laszlo's angle in court, if it ever gets to court, which it won't. We'll probably have to settle."

Chip reenters, hunting for lilies, so Gil returns to his normal tone of voice, bossy and loud.

"So, Hubbard. I want you to go back to the office and retrieve all of my messages and mail, then I want you to come back here to return some calls. But first I want you to take these fruit baskets and send them off as thank-you gifts to my supporters. Just make sure you don't return them to the same people who sent them to me. Well, you know how to—"

"Uh-uh-uh," says Chip, wagging his finger. "Remember what the doctor said? No worky-worky. And if you're here to enable this man's compulsion, I'm going to have to toss you out with the lilies."

"Would you please?" says Lizzie, suddenly realizing Gil's ulterior motives for calling her here.

"I'm not working," says Gil. "She is. She's my assistant."
"I am not!"

"Oh, my development person, or whatever . . ."

"I am *not* your development person either," Lizzie fumes. "Remember? You fired me. Without benefits."

"Well, now I'm rehiring you. With benefits, Hubbard."

"You don't even have a deal!"

"I will pay your salary out-of-pocket until I get one."

"Work!" Chip referees, but they both ignore him.

"I can't believe that you dragged me here under false pretenses thinking that I would go back to work for you! After you strung me along for years, underpaying me, overworking me, verbally abusing me, throwing things at me, always with the promise that the next movie would be a hit, the next deal a winner. So where are the hits, Gil? Where are the winners?

Wake up and smell the lilies! You're not going to get another deal!"

"Hmpf!"

"And even if you could, I want no part of it. I am not lifting a finger for you ever again. Those days are over. Shall I spell it for you? O-V-E-R. There is only one crazy person in this room, and it's not me."

As Chip applauds her performance, Gil reaches for a potted orchid and aims it at him, but Lizzie grabs it away just in time. Chip goes back to making busy and eavesdropping, as Lizzie places the orchid far out of Gil's reach.

"You're turning your back on me, Hubbard?" says Gil, looking wounded. "Now?"

"No, not now. First I'm going to finish this apple," she says, taking a big, crunchy bite.

While Lizzie tries to enjoy her perfectly art-directed, meretricious apple, Chip monitors the conversation like a federal agent, and Gil sulks.

"You don't get it, do you, Hubbard?"

"No, but why do I have the feeling that I'm about to?" she snarks.

"Look around, Hubbard. What do you see?"

"Too many plants and one large, mentally disturbed gay man in a hospital gown."

"Funny, Hubbard. Side-splitting. You know what I see when I look around this room? Momentum. Every piece of fruit, every flower, every sprig of fern, every spray of baby's breath represents real momentum," he orates. "I'm a hero to these people, Hubbard. I did what they all only dream of doing. Do you think it's easy living according to the whims of people like Louth? Every single one of these people goes to bed at night wishing they could strangle the stars they depend on for their livelihood, but I really did it, Hubbard, and I dared to strike out at one of the biggest. I'm in their good graces now and I need to capitalize on my new standing.

"That's the difference between us, Hubbard. You look around the room and see a bunch of plants, but I look around the room and see a long, wide boulevard lined with green lights as far as the eye can see. I've got what everybody wants, Hubbard—real momentum. And I'm willing to share it with you.

"C'mon, don't you want something to show for all your years of hard work?"

"I do, but all I have is this lousy apple," stonewalls Lizzie.

"Okay, now that is enough work for one day," says Chip. "You heard the lady, and it's time to take 'no' for an answer."

Gil realizes that he's getting nowhere with Lizzie, or his nurse, and he sinks into his pillow with a heartbroken sigh.

"Do you know whose fault this is, Hubbard?"

"Steven Spielberg?" says Lizzie, dreading what's coming next.

Gil nods. "All that talent, all that showmanship, and no taste whatsoever," he laments, then he launches into a monologue that Lizzie has heard many times before, one Gil often indulges in whenever he's faced with a major setback and is feeling fatalistic.

"I used to love movies, Hubbard. Really love them. They

were so exciting in the seventies. I wanted to be one of those maverick producers. I wanted to bring the world the next Bogdanovich, the next Scorsese, the next Altman, the next Malick. I really did. I wanted to be the guy who made important movies that said something and challenged the audience. It's what I spent my entire youth preparing for."

Lizzie picks up one of the trades and begins flipping through it. Absorbed in his own personal myth, Gil doesn't even notice.

"All I did when I was a kid was go to movies," he says. "I hated everything else about childhood: games, sports, dogs, camp. What a trap! But I loved the movies, Hubbard. Really loved them. Unfortunately, by the time I got to make them, Spielberg had come along and pissed all over everything. Him and that goddamned white light. I hate that white light and every single one of those damned dust motes. It's so tacky. And that schmaltzy John Williams. Don't get me started on him!"

"Don't worry, I won't," says Lizzie, knowing there's no stopping him.

"Over the years, that man has ruined more movies for me than the beehive, the afro and the mohawk put together."

Recognizing the end of the anti-Spielberg spiel, Lizzie closes her magazine, sticks her apple core in the potted orchid, and stands to go.

"I think it's time for his sedative now," she says to Chip, but Gil looks up from his pillow and says something that truly surprises Lizzie.

"Hubbard, am I a bad person?" he asks in a small, frail voice she has never heard before.

It catches Lizzie off-guard and she stands there for a while, stumped and searching for an answer. Even Chip is eagerly awaiting her reply, curious to see how she's going to handle this one.

"No, Gil . . . you're not a bad person. You're just . . . not . . . a very *nice* person."

"Bingo-o-o," Chip sing-songs. "It's exactly what I told him. Maybe if he tried being a nicer person; he'd be a happier person."

Lizzie fires a look at Chip, who puts up his hands in surrender and escorts another bunch of lilies from the room. She turns to Gil, who looks weary and empty and as sad as a fallen cake. There's even a tear leaking from the corner of his eye. It suddenly dawns on Lizzie that Gil's diagnosis isn't a legal ruse at all; she is looking at someone who has suffered a very real crisis, a total breakdown of the spirit.

"Well, I'm sorry, Hubbard," Gil mutters softly, almost inaudibly.

"What's that?" asks Lizzie, still getting used to this version of Gil.

"I said I'm sorry, Hubbard. I used you. No, I *usurped* you. I knew things were starting to go south when I hired you and I needed someone with your smarts and your talent and your conscientiousness and your toughness. *And* your hunger and inexperience. I shouldn't have done it and I don't blame you for hating me.

"I never really intend for people to hate me, Hubbard. I really don't. But I don't know how to make them like me either, and I never have. At least when I could make movies,

243

I could make them appreciate me, and respect me and *need* me. But now . . . I'm tired of trying, Hubbard. I'm tired of the game, and I am so tired of . . . myself," he says, breaking into tears.

"Oh, you big mess," says Lizzie, feeling genuinely sorry for Gil for the first time in her life. "I don't hate you, Gil."

She sits back down and takes his hand, but Gil looks away, unused to such gestures of tenderness from Lizzie, or anyone.

"Look, I took out a couple of those K-Lads for you, didn't I?" she says, but Gil can only look away and stare glumly out the window.

"And I don't blame you for the years that I spent working for you," she adds. "I really don't. I could have walked out at any point, and I didn't. In fact, I'm grateful to you for a lot of it, Gil. I learned so much about the business, and movies, and writing, and ambition and myself. I just stayed too long at the fair, that's all.

"I'm a writer, Gil, and the hardest lesson I learned is the simplest one. Writers need to write. That's why I can't come back to work for you. I sold myself out once, and I can't do it again. It's not fair to either of us."

Gil nods, full of resignation.

"Well, I wish you luck, Hubbard. Just try to hang on to your passion. I had so much passion once. Everyone does when they come into this business, but then the business slowly sucks it away, and now . . ."

"Gil, you can get it back. You *will* get it back."

"You know there are no second acts in American lives, Hubbard."

"Oh, fooey!" says Lizzie. "What about John Travolta? And Ronald Reagan? And how many acts has Jane Fonda had? At least five."

Gil almost smiles.

"Thank you, Hubbard. Thanks for everything. I'll try to do whatever I can to make it up to you. As soon as Nurse Ratched goes home, I'm going to call my accountant and tell him to make up for the severance package you should have gotten and I'll pay your insurance for the rest of the year. I'll do whatever I can to help you out."

"Well, thank you, Gil. I really appreciate it."

"You deserve it, Hubbard. I really admire you for what you're doing, and you need to do it before you get too set in your ways."

Chip, the most conspicuous spy in the world, saunters back into the room and begins clipping the heads off lilies with a pair of scissors. Lizzie takes this as her cue to leave.

"So, Hubbard, what are you writing?" Gil asks, blowing his nose again.

"Well, I'm still in the early stages and I'm not ready to pitch it just yet, but as soon as I have it figured out, Gil, I'll let you know."

"Just give it to me in a few sentences," he pushes, still the producer.

"No! No! No!" says Chip, stamping his foot. "That sounds like business to me. This is a no-work, no-stress, re-covery zone and there will be no Hollywood wheeler-dealing on my watch."

"You heard the man," says Lizzie. "Before you take care of

business, Gil, you have to take care of yourself. Promise me that you'll listen to your doctors."

"Ahem," says Chip.

"And your nurses," she adds. "And maybe your heart, too. Okay?"

"I think I coughed it up," Gil says weakly.

"I'm sure you didn't," she says, planting a kiss on his head. "I'll check in on you later."

"Thank you, Hubbard. And do me a favor? Take some of this damned fruit out of here. You know I hate fruit."

"Gladly," says Lizzie, who begins shopping for produce as the telephone rings.

Gil lunges for it, but Chip beats him to it.

"Room 409. Mm-hm. What's the nature of the call?" he demands. "Uh-huh. Well, Mr. Gorman isn't taking any business calls. Doctor's orders."

Gil starts tugging at the phone cord, so Chip turns his back on him, yanking it out of his reach.

"How do you spell that?" Chip asks. He begins writing the message on his clipboard. "S-as in Sam-P-I-E-L-B—"

"What are you . . . ?" Gil says through his teeth, desperately tugging at the Smock of Pride.

Lizzie finally settles on a towering pyramid of fruit and she tiptoes out, just as Chip, all business, wraps up the call.

"Well, I'll give Mr. Gorman the message and he will have to get back to Mr. Spielberg at his convenience. Okey-dokey? Oh, there's no telling. Yes, that's right . . ."

Loaded down with her bounty, Lizzie rushes past the nurses' station as a horrified *"N-o-o-o-o-o-o-o!"* howls through the air. The nurses and orderlies bolt past her toward Gil's room, and Lizzie stops. She shifts the weight of the fruit to her other shoulder and considers following them, but then she remembers that Nick is waiting for her at home, along with all of the work she has to catch up on.

"No! No! No! No-o-o-o-o-o!" Gil's cry echoes down the hall, as Lizzie, arms heaped with fruit, keeps moving straight ahead, with purpose, with hope, with a premise.

12

Flash forward one year and reprise Lizzie's ominous heartbeat one more time. Pan the glamorous audience at the Kodak Theatre past the over-familiar faces of the overpaid celebrities in the front rows and find Lizzie, not so far back herself. She is wearing her borrowed Cerruti gown, but this time, it is Nick holding on to her hand as Meryl Streep glides out to announce the nominees for Best Original Screenplay. Lizzie is amazed at how similar this moment is to her dream. The actress is even wearing the same dress and she finesses the same weak joke. It all adds an element of spooky déjà vu to Lizzie's anxiety.

Angle on Nick, and add another heartbeat to the mix, as Meryl Streep announces the nomination for the screenplay that he and Lizzie have written together.

La Streep fumbles with the envelope, playing the same adorable schtick from Lizzie's dream, and the audience eats it up.

Lizzie turns to look at Nick. In the time that they have been living together and collaborating on this script, she has grown to love him more and more every day. She squeezes his hand, and he turns and smiles at her.

Nick feels luckier than any man in the world at this moment. It doesn't even matter to him whether he wins the Oscar that he has always dreamed of winning, because he has already won Lizzie.

"And the Oscar goes to . . ."

Turn up those heartbeats, beating in perfect syncopation now, pounding as one.

"Lizzie Hubbard and Nick Inkersham!"

Lizzie and Nick jump at each other and kiss much longer than most screenwriting teams ever would, as the theme music rises up all around them . . .

"Hey," says Nick, pulling out of the kiss. "Good morning to you, too."

"Oh," says Lizzie, embarrassed at having mauled her boyfriend in his sleep.

There are no Cerutti gowns, no Oscar-rich actresses and no theme music at all in Lizzie's bedroom, which is far more humble than the Kodak Theatre.

"Dreaming?" Nick murmurs.

"Yeah," says Lizzie, as she rolls over onto her other side.

"What about?" asks Nick, assuming the spooning position that has become second nature to them both.

"Sap," says Lizzie.

"You're dreaming about sap?"

"Ugh," she grunts, backsliding into dreamland.

"Y'know, we should really get up and nail that scene down," Nick says.

"Let's stay like this a little while longer," says Lizzie, clutching his hand under her chin.

"Okay," says Nick, getting cozier. "But just for five mintues."

"Ten," she bargains.

"Fifteen," he says. "But not a second more."

"You're the best," Lizzie murmurs.

"Yes, yes I am. And don't you forget it," he says with a little oomph from his hips.

It is not something Lizzie is likely to forget soon. Even after a year of sharing her small apartment with Nick, she is still getting used to his size thirteen sneakers, which seem to be everywhere she steps. Lizzie is still learning to navigate around him in her tiny kitchen and her cramped bathroom. She is still getting used to sharing her computer line, her television, and her precious closet space. Lizzie and Nick argue with great regularity over whether the apartment is too hot or too cold, too bright or too dark, whose turn it is to wash the dishes and whether they should stay in or go out for dinner. They are, in short, a typical, functioning happy couple who are very much in love and doing their best to make it work.

Some things they have figured out quite efficiently and co-operatively. While Nick is off attending his Filmmaking class at the School of Visual Arts, Lizzie works on a new novel. While she is off catering, he works on the story boards for his short film. On weekends, they have been collaborating on *My Fair Loser* together.

Once Lizzie let her defenses down and fell for Nick, she could not deny the happy ending of her romantic comedy and it seemed only right to collaborate with Nick on the screenplay. For both of them, writing the story has been almost as difficult, and almost as sweet, as living it. If they can survive the grueling test of collaboration, Lizzie is convinced that she and Nick can get through anything together.

Later that day, after they have rewritten their final fade-out, even the frugal Nick is more than ready to indulge Lizzie's take-out habit with a bottle of champagne. While Lizzie has been adjusting to the enormous changes in her life with a grace, patience and maturity that even surprises her at times, the waiter at her Chinese restaurant isn't adapting so easily.

"Okay, a double order of Special Double Happiness. So, four orders of Double Happiness?" he says when Lizzie calls in her usual selection.

"No, I just want one double order of Special Double Happiness," she says.

"For four people?"

"No for two. Just one big order of Special Double Happiness for two people."

"O-o-o-oh," says the waiter, sounding troubled and perplexed. "Okay, fifteen minutes. Bye-bye."

When the delivery man shows up later, he is loaded down with enough food to feed a hungry rock n' roll band. "Special Double Happiness," he says brightly.

"Oh, yes," says Lizzie. "But I think the guy on the phone misunderstood me. I only wanted one double order."

"Yes, one large order Special Double Happiness for number five-A. One large order Special Double Happiness for number five-B," he says, as Sandy Dennis from across the hall opens her door.

To Lizzie's surprise, the Don Knotts character from downstairs is fidgeting at her side, anxious to pay the delivery man.

"Same order," says the delivery man, tickled by this strange coincidence.

"Oh, oh, I see. Isn't that something?" says Lizzie, also tickled, as she trades him her money for one of the bags.

As she closes the door, Lizzie catches her neighbor's eye, and for the first time ever she smiles at Lizzie. It's a warm smile, a little tentative at first, but it is heartfelt and content and wide enough to poke a hole in Lizzie's theory about the Sandy Dennis syndrome, sinking it once and for all.

"All the confusion cleared up?" asks Nick, uncorking the champagne as Lizzie sets the food down on the table.

"Beautifully," says Lizzie. "Just beautifully."

Establish a pretty Greenwich Village block, Perry Street between Bleecker and West Fourth, if the city permits will allow. Find Lizzie and Nick walking arm in arm past the quaint sun-dappled townhouses on this perfect September day.

"This is it," says Lizzie, approaching Gil Gorman's house.

"Which floor does he live on?" says Nick.

"All of 'em," says Lizzie. "It's his Xanadu."

Gil Gorman has emerged from his legal scrape with Killian Louth minus one housekeeping deal, some medical expenses, and an undisclosed legal settlement, which was, of course, fully disclosed on The Smoking Gun. To pay for the damages, Gil has sold off his Ray Kappe mid-century modern house in Santa Monica Canyon, which was really more a trophy than a home in the first place. Still, he hated to see it go.

Despite these losses, Gil has not been defeated absolutely. He has not lost his beloved townhouse, where Lizzie is leaning on the doorbell at the moment. It's a place heavy with sentimental value for Gil, who purchased it with the returns on his first hit several real estate booms ago. Gil has also started a new, scaled down, and truly independent production company out of his home office. Although there's not as much security in it, it is a real challenge for Gil, who still can't resist a good challenge. He has also taken on a new partner, one more genuinely engaged with the running of the company than Lizzie ever was. It was a difficult adjustment for Gil to make at first, but much to his own surprise, he is enjoying this new arrangement more than anything.

Although Lizzie hasn't seen Gil since he was released from the hospital a year ago, they have talked on the phone, and as promised, she has sent him a copy of *My Fair Loser*. She expects that Gil will be mercilessly critical toward it, and possibly even litigious, and she has been trying to prepare Nick for this for weeks. What Nick lacks in patience, however, he makes up for with unbridled trust in his fellow man and the universe.

"Press the bell again," he says eagerly.

"Down, doggie. You have to give Gil some time," says Lizzie. "It's a big house and he's a big man."

With that Lizzie turns to face Gil, who is standing there

holding the door open. He has shed more than fifty pounds since Lizzie last saw him, and he is not so big at all anymore. He is also wearing jeans for the first time ever, not because he likes them, but because now he can.

"Hello, Hubbard," says Gil, ignoring her comment. "Nick. It's so good to see you both." He reaches out and gives Lizzie a warm embrace that takes her by surprise. He even hugs Nick.

"Gil, you look great," says Lizzie, still processing the shock.

"Thank you, Hubbard. So do you. Come on in."

Lizzie, who in the past has been forced to arrange Gil's sock and underwear drawers, knows the layout of his townhouse all too well, and she begins to make her way to his office on the third floor.

"Oh no, Hubbard, it's such a nice day. Let's meet in the garden."

"What garden?"

"*My* garden, Hubbard. My partner is waiting for us there."

"What partner?"

Mystified, Lizzie shrugs at Nick as they follow Gil to the rear of the house and out the back door. They step into a radiant garden rich with ferns and ivy and caladium and hostas and all manner of shade-loving greenery. Here and there are carefully placed stones furry with moss, and there's even a little fountain bubbling out of the center of a small koi pond.

Lizzie gapes at it in wonder. "Gil, when did you do all this?"

"You know I don't have a green thumb, Hubbard. My partner did it."

Lizzie is about to ask when she might actually get to meet this miracle worker when she hears someone say, "Well, hello there! Long time no see!"

Enter Nurse Chip, carrying a tea tray out from the basement kitchen.

"Nick, I'd like you to meet my partner, Chip Farrabee. Hubbard, you remember Chip, don't you?"

"How could I forget?" says Lizzie, thrown off again as she shakes Chip's hand.

"I just *loved* your script," says Chip.

"Really?" says Nick.

"Oh, I thought it was so sweet and romantic. But I don't want to talk about it. That's his department. This is mint tea, but it's decaffeinated," says Chip, tossing a look toward Gil, who is only allowed one serving of caffeine a day.

"I love what you've done with the garden," says Lizzie. "And no lilies."

"Oh, thanks. I can't believe Gilbert was just letting this space go to waste. In Manhattan! He really needs a refuge to balance all of his energy. Otherwise, he'll just work himself right into the ground."

"Gilbert?" says Lizzie.

"That's my name, Hubbard."

"Say when," says Chip, pouring Gil's tea.

"Okay, honey," says Gil. "That's good."

Suddenly, Lizzie realizes that Chip isn't just Gil's partner; he is Gil's *partner*. To Lizzie, Gil has always seemed gay in theory only, someone who would date men, if he had the time or the interest in dating at all. She is still trying to wrap her mind around the idea of Gil as someone's lover, and she feels the way many adolescents do when they discover that their parents actually have sex, and possibly even enjoy it.

"So, Hubbard and Nick, huh?" says a beaming Gil, his hands folded behind his head. He is taking them in as a couple for the first time as well. Gil feels some responsibility for the match, and he always takes great pride in making anything happen.

"That's right," says Nick, taking Lizzie's hand. "Can't live without the ol' ball-and-chain."

"So, Gilbert and Chip, huh?" says Lizzie, reflecting Gil's beam right back at him.

"That's right, Hubbard. It's funny the way things turn out."

"Isn't it," she agrees.

"Did you happen to see this?" says Gil, handing over a copy of *Variety*. "It's today's."

Angle on a headline: *Don Flynn Loses His "Way."*

"Killian pulled out," Gil explains. "He didn't like the direction they were taking the script—with the writers *he* demanded, of course. Don's closing his New York office. Jenna's out of it, too. Last I heard, she was working at Kinko's."

"Wow," says Nick, scanning the article and enjoying the warm rush of schadenfreude sweeping over him.

"So, we can all die happy now," says Lizzie, reading over his shoulder.

"Well, I really liked your script," says Gil, forging straight into work. "I think you did a bang-up job. I know that movies about movies can be hard to sell, but I'm not afraid of that. I don't know about the title either. It's a little negative, but they'll test it and call it something else if they want to. There's nothing we can do about it, really. I do think the producer is a little shrill. . . ."

"Now, now," says Chip. "Is that really the way that we want to start?"

"Maybe we went a little too far with the producer," says Nick. "We can always tone him down."

"Nonsense," says Lizzie. "I think he represents all the producers I've ever known pretty darn well. . . ."

Pull back and crane up, higher and higher, leaving them gathered in the middle of their little emerald oasis, pitching, chatting, debating and interrupting, keeping one another in check and balance. Fade to black slowly, as the conversation turns to soft indiscernible patter, no louder or more distinct than the trickle of the fountain, the sparrows chattering in the leaves or the faraway sounds of the city. It is punctuated here and there by the tinkling of cups on saucers, the occasional burst of four people laughing together and a bit more frequently, the jab of a spirited "Hmpf!"

Roll the Credits

THIS BOOK WAS WRITTEN OVER AN EXTREMELY ITINER-ant year of willful homelessness, and for the generous loan of their spare keys, guest rooms, sofa beds and inflatable mattresses, I must thank the following people: In Provincetown, Tim Hazel, Ben Thornberry and Ross Sormani. In Boston: Laura Walsh, Jim Chamberlain and Tom Gillis. In New York, David Rakoff, Joanne Dolan and Doug Montgomery. In San Francisco, Robert Francoeur, Jose Lopez and Paco Cifuentes. In Los Angeles, Alexa Junge and Doug Petrie. In Porto Alegre, Brazil, Benjamin Junge.

Thanks also to my family and friends for their constant support and for being so patient with my wandering ways. I am especially grateful to Danielle DeKoker and Suzanne Collins for their help in the early stages of writing this story, and to my agent, Wendy Silbert, for all of her hard work, insight and sushi.

Thanks to Kelly Notaras for helping me get this story off

the ground, and to Emily Haynes and everyone at Plume for helping to see it through. Finally, epic thanks to my editor, Trena Keating, who suggested that I delve into my own unhappy backstory in feature-film development and led me to the happy ending I'd been missing all along.

About the Author

The author of *Wanderlust* and a battle-scarred survivor of too many feature-film development wars, Chris Dyer has worked as a script reader, story editor, creative consultant and development executive. For fifteen years Chris Dyer has also successfully resisted moving to Los Angeles, and lives in Brooklyn, proudly.

also by chris dyer...

a novel of sex and sensibility.

AVAILABLE WHEREVER PAPERBACKS ARE SOLD

 Plume
A Member of Penguin Group (USA) Inc.
www.penguin.com